ALISON DeLAINE

A Gentleman 'Til Midnight

A Promise by Daylight

A Wedding by Dawn

A *Promise* by Daylight

ALISON DeLAINE

Published in Great Britain 2015
by Mills & Boon, an imprint of Harlequin (UK) Limited,
Eton House, 18-24 Paradise Road, Richmond, Surrey, TW9 1SR

© 2014 by Black Canyon Creations

ISBN: 978-0-263-91550-1

012-0915

Harlequin (UK) policy is to use papers that are natural, renewable and recyclable products and made from wood grown in sustainable forests. The logging and manufacturing processes conform to the legal environmental regulations of the country of origin.

Printed and bound in Spain
by CPI, Barcelona

ROM
Pbk

Alison DeLaine lives in rural Arizona, where she can often be found driving a dented old pickup truck out to her mining claim in the desert. When she's not busy striking it rich, waiting on spoiled pets, or keeping her husband in line, she is happily putting characters through the wringer.

To Christie Craig and Faye Hughes,
in honour of the Quiet Room

CHAPTER ONE

THE INFAMOUS DUKE OF WINSTON'S brush with death had been on every tongue in Paris for days, and as Millicent Germain waited to be shown upstairs to his chamber, she half hoped the crumbling building that nearly killed him might have also damaged his privates.

The duke's Parisian salon was empty of people but filled with gilded furniture and nudes, nudes, nudes. *Everywhere* nudes: statuettes, portraits, vast paintings and plasters on the ceiling. There was nowhere to rest one's eyes.

Winston does like to have his fun, Philomena had laughed, even as she'd waved away Millie's violent objections to the employment Philomena had *found* for her. Forced her into, rather, but that was neither here nor there now. The employment would be a disaster—there was no doubt about that—but by the time it was finished, Millie would have what she wanted.

A bawdy statue of frolicking nymphs on a nearby table, and the duke's renowned penchant for debauchery, mocked Philomena's description of him:

Intelligent. About what subjects? Copulation?

Respected. By whom? Libertines?

Wealthy. And therein lay the crux of the matter. His

money, in exchange for her medical services during his journey to Greece.

Well, in exchange for *Mr. Miles Germain's* medical services. She may be desperate, but she wasn't mad. His Grace's household was no place to be perceived as female. Thankfully, her simple features became entirely nondescript against the background of a bagwig and coat.

This wouldn't be the first time she'd passed for a man.

She smoothed her palms across her breeches, anticipating the butler's return at any moment, and glanced up at a pair of entwined lovers on the ceiling. It seemed almost certain she would be required to witness one disgusting exhibition after the next, all the way to Greece.

Beggars can't be choosers. And she was very much a beggar. But in a matter of weeks she would be a stone's throw from Malta and the surgical school that waited there, with enough wages from this employment to begin the life that only days ago she'd believed was lost to her forever.

All she had to do was restore a spoiled, depraved peer of the realm to health. Which would be a simple matter, because he'd probably exaggerated his injuries in the first place.

If he hadn't, she would end up coddling His Grace's ego, even as she attempted to prevent his condition from declining, which she could never accomplish if he was constantly indulging in wild fornication parties, as he was rumored to do—

"His Grace will see you now, Mr. Germain," the butler announced from the doorway behind her.

Millie bolted from the chair and turned to face the tall, fair-skinned man who'd introduced himself as Mr. Harris. There was still time to change her mind, flee to Philomena and beg for help finding a different employment.

You don't want a different employment. You want to go to Greece.

"Very good," she said a little hoarsely, and cleared her throat. "Thank you."

She tugged the sleeves of her jacket, glancing down, double-checking that her waistcoat was properly buttoned and her curves were truly concealed. Then she picked up her medical bag and followed the butler out of the salon.

They were halfway up the main staircase, with its elaborate, polished stone balustrade, when a shriek of laughter drifted from somewhere in the recesses of the upper floors.

Mr. Harris didn't seem to notice.

"I understand the stones from the crumbling building facade resulted in numerous injuries to His Grace's person," Millie said to him.

"Indeed," Mr. Harris confirmed. "His Grace was most fortunate not to have received the kind of fatal blow that other poor soul received."

"Yes. Very fortunate." According to the stories, the man walking just behind the duke had been struck directly on the head and died immediately, God rest his soul. "Are you aware of whether any of His Grace's injuries in particular have…affected his mode of living?"

There was another shriek, louder now that they'd

reached the top of the stairs, followed by an eruption of laughter.

Mr. Harris's pleasant face sank into a frown. "His Grace was abed with fever for three days, Mr. Germain. I can assure you it has affected his mode of living enormously." He lowered his voice and added confidentially, "I only hope you can aid the situation more effectively than the other physician."

She heard the voices now—a growing hubbub of them as Mr. Harris led her down a corridor past carved doors of rich, burnished wood.

From the sound of things, the situation had been aided already.

"This way, please, Mr. Germain." Mr. Harris ushered her through a door and into a room teeming with activity—His Grace's dressing room, apparently, where a pair of lavishly dressed women were peering at their faces in a glass, a trio of sporting men were making a game of tossing coins into a whore's cleavage from half a room away, and a man with a laughing woman pinned beneath him was on the verge of tumbling off a love seat and onto the floor.

Mr. Harris led her through another doorway into the adjoining bedchamber just as a familiar shriek and burst of laughter came from a table by the window, where a man with a buxom brunette on his lap was apparently playing at more than just cards. A chambermaid collected dishes, a maidservant poured tea, another fussed with the fire in the fireplace. A monumental bedstead of intricately carved wood and lush midnight-blue draperies dominated the far wall. A man paced near its foot, holding forth in rapid French, while two elaborately coiffured courtesans chatted nearby on a chaise longue.

Finally, Millie's attention landed on the man who lay sprawled against a mountain of pillows.

"You'd best reform your behavior—" he was laughing, calling to one of the courtesans on the chaise longue "—or I might decide you need a punishment." His smile was a wicked flash of white teeth in a face that rendered the word *handsome* entirely inadequate— except for a nasty scrape down his right cheek and faint smudges beneath his eyes. He wore a banyan in blue patterned silk and a pair of trousers that rode up just enough on his right leg to give her a glimpse of dark hair sprinkling a thick, solid calf.

The courtesan fluttered her fan near the edge of her décolletage and smiled at him, leaning forward so that her breasts practically spilled from their stays. *"Viens- toi,"* she taunted, *"si tu peux."*

But the duke made no move to get up and carry out his threat.

Mr. Harris guided her forward and stood with her at the bedside. "Mr. Miles Germain, Your Grace."

And now, eyes black as sin flicked over Millie with calm disinterest. "I should have known any medic recommended by Philomena would be of the youthful variety," he drawled, and amusement touched the corners of his mouth. "Tell me, Mr. Germain…do you have any medical experience beyond the careful examinations you've doubtless conducted in Lady Pennington's bed?"

A sharp answer leaped to her tongue. He thought she was inexperienced?

"Your Grace." She swallowed back her initial reply

and bowed, even though he hadn't bothered with courtesy himself. Her eyes glanced off large hands that had doubtless groped any number of chambermaids and went to his left arm, which lay in a sling. "My condolences for the situation in which you find yourself."

This self-indulgent profligate could question her credentials all he liked, but she was going with him to Greece.

He accepted a glass of something—cognac, perhaps—from one of the courtesans and let her fuss with some nonexistent problem with his banyan. "How old *are* you, Mr. Germain?"

"Three and twenty."

"Three and *twenty*." Amusement deepened in his eyes. "I might rather have suspected three and ten, would you not agree, Deschamps?"

The man who'd been pontificating at the foot of the bed laughed. "*Tenez,* I fear you offend," he said, gesturing toward her magnanimously.

"Not at all," Millie said evenly. "Perhaps it will comfort you to know that I served four years as a ship's surgeon. I can assure you, I've tended men in far worse condition than yours."

"And do any yet live?"

"All that could be saved, Your Grace." She thought a shadow passed across his eyes, but it was there and gone so quickly she couldn't be sure.

"Hold out your hands," he instructed.

Her hands? She did as he asked, holding them palms down in front of her until he bade her stop with a wave of his hand. "At least you don't shake like the last one. Bloody drunkard—I endured twice the pain from all of his bumbling around." He grimaced and put a hand to his shoulder. "Come and see what's wrong with this sling. Damned arm's been aggravating me all day."

She could already see the sling was tied too tightly. She put down her medical bag, and the courtesan returned to the chaise longue to allow Millie room at the side of the bed. Mr. Harris withdrew to an unoccupied space by the wall.

"I understand Your Grace has just recovered from a fever," Millie said as she reached across him. Up close, she could see the thick lashes that framed his dark eyes and the laugh lines that creased their corners as he exchanged a few loaded remarks with the women.

"Give him something to increase his desire," one of them instructed her in French, laughing.

"You could never endure it if he did," the duke shot back, and then, to Millie, "The fever? Three days of utter misery. Yes, that's right."

"And the wounds? How are they progressing?"

"The wounds are on my back, Mr. Germain. I couldn't possibly tell you."

She glanced at him as she loosened the sling. "Did you ask no questions of your physician?" If he was going to act as if she were stupid, she'd be happy to do the same. "He must have given you some report. Is there any sign that pus has developed?"

There was a horrified squeal from the chaise longue.

"Good God, Mr. Germain," the duke said. "That kind of talk will drive away my company."

Which had just become her first order of business. She adjusted the sling, eased his elbow out a smidgen.

"I don't suppose Your Grace has considered that solitude and rest might be enormously beneficial."

He laughed at that. Deep lines cut at the sides of his mouth, and those blackish devil eyes came alive with alarming intelligence.

A sensation whispered through her body: a slight heaviness in her breasts. A faint stirring at the juncture of her thighs.

Dear God.

"Mr. Germain," he said, "if you were in my place, would you be anxious to rid yourself of this particular company?"

She fixed her attention on his arm. After a moment, the unexpected sensation passed. Yes…it passed completely.

"Were I in your position," she replied, "my foremost concern would be the fastest possible recovery of my health." Another quick adjustment, but then—

She leaned closer, sniffing, and frowned.

"What is it?" he asked.

"Oil of turpentine."

"My physician has been using it on the dressings."

Aha, so he *had* received a report. "Yes, of course, but…" Still?

"But *what?*" he said irritably.

"I shall need to see the state of the wounds, but I rather suspect a different ointment would be more to your advantage at this stage. How does the sling feel?"

He shifted his arm the tiniest fraction, frowning. "Much better."

Suddenly she was more aware of his arm flexing beneath her fingers than she'd been a moment before, of warm muscle and sinew warming her fingertips through two thin layers of silk and linen. A tiny nerve pulsed way down low in her belly.

"I must warn you," she said in her direst tone, straightening and stepping back from the bed, "that rest is important above all else." She thought of the only medical volume she owned, a surgical treatise that was tucked away in her bag at this very moment, and how accurately its advice matched her own experience.

"Mr. Germain," he said irritably, "I've been abed these four days."

"A proper diet and a healthy air are important, as well, naturally," she went on gravely, still too aware of her own fingertips, "but there should be no excitement of the senses. Nothing to arouse the passions."

A commotion went up from the card table, and one of the women bolted from her chair on a peal of laughter, only to be brought firmly down onto the lap of one of His Grace's friends.

"Perish the thought," the duke said dryly, and reached for his drink.

"I'm quite serious, Your Grace. 'Disturbances of the mind are great enemies to the health of the body,'" she quoted from the book.

"You medical types are all the same, with your morbid admonishments. But you may rest easy, as nothing would disturb me more than to be deprived of entertainment." His lip curled a little, and her eye went straight to it, and now she noticed the shape of his mouth in a way she hadn't before even though there was nothing unique about it—nothing at all.

"And you should know that I cannot work with onlookers," she added now, in case he imagined she would conduct an examination of his person with all of these people milling about.

He laughed. "No? *I've* been known to perform rather well with an onlooker or two." He tossed a wicked grin at the women on the chaise longue, then took another drink.

Millie watched his tongue catch the moisture from his lips as he lowered the glass. Realized she was holding her breath.

His eyes found hers.

She couldn't look away.

"Harris," he drawled, lifting his glass to his lips once more, "show Mr. Germain to his rooms. Find out his fee and pay him a month's wages in advance."

"You'll have a difficult time convincing His Grace to follow a straight and narrow path, even when his health is at risk," Mr. Harris told her with a knowing grin when they had returned to the corridor. "But I daresay you'll find his sporting activities lead to any number of beneficial consequences, if you understand my meaning."

She glanced over her shoulder and through the doorway just in time to see one of His Grace's friends catch a courtesan around the waist and plant a dramatic bite on her neck.

Oh, yes. She understood all too clearly.

"He keeps less company now than before the accident, I regret to say—" That was *less* company? "—although hopefully, now that you're here…"

They exited the anteroom and returned to the corridor, only to be stopped by a footman.

"Mr. Germain's bags have just arrived," he said to the butler.

Her bags? "That isn't poss—"

"And this letter, for you, sir." The footman handed her a note and bowed.

Millie recognized Philomena's writing immediately and tore open the letter, skimming fast.

...decided to leave Paris today instead of Thursday...

No. No, it wasn't possible.

"Put Mr. Germain's things in the yellow room," Mr. Harris was saying to the footman.

...certain you will find yourself very comfortably appointed with the duke...

"Very good." The footman turned back toward the stairs.

Philomena had left Paris. She'd sent Millie's bags without waiting to learn how the interview had gone, and she'd *left Paris.* For a moment Millie experienced that same sensation as when a ship fell after rising on a large swell—as if the deck was falling from beneath one's feet.

Not that she had any intention of throwing herself on Philomena's mercy again—not when she had done more than was required in securing Millie this position in the first place. But...

"Is there a problem?" Mr. Harris asked.

There would be no question now. "No," she said slowly, refolding the letter and tucking it inside her jacket. "No, not at all."

Mr. Harris nodded and led her a short distance away, opening another door. "Here you are, then. These will be your rooms."

Her attention shot to the left, toward the direction they'd just come from. Her chamber was just down from His Grace's rooms. *Adjacent* to His Grace's rooms, if she estimated correctly.

She didn't like that. Not at all.

She followed Mr. Harris inside, endeavoring to remain calm. There was no reason *not* to be calm, really. "Surely there must be accommodations below stairs that I could occupy," she suggested. A memory snaked in— the reason she'd left service in the first place, and one of the many reasons she'd balked at the idea of returning.

"His Grace has ordered that you be installed here for his convenience," Mr. Harris said. "You wouldn't want to be down there, anyhow. The opportunities are fewer and of a quite different caliber."

She managed a halfhearted smile—it wouldn't do for him to think her completely uninterested in the *opportunities* he valued so highly—and looked at the wall she almost certainly shared with His Grace's bedchamber. There was no adjoining door, but a large curio cabinet stretched across half its length and rose at least seven feet.

"In any case, as I was saying, I'm already seeing signs of improvement, and I expect His Grace's social calendar to return to full capacity very shortly." Another grin, this time accompanied by a wink. "Not to put you on the spot, but Sacks and I are counting on you."

"Sacks?"

"His Grace's valet. And not to worry…I've no doubt there'll be plenty of, shall we say, *incentive* in it for you, as well." The footmen returned upstairs with her things—just a small trunk and a bag—and deposited them on the floor in the lavishly furnished dressing room done in three shades of gold and yellow.

She cast her eye about the room, into the adjacent chamber that included a bed draped in gold damask, and suddenly had trouble breathing.

"His Grace asked me to discover your fee," Mr. Harris said now.

Her fee. Of course. Her mind raced for a figure that might make this all bearable and named an outrageous sum.

Mr. Harris didn't bat an eye. "Very good. I shall return with your advance wages."

And then she was alone in her new accommodations, with the sounds of the duke's entertainment filtering through the wall and not a single alternative in all the world.

She strode to the window. Looked out at Paris with its mishmash of buildings, houses, cobbled streets, wagons, pedestrians, all bathed in a gloomy drizzle. The truth was, she did have an alternative, and she was looking at it now.

The streets of Paris. Penniless, to make her way alone in a city that would show no mercy. Out there, without any references or money, the only position she would find would be in a brothel.

In here, on the other hand…

She looked over her shoulder at the room's grand furnishings, paintings, statuettes, trinkets. Just one or two of the pieces here would go a long way toward financing her education. Not that she would ever consider stealing from him.

But he had what she needed—money—and he would

pay her an exorbitant wage to attend him. Before she left his service, she would make sure that he wrote Miles Germain a letter of introduction, as well.

She tightened her hand around the windowsill, looking out at Paris but imagining the Mediterranean's great cities: Venice, Athens, Constantinople.

With the duke as a reference, her identity as Miles Germain would be cemented for as long as she could maintain her disguise. She could come and go freely, unaccosted, because all the world would believe she was male.

Within a few years, armed with knowledge from Malta's renowned School of Anatomy and Surgery, Miles Germain would be a well-respected surgeon in practice for himself, and nobody—*nobody*—would ever take that away.

All she had to do was continue in his employ and make sure he made a full recovery.

A sudden knock startled her, and she turned quickly from the window to find another of the duke's servants—a very young man wearing a tidy wig and an expectant expression.

"Monsieur," he said with a bow. *"Je suis à vous."*

But she didn't *want* him at her disposal! She started forward. *"Merci,"* she said, "but—"

"I shall put away your things—" He started toward her trunk and bag.

"No," Millie said quickly, hurrying to block his way. "No, that won't be necessary," she told him in French. "I shall put them away myself." The duke had assigned her a valet?

"I have been placed at your service, *monsieur,*" the

man said firmly. "You have only to tell me what you need. A change of clothes, perhaps…"

"I don't need a change of clothes. And I won't need anyone at my service."

Just then, Mr. Harris walked in. "Ah, excellent. Bernet has found you."

Already she was imagining the man lifting away her wig to find her shoulder-length hair stuffed inside— damn and blast, she should have cut it completely off— whisking off her shirt and discovering the cloth she'd wound around her breasts beneath her shift to flatten them, and realizing that a maid, not a valet, was the appropriate help.

"Mr. Harris, I absolutely will not require any assistance. I am perfectly capable of looking after myself. In fact, I'm used to it."

"Of course you are," Harris said, handing her an envelope that doubtless contained the ridiculous sum she had demanded. "But there's no need, while you're here. Bernet's been only too anxious for an upstairs assignment," he added with a wink. "I'm sure you'd hate to disappoint him."

"Perhaps he could look after one of the guests— *Attendez!*" Bernet was kneeling in front of her trunk with his hands on the latches. She rushed to stop him. "I've got half of an apothecary's shop in there," she said now. "Very delicate—I shall need to unpack it myself. Truly."

That seemed to satisfy him. He inclined his head, stood up and backed away.

Now she lifted her chin and summoned a tone she'd

heard Philomena use often enough to dismiss servants. "That will be all for now."

"Très bien," Bernet said with a bow.

"You may give me a list of any supplies you'll need for His Grace's care," Harris said now. "Otherwise, you have only to ring if you need anything, and Sacks will let you know if His Grace requires your attendance."

The moment they were gone she dropped to her knees in front of the trunk, jerked the lid open, dug through shirts, waistcoats and pairs of breeches and men's stockings. Yanked out the shifts she should never have kept. And at the very bottom, a tiny box with a pair of dangling silver earrings, and the two colorful scarves she hadn't been able to part with. She paused, running her hand over their silken texture, letting her fingers play with the bright blue fringe at the ends, remembering that day at Constantinople's grand bazaar— she, Katherine, Philomena and India.

The scarves and earrings had been a silly indulgence. She'd never even worn them.

With the shifts and scarves wadded in her hands, she hurried into the bedchamber, threw back the drapery at the back corner of the bed and stuffed them beneath the mattress.

It would do until she could find a better place, which she would have to do before the maid came tomorrow morning to make the bed. She returned to the dressing room

Now what? Would the duke expect her to return to his rooms or wait to be summoned? Would his guests ever leave? And what would happen if they did?

He would be alone, and bored, and may well seek out more company or an impromptu medical examination.

She touched the hilt of the smallsword at her hip. What good fortune that a fashionable man wasn't dressed without one. But if the duke sought her out at night, perhaps finding his way into her rooms while she was abed and not fully dressed...

That simply could not happen. She would not give up the freedom of her disguise that easily, not even if she had to sleep fully clothed. Still...

She went to the door and turned the latch. But, of course, he would have a key.

She spun on her heel. Surveyed the room: one door led out, another led to her new adjoining bedchamber, where there was yet another door she would need to consider.

Moments later, she dragged a chair over and shoved it against the door that led from the dressing room to the corridor, and then stood back. Tonight, after she'd gone to bed, that might work. But...

She looked suspiciously at the curio cabinet. Some grand houses had secret passageways, or so she'd heard. Furnishings that were merely false fronts. She inspected the edges of the cabinet, running her finger along the seam where it met the wall, finding no discernible space. Muted laughter drifted from the other side. Was not his bed directly opposite? So there couldn't possibly be any kind of...

Of course there could. The entire house could have a network of secret passageways through which His Grace made surprise visits on unsuspecting guests.

She got another chair, dragged it next to the curio

cabinet and climbed up. Reached to the back paneling and tapped—lightly, so she wouldn't be heard—
but could determine nothing. She reached to remove
a bronze obstacle but snatched her hand back, seeing
now that it was a sculpture of a man with his face buried between a woman's—

Ugh. Disgusting.

Tap-tap-tap. Did the wall sound hollow?

She moved a benign porcelain horse instead and tried
a different section of paneling.

Tap-tap-tap.

Behind her, a man cleared his throat.

She whirled around, losing her balance, grabbing
for the cabinet to keep from falling. The duke stood
in the doorway to the bedchamber, watching her with
amused interest.

"Please," he said, holding up his hand. "Do not let
me interrupt."

CHAPTER TWO

Mr. Miles Germain was apparently debating whether to climb down from the chair.

Yes, Winston had definitely expected someone older. And someone *male,* which he had a strong suspicion *Mr.* Germain was not.

Apparently he hadn't asked Philomena enough questions.

He studied his new medic now—average features, nothing to draw a man's eye. No hint of breasts. Even lips, plain, straight nose, ordinary rounded chin. Slightly arched brows, thick lashes that weren't too long, weren't too short. All of which, set above a modest suit and topped off by an awful bagwig, did little to betray her sex.

But he'd been a breath away from too many graceful female necks not to have noticed the smooth, curving throat when his new medic had adjusted his sling.

And there was the matter of Mr. Germain's ear.

It was a small ear. Delicate. Dainty, really, with a tiny, almost imperceptible hole in the lobe, which didn't mean anything—Sir William Jaxbury and his gold hoops were proof of that—but that was no male ear.

"I once had a cabinet fall," Mr. Germain said now, as if it were the complete truth. "Toppled to the ground.

Very dangerous." He—almost certainly *she*—even looked Winston in the eye when she said it.

Interesting.

Winston glanced at another chair that had been shoved against the dressing room door in an apparent attempt to keep someone out—that someone, he assumed, being himself. "You've also had trouble with doors flying open, I see."

"Occasionally."

It explained why he'd had to come in through the bedchamber. "Perhaps, to put your mind at ease, you'd like me to call a carpenter."

"That won't be necessary." A small crease appeared above her upper lip—a lip that, on closer inspection, was a bit too full to appropriately frame the mouth of an average male medic.

"I want you to feel entirely safe here, Mr. Germain," he said.

"I can't think why I wouldn't," she said evenly, finally climbing down from the chair. It was too bad her coat prevented any view of her arse, or his suspicions would certainly be proved.

"If it's my guests that concern you, a simple turn of the key will deter any unwanted visitors."

"At the moment, Your Grace, my only concern is for your health. I can't believe standing is good for your condition. I would advise a hasty return to your bed."

"I'm hardly an invalid."

"Obviously."

He'd irritated her. How intriguing. Although now that he was standing here, he wished he weren't. The gash on his thigh throbbed, and it hurt like the devil to put his weight on that leg, and his back felt as if some-one had taken a knife to it.

"When do you expect we shall depart for Greece?" she asked now.

"Oh, I don't know," he said, and leaned against the doorjamb to take some weight off his left leg. "I'm in no particular hurry. I suppose it will depend partly on your assessment of my fitness for travel."

"Mobile as you are, I expect you will be fit very soon," she said almost immediately.

He raised a brow. "One might almost think you were anxious to be under way. Are you not enjoying Paris, then? If you like, I could make some suggestions for your entertainment while we're still here."

"That won't be necessary."

"Are you sure? There are any number of pleasur-able hideaways that should not be missed. I suspect you enjoy a good debauch now and then, isn't that right, Mr. Germain?"

That little line appeared again on the left side of her upper lip, and she gave him a look of grave reproof. "I am in the business of staying *free* from disease, Your Grace."

He laughed. "I can think of several ways to do *that*. One has only to take precautions. Surely a man of your age is well versed in that subject."

That line above her lip deepened.

"I shall have plenty to keep me occupied looking after Your Grace's health. I understand that Your Grace is extremely fortunate not to have been more seriously injured."

He thought of the accident, and a quick, sucking

sensation grabbed his chest. "Indeed. Very fortunate." Thoughts forced their way in—images of the man who'd not been so fortunate, who had died mere feet away from Winston, whose blood had pooled around Winston's fingers as they both lay on the street.

Her brows dove. "Is something the matter?"

"Not at all." Nothing except the fact that he did not wish to discuss anything about the accident. "Unless you consider that I've lost use of my arm, and my shoulder aches like the devil, and I have a number of nasty cuts. Of course, you'll be able to determine all the facts upon examination." An examination that, if her manner in his bedchamber were any indication, she would not hesitate to perform.

And wasn't that going to be an interesting opportunity.

"Of course," she agreed.

And he couldn't help himself. He gestured with his good arm toward a chair by the window. "Perhaps you'd like to perform it now?"

A spark of objection came into her eyes. "I haven't yet unpacked all of my instruments."

"Good God. I should hope you won't need any *instruments* to perform a simple examination."

"Mmm, yes," she said doubtfully. "One would hope. But I have no idea what I might find. I shall want my scissors and probe at the ready, and my incision knife, certainly—"

"*Incision* knife."

She looked at him as though he were a child. "I must be prepared to immediately address whatever I might find. Which is why I shall need to wait for the basic supply of lints, plasters and bandages I asked Harris to send for, in case any kind of procedure is required— and even if it isn't, as Your Grace's wounds will almost certainly require fresh dressings, if for no other reason than to apply a medicine more appropriate than oil of turpentine."

"How very…thorough."

"Your Grace, if you were struck by mortar and stone, there's no telling what manner of grit could have escaped the eye of the surgeon who first attended you. Given your mobility, and the fact that you don't appear to be feverish at the moment, I'm inclined to think that all is as it should be. But only when I've had a chance to see exactly where the stones struck you and precisely what damage occurred shall I be able to fully—"

"I understand your point, Mr. Germain." And he'd had more than enough of it. He pushed away from the door frame, and an arrow of pain shot from his shoulder to his left buttock.

"By all means, let us delay the examination." He bowed. "Until later, then."

HIS ENTIRE BODY ached as he returned to his rooms. It was tempting to toss everyone out and go to sleep.

He eased himself back onto his bed and replied to a ridiculous political assertion Favreau was making, laughed at a joke Perry tossed out from the card table, called to Seville in the other room to inquire whether Linton had arrived in Paris yet.

"Doctor's a right young piece of stuff, isn't he?" Perry said, wandering over from the card table. "You know who'd like him...Kern. Always did enjoy that sort of thing."

"If Kern tries to distract my medic, he'll answer to me." And he would be very disappointed once he discovered that the protrusion at the front of Mr. Germain's breeches was just for show. He smiled to himself, thinking of it now.

His woman doctor may not have any discernible breasts, but she was bloody well hung.

Just then, Harris came in and leaned close to his ear. "She has been found, Your Grace."

The room seemed to fade, and Winston fixed his full attention on Harris. "Where?"

"A small house at the edge of town." Harris hesitated. "It is my understanding that there are five children."

Bloody hell. "You're certain?"

"It's been confirmed."

Five children and a widow. Winston rubbed the back of his neck. "See that they receive a hundred pounds," he murmured. "No. Five hundred."

"Very good, Your Grace. I'll see to it straightaway."

Winston exhaled, leaned his head back and closed his eyes, but that only made the problem worse. That face was always there—those sightless eyes staring at him while the man lay lifeless, his head cracked open by a piece of masonry that could just as easily have struck Winston. He could hear the screaming, the chaos of those crazed moments.

Now, a female hand smoothed over his chest. *"Ça va?"*

For a moment the courtesan's perfume cloyed nauseatingly in his nostrils, but then he opened his eyes, drew his finger lazily across the top of her bosom. *"Oui."*

She smiled and eased a hip onto the bed next to him.

Everything was fine. Or it would be, as soon as they were under way to Greece. He imagined the heady taste of Mediterranean wine, the even more intoxicating distraction of Grecian women and the exotic fantasies they would bring to life.

You vowed to put an end to all that.

Indeed. That was the other part of this entire debacle that would not let him alone: his private vow to reform. *By God, I'll be the man Edward wants me to be.* The vow had exploded through his mind as he lay there in fiery pain, while people ran frantically around him, and even more masonry broke loose from that blasted building, crashing to the ground.

As long as he lived, he would never forget the sound of stone hitting the street inches from his head.

He forced himself to smile when Hélène joined Marie on the edge of his bed, exchanged a few loaded remarks with the two of them, considered several possibilities for other ways they could entertain him.

Instead, he told them his side hurt. Told everyone he needed to rest. Instructed Harris to turn away any new visitors.

Ten minutes later, his rooms were empty. And now he lay there, irritated, wishing everyone back.

This was ridiculous. It was a freak accident—anyone could have been passing by that building when the facade fell. That falling masonry was not a sign from above. It was not a heavenly indictment of Winston's life. The danger of those moments had gotten the better of him, that was all.

He'd made the kind of vow sailors made in a hurricane. The kind soldiers made on the battlefield.

They weren't the kind of promises a man was meant to keep.

He was being superstitious. His best friend had been admonishing him since school days. Little surprise there, given that Edward was a vicar and couldn't be expected to know about real life—the pleasures to be had that were just pleasures, nothing more, but made life worth living.

Consider your ways, Winston. That's what Edward had always said. For God's sake, what did that even mean?

Only a saint could live up to Edward's standards.

He ought to have Harris summon his company back. Now, before he could change his mind again.

Instead, he called Sacks. "Bring Mr. Germain," he said irritably. "I want my bandages checked."

He thought of those pursed lips and almost smiled. Perhaps there was entertainment to be had, after all.

BY THE TIME the duke's valet came to tell her that His Grace required her assistance, Millie had decided that if the mere mention of an incision knife was all it took to make the duke recoil, it would be a simple matter to keep the advantage over him for the remainder of her employment.

Mr. Sacks, the valet, was a short, brawny man with giant hands and dark bushy brows, and he stood expressionless as he waited in the doorway. Millie gathered up her medical bag and followed him to the duke's rooms.

Where—unbelievably—the duke was alone.

Wearing nothing but his shirt.

"Mr. Germain, Your Grace," Mr. Sacks announced unnecessarily.

"Excellent." Reclining against his pillows, with a glass of liquor in his hand and the tails of his shirt covering him only to midthigh, the duke smiled. "That will be all."

Mr. Sacks withdrew, and Millie plunked her medical bag on the card table by the window and reminded herself that the duke was just a man like any of the sailors she'd doctored aboard the *Possession*—no more, no less.

"A number of cuts and an immobilized arm that isn't broken," she recounted briskly from their earlier conversation as she dug through her bag for heaven knew what except a few moments to delay the inevitable. "Is that the complete list of your complaints?"

"Hardly," came his cognac-roughened voice from the bed. "Among other things, there isn't a single comfortable method of copulation."

She paused for only a second. And, for that, she deserved a medal.

"I shouldn't think there would be a single comfortable method of eating, sleeping, defecating or any of the body's other natural functions, either, in your condition," she said matter-of-factly. If he thought the young Miles Germain would be startled by the duke's excesses, he would soon learn otherwise. "But I was asking about your injuries, Your Grace."

"Forgive me—when you said *complaints,* it was my most pressing grievance that came to mind."

"As well it should." She turned from the card table. Hardly a surprise that he considered slaking his lust a more serious issue than an immobilized arm.

"Bad enough that a woman has two breasts while I only have one good hand," he complained

She smiled, tight-lipped, because a man would smile at such an idiotic statement. And she approached the bed, hoping that if she didn't encourage him further they could be finished with talk of copulation and breasts.

One of his legs was severely bruised—black and purpling, wrapped in two places with bandages.

Without all his clothing, she would have thought he'd seem smaller.

"Of course," he mused, raising his glass to his lips, "there is much one can do with a breast and one's mouth."

And no, of course they weren't finished with lewd talk. Because they were supposedly two men, and men were never finished with lewd talk.

"What a miracle that your injuries have not entirely kept you from enjoying your company," she said in her blandest tone.

"But they have kept me from enjoying it in an entirely satisfactory way, if you understand my meaning, Mr. Germain."

"Perfectly, Your Grace. But you needn't fabricate the situation to me."

"Was I fabricating?"

"The body is less able to respond to stimulus when it is putting its efforts into healing itself. But rest assured that as the healing process continues, you'll find yourself once again able to copulate to your full ability."

"Oh, but you misunderstand, Mr. Germain. I don't have a complaint of ability."

She let her brows edge upward, as if just comprehending something new. "Oh. I see."

"Good."

"In that case, I shall prepare a concoction straightaway. We should foment the organ very often—perhaps even apply a poultice in a suspensory bandage—and with a strict regimen, things should clear up for you eventually—"

"Mr. Germain, that is *not* the issue."

"You needn't be embarrassed. And rest assured that should there be anything present that requires lancing, I will use my knife most delicately."

"You will not come near my privates with a knife, Mr. Germain. Is that clear?"

She almost smiled. "Certainly."

"And there is nothing in need of clearing up. Or... *lancing.*"

"I trust your word completely, Your Grace. And *you* may trust *me* not to reveal this conversation to a single soul. We shall simply pretend nothing was ever said about it."

"Nothing *was* said about it," he said with a hint of frustration.

"Exactly." She continued her cursory examination, close enough now to detect a spicy kind of musk on his skin and feel the whisper of breath on her cheek as she leaned forward to check his sling once more. And there was that sensation again—a quiet response to him, stirring in a deep, intimate place. She inhaled to cleanse it away, only managing to breathe in more of him.

"It's a miracle no bones were broken," she said, focusing intently on his shoulder.

She could sense him debating whether to press the point about the state of his manhood, but instead, "Indeed," he said shortly.

"I shall need to see the wounds." She backed away from the bed. He would have to sit up to remove his shirt.

When he did, he would be nude.

One male body is the same as the next. God knew she'd tended enough of them aboard the *Possession*.

He reached to set his glass on the bedside table, and his shirttails edged upward on one powerful thigh. A sudden frisson of anticipation had her turning toward her medical bag. But then, before she realized what he intended, he swung his legs over the edge of the bed and stood up. Turned his back to her. Grabbed his shirt with his good hand and pulled upward, revealing a solid pair of buttocks.

"Mr. Germain…"

"Of course," she said quickly, tearing her eyes away from where they should not have strayed, helping him off with his shirt, seeing now that his other physician had dressed a handful of wounds down the left half of his back and his left thigh. Much of his torso was wrapped completely around with bandages and plasters to keep the compresses in place, and where the skin wasn't covered, it was badly bruised.

Dear God.

She lifted the edge of a bandage on his back and

sucked in a breath at the ragged wound beneath. He had to be in considerable pain. Gently she checked the others, found thankfully that the first was the most serious. "What a miracle none of the pieces struck you on the head or neck," she said, more sincerely than she'd intended, and felt him tense.

She touched his skin, lightly, and heard him hiss. "How long before I'm fully recovered?" he asked.

"Weeks, certainly."

"*Weeks*. What can you give me to hasten the process?"

"Only the natural course of time and healing will do that, I'm afraid." Assuming the wounds didn't fester and bring on a new fever.

Holding up his shirt like a shield in one hand, she moved around him and reached up to press the back of her fingers to his forehead. "Have you felt warm? Any sign that the fever is returning?"

"No warmer than usual," he said.

She let her hand fall. And now she became too aware of his bare chest, the dark hair dusted across it, the bare hips visible on either side of the shirt hanging limply from her fist.

She looked him in the eye. "When was the last time you were bled?"

"Good God. Yesterday."

"Hmm." Perhaps she ought to bleed him again, just to be safe. But if it had only been yesterday...

She moved behind him again, leaned close to sniff the poultices. Yes, definitely turpentine. "I'd like to redress the wounds, as I suggested earlier. But I'll need to prepare the dressings first. It shouldn't take long." She ran her fingers along a length of gauze that stretched across his lower back and heard him inhale sharply.

She pulled her hand away, and a warm sensation skittered up her arm.

His hand reached back. "My shirt."

She gave it to him. Had to help him again, because he could not put it back on one-handed. He walked a few steps to the bedside table, keeping his back to her, and picked up his drink.

"Prepare the dressings," he said a bit shortly. "I shall be ready."

AND WHEN SHE RETURNED, Winston thought as she left, his body would have stopped responding to her touch and begun responding to the liquor he would need in order to bear the pain when she changed the bandages.

He glanced down at his tented shirttails and knocked back a swallow of liquor, a little disgusted with himself. He'd sent away all the beauties, so his anatomy was making do with what was available.

And what was available was a medic whose cheeks had pinkened during the examination, who had inspected him with eyes averted from his crotch, and whose small, capable fingers were too easy to imagine wrapped around his cock.

Or around a surgical knife. Good *God*.

He'd do well to dismiss her. Today, now, before she could do any damage.

But already he preferred her methods to that Parisian doctor whose thoughtless handling had nearly hurled him into unconsciousness from the pain. And something in her tone had him suspecting that whatever she planned to use on his wounds actually stood a chance of having some effect.

Miles Germain would stay. He would take her to Greece, perhaps even continue to entertain himself at her expense. But he'd be damned before he'd let her near his privates again.

CHAPTER THREE

"THIS ISN'T LIKE HIM, you know," Harris said early that evening, taking a quick sip from a glass of wine before lowering himself into an armchair in Millie's dressing room. Across the room, Millie busied herself arranging her medical supplies inside a small cabinet whose contents she'd transferred to the cupboards below the bookcase. "Not like him a'tall, and it's making me bloody nervous." He stretched out his legs in front of him and crossed them at the ankles. "And you getting to be upstairs. Wish he'd put me upstairs. Make it a good deal easier to access the side benefits."

It wasn't difficult to imagine what those *side benefits* might be.

Sacks, the duke's valet, refilled his own glass. "You're certain he said *no* visitors?" Sacks asked.

"*No* visitors," Harris said emphatically, sipping his wine and frowning. "What can he be about?"

"Only let that princess present 'erself below, and ten to one 'is Grace would—"

"*None*. He said no exceptions."

Millie smiled to herself as she arranged her new lints and bandages. Apparently His Grace was finally taking her advice seriously. He'd been appropriately clothed when she'd returned to change the dressings—at least, as much as was practical, given that he'd needed to disrobe almost entirely in order for her to remove and replace all the bandages. But there had been no more talk of copulation. In fact, he'd scarcely talked at all.

He'd flinched only a little and, during the worst parts, she'd heard him hiss.

"Perhaps," she said over her shoulder to the two man-servants, "what he's about is rest. His wounds are quite serious," she said. "They'll be some time in healing, and I've advised him against all activity."

"And all company?" Harris sat forward. "Good God, man, you'll drive us to the madhouse!"

"Understand," Sacks told her, putting his glass down and walking to the chamber stool in the corner, "'tis more than just the injuries. He hasn't been 'imself."

Millie turned back to her medicines when Sacks reached for the front of his breeches.

"His Grace not being himself is bound to have a negative effect on my *own* self," Harris groused.

Sacks made a noise while he rearranged his breeches. "Side benefits are bound to be significantly reduced. You've got to restore 'im quickly," he said to Millie, as if it were that simple.

"I'm not a miracle worker," she said.

"'Twas *your* news about the widow that got 'im started on all this," Sacks accused Harris now.

"I could hardly keep the news from him," Harris said irritably.

"What widow?" Millie asked.

"Wife of 'im that died in the accident," Sacks told her. "'Is Grace keeps asking after them. Finally learned her whereabouts today—her and 'er five young 'uns."

He shook his head. "Pity, that is." And then, to Harris, "But you could've waited a day or two."

"The burial is tomorrow."

"He's not going anyhow."

"But we couldn't have known that, could we?" Harris snapped. "He ordered five hundred pounds sent this afternoon."

"Five hundred!" Millie exclaimed, and almost knocked over a bottle of linseed oil.

"His Grace seems fixated on that accident," Sacks said. "And now—" he shot a frown at Harris "—on the widow and young 'uns. If you ask me, it's interfering with 'is recovery. What if he decides to go to that burial, after all?"

"His Grace will *not* be attending the funeral of an accounting clerk," Harris said irritably, then tilted his glass toward Millie. "And you mustn't allow him any manner of activity that will prolong the healing process."

"Get him back to 'imself quickly," Sacks said, "and you'll have no end of interesting pastimes in these rooms."

"I haven't the least—" She caught herself and, instead, raised her brows in what she hoped was a semi-interested expression.

"No need to worry about the dangerous side of things. Just look in that drawer there." He pointed to a side table with one small drawer. "Go on," he grinned. "Find all the armor you need, just in case His Grace's entertainments conveniently spill over into the adjoining rooms."

Millie opened the drawer. Found a slender case containing—

A protective sheath for an anatomical organ she did not possess.

She snatched her hand away before thinking better of it, glanced over her shoulder to find Sacks grinning at her.

"Got a feeling our young medic 'ere is a virgin."

Oh, dear God—it would never do for these two to think *that*. "Don't be ridiculous," she said evenly, and gave the sheath another look for good measure. "Just took me by surprise, that's all." She smirked and replaced the cover. "Much obliged."

"You won't be sorry you took this employ," Harris said, leaning back in the armchair, raising his wineglass to his lips. "And if you can return His Grace to his former spirits quickly, neither will we."

WINSTON LAY WITH a glass of cognac in his hand, nary a sound in the entire house, thinking about the accident, that bloody vow, that dead man's widow and fatherless children.

He looked at the vast room—empty chairs, bare tables, closed drapes.

This is what it would always be like if he became the man Edward wanted him to be. Every bloody night for the rest of his life, if he kept that promise.

He got out of bed, took his drink off the night table and limped across the room to the card table. Sat down. Reached for the cards, shuffled, dealt a hand of solitaire.

Lost.

Lost again, and then a third time.

Finally he snatched the cards off the table and tapped them into a neat deck, knocking back several swallows of cognac, looking angrily around the room.

This was what considering his ways would entail. He would have to abandon his women, his friends, his entertainments. He stood up, felt a painful tug beneath his bandage and had to sit down again.

Devil take it.

He'd always done as he damned well pleased—every night, if he had a mind for it, which he usually did. Nobody even knew about that vow, least of all Edward. It wasn't as if he'd pledged his support to a bill in the Lords or promised to protect a friend's indiscretion. He'd merely made a tiny vow. One only he really knew about.

He was being nonsensical. A nonsensical, superstitious faux-puritan with a raging desire for a woman.

He stood up again, more carefully this time, and called for Sacks. He would dress and go out. Perhaps to Madame Gravelle's. Plenty of opportunity there, and if he found himself a quiet corner—perhaps lounged himself on a chaise longue—he could indulge in any number of satisfying pastimes without risking further injury.

But struggling into his evening jacket was a devil, and standing made the wounds on his leg throb, and even after he sat down they continued to ache, and he finally had to accept that there would be no going to Madame Gravelle's tonight.

"Call Mr. Germain," he snapped, breathing deeply against the pain, sitting in an armchair in his dressing room after Sacks had removed the jacket.

His prune-lipped doctor appeared moments later.

When she saw him, her expression softened in a way she would need to learn to control if she wanted her disguise to be effective for any length of time.

"What have you done?" she asked with something like irritation.

"I shall be doing nothing, as it turns out."

"You can't possibly have imagined you're fit enough to go out. Oh, for heaven's sake. You should return to your bed at once."

"I need some entertainment."

"Entertainment is the last thing you need. Rest and abstinence is what's called for, and you've made an excellent start by getting rid of your guests."

"Rest and abstinence are the problem," he snapped. "My existence has become downright monastic in a matter of hours."

"Do monasteries *have* statues of copulating couples?"

Those words, coming from her prunish lips, nearly made him laugh. "Now there would be a cruel form of torture," he said irritably. "Poor bastards."

He tried to imagine himself truly living a monastic life. For God's sake, even Edward didn't live that way. He had Cara, and—

Christ. Cara was the last person he wanted to think of now.

He stood up, starting for his bedchamber, his bed, but got an idea and veered toward the card table instead. "Sit," he ordered.

She frowned. "Why?"

"Why does anyone sit at a card table?"

"I don't wish to play cards."

"I *do* wish to, and you are the only one here aside from Sacks and Harris."

"I'm quite certain either of them would be happy to oblige."

Sacks and Harris were happy to participate in most any kind of amusement, but that was hardly the point. Winston paused. Stared at her. "You *are* in my employ, are you not?"

"Indeed I am, Your Grace, but I'll not allow you to win away my advance earnings."

"Ah, I see." He pointed across the room. "Go look in that box. Bring it here." He sat down and shuffled the deck, letting himself watch her legs as she walked over to the side table and retrieved the gilt box where he kept his coins. He watched her peek inside, thought he saw her physically react to the sight of the contents. Interesting.

"We'll use those," he told her. "I shall even allow you to keep your winnings." He would probably do well to let her win a few rounds, if only to avoid upsetting the person who held the incision knife. "We'll consider it extra wages."

She carried the box to the table, struggling visibly with its weight in a way a man would not have.

"You shouldn't be sitting up," she said sourly as she took the seat across from him.

He gestured to her to cut, and he followed, cutting the high card. Dealing put him at a disadvantage, but that was no matter in this case. "Tell me, Mr. Germain," he said as he dealt the cards, "what exactly are the supposed benefits of your strict regimen of boredom and sexual frustration?"

"If you're frustrated, it's only because you surround yourself with reminders." Her eyes stayed on her cards as she deftly sorted her hand. "Put away your knick-knacks, and you will forget all about whatever you might be missing."

"Much as they do in monasteries, hmm? I have to wonder how effective that strategy really is. Lust is a powerful force—certainly you've found that to be the case."

"Indeed." Her gaze fixed on his face, and he found her directness a bit unnerving. "I've found it can quite consume a man whose mind does not naturally lean toward substantive lines of thinking."

He felt his lips twitch. "Perhaps you could share some examples of substantive thinking."

"I would never presume to advise you on that subject." She selected three cards from her hand, placed them facedown, and drew three replacements. "Certainly you are creative enough to find ways to occupy yourself until you've recovered."

"Mmm." He exchanged four of his own cards, deliberately discarding one that might have proved helpful. "Yes, I would say I've been described as somewhat creative."

She raised her eyes from her cards. "*Healthful* ways of occupying yourself."

"Such as?"

"I cannot pretend to know how men of leisure amuse themselves, but no doubt they have any number of interests and pastimes. Reading, for example."

"Indeed. I read an amusing little novel last week about a young woman who fell prey to a libertine's seduction and found a new life that she enjoyed to the fullest—although *read* may not be precisely the right word. There were an abundance of illustrations."

"Some men read about scientific topics," she said sternly, "or they read literature."

"Do they."

"Or they engage themselves in political subjects. You must have any number of political obligations demanding your attention."

"I suppose I do, occasionally. It would seem you know more about men of leisure than you thought, Mr. Germain."

"Some men enjoy horticulture, collecting insects, observing the fauna of a particular region," she continued, completely ignoring his remark. "You could make a study of the natural world during your journey to Greece."

"And yet I'm told at every turn that my efforts to… *study the natural world* are detrimental to my health and my soul."

"There are any number of fascinating birds that dwell around the Greek isles."

He couldn't resist a grin. "Or on them."

"I was not speaking with a double entendre, Your Grace."

"Pity."

They finished the hand. She came away the winner— and would have done even had he not exchanged that high card. On the start of the next hand, she had the dealer's disadvantage.

She dealt the cards with an efficient familiarity, and

he decided perhaps he would keep his advantageous cards this time.

"Tell me, Miles—you don't mind if I address you as Miles, do you?—despite your disapproval of lusty pursuits and the double entendre, I'll wager you've enjoyed a few women while you've been in Paris."

"That isn't something that I normally discuss—"

"Confess. At least one Parisienne has welcomed you to France with open thighs."

"Not one, sir."

"Not *one?* I find that very odd for a man of your obvious youth and vigor."

"Not every man is entirely preoccupied with women—"

"Ah, I see. You prefer men. I do wish you'd told me before I sent Perry away. He had some thoughts about a possible companion whose company you may well have enjoyed—"

"That is *not* what I meant." And now her temper was starting to rise, and her brown eyes that seemed so plain earlier took on a tigress sort of luster. "If you must know, in fact, I have enjoyed a woman or two in Paris."

It was a blatant lie, of course, yet the very idea of it sent a lick of flame through his groin. He'd wager his entire collection of statuary that she'd never even enjoyed a man, let alone— Good God.

He reached for his drink. "Well, well, Miles, I daresay all this puritanical advice of yours is hypocrite's talk."

"*Medical* advice," she corrected. "Besides, I am a man, after all."

No. She was a woman, and a fairly young one, and

despite her apparent skill at cards, almost certainly an untried one. Which meant he would not be having any *real* entertainment with her—not that he had any real desire to—because contrary to popular belief, he did have a code of ethics: no virgins.

It wasn't as if he was seducing his way through England's crop of young hopefuls and leaving a trail of ruination in his wake. Which was more than could be said of any number of men he knew.

The truth was, he was *already* a moral citizen. Edward ought to have been praising Winston's restraint all these years instead of quietly suggesting that Winston reevaluate his priorities.

Change—and that vow—were entirely uncalled-for.

They finished the hand, and once again she bested him. Four more, and she'd won the game. Utterly trounced him.

She watched him with impassive eyes as he pushed a pile of coins across the table.

He raised a brow at her. "It would seem you learned more than just sailing during your four years at sea, Mr. Germain."

IT WAS LATE when Millie finally returned to her room with a pocketful of coins.

The house was quiet, all the servants asleep.

But there was one person who was not asleep. She stared at the wall of her dressing room and imagined him just on the other side, preparing for bed, and a sensation fluttered deep in her belly.

She should have absolutely refused the card game. Two hours of bantering with him, of watching him from across the table, with that wicked smile that hypnotized her every time it touched his lips—watching him watch *her* with those dark eyes that glittered like obsidian with a wit and intelligence far deeper than his bawdy talk would suggest...

She went into her bedchamber, dumped the coins on the bed and counted them briskly, pushing away the image of him in her mind.

There was nothing deep about the duke. Quite the contrary. It was only too clear that she'd accepted employment with another Lord Hensley, after she'd sworn she would die before she would enter service to another disgusting lecher.

Disgusting? That's not what you were thinking moments ago.

What she'd been thinking moments ago, she told herself sternly, was that this time she wore breeches, which would be a fair sight more difficult to reach into than her skirts had been to reach beneath—and this time, she was not the fearful, compliant girl she'd been while in Lord Hensley's employ.

If His Grace attempted anything like what Lord Hensley had done, she *would* use her incision knife, and in a manner he would not soon forget.

She finished counting and sat for a moment with her hands around the coins, silently adding the sum to the wages she would receive.

With enough time in the duke's employ, perhaps she could recoup the sums she'd lost. It made her ill just to think about all that money, gone. Five hundred pounds, stolen, ripped from her very hands. Slightly less than that left hidden aboard the *Possession*. And she would not be able to retrieve it, because she would never again be allowed to set foot aboard the ship.

Guilt stabbed her hard, and she squeezed her eyes shut against a past she could never undo. Friends betrayed. *All* of them—each and every one.

There was no one left.

For a moment the pain drove so deep she couldn't breathe. But then she managed to inhale—a thin, reedy breath that barely filled her lungs.

She didn't need anyone. She could survive on her own—she'd done it before.

Besides, a man wouldn't need anyone to help him survive.

She scooped the coins into her hands, slid off the bed and carried them to her trunk, hiding them in the secret compartment at the very bottom. And then, snuffing the candle, she climbed into bed fully clothed. The wig felt lumpy and hard between her head and the pillow. But if she put on a nightshirt, and the duke had an emergency and found his way into her rooms...

Even a man's nightshirt wouldn't conceal the truth.

It wouldn't be long. Only a matter of weeks before they arrived in Greece. And already, things had changed for the better because she'd left Millicent behind and become Miles. *Miles* Germain would not have to endure men taking lewd advantage. Miles would be taken seriously. He would be able to come and go freely. Miles would be welcome at the School of Anatomy and Surgery.

How much more would she be able to help people if she truly understood the body? If she could only see it—dissect it, explore it—so much more would make sense. Mysteries were hidden there. Treasures of knowledge that she wanted more than anything. All she had to do was imagine being at the school, participating in learned discussions about the latest medical theories, having access to thousands of texts, observing the dissection of cadavers—perhaps even participating in those, too—and she knew she could do anything the duke required of her.

If she were fortunate, she could make connections through the duke that would help establish her reputation after she'd finished at the school. Miles Germain, learned surgeon, would earn a handsome wage and be respected for his skills.

And when that day came, Millie would have no more reason to be afraid.

CHAPTER FOUR

"I MUST ADVISE against carriage travel, Your Grace," Millie warned the next morning as she followed the duke down the main staircase. His greatcoat sat around his shoulders like a cape, unable to be worn properly because of his sling.

"Advice noted," he said.

"Your wounds could easily be aggravated in a way that could cause your condition to worsen and your journey to be further delayed."

"Advice *noted,* Mr. Germain."

They exited the front door and climbed into the waiting coach—the two of them, alone, sitting across from each other as the coach lurched into motion. Millie grabbed for her medical bag to keep it from tumbling to the floor.

"If you *must* have your entertainment, then I *highly* suggest you have it at home," she said irritably. If he thought he could drag her around Paris and force her to attend him at the city's various houses of pleasure, he was very much mistaken. "I never agreed to provide my services at a brothel."

He looked at her—expression blank, eyes inscrutable—and returned his gaze out the window, dark and pensive.

The coach clattered through the streets, grand and ornate with velvet cushions that felt like being seated on a cloud. She watched him brood in silence, noticed his jaw clench each time the coach hit a rut.

For heaven's sake, what entertainment could possibly be worth what he must be suffering? The damage he would likely do to his wounds? She'd read about this kind of abnormality—men for whom no pleasure was ever enough, who exposed themselves to any kind of danger in pursuit of ever greater stimulation, until…

The coach slowed.

The duke's lips thinned.

The coach came to a stop—

Next to a cemetery.

"Wait here," he ordered when the coach door opened.

Dear God. Harris and Sacks had been mistaken. Lord Winston was attending the burial, after all.

She watched him climb out, clearly in considerably greater pain than when he had climbed in. A footman opened the cemetery gate, but he waved the servant away. Beyond, among the headstones, a group of people was already gathered. A fine mist put a sheen on every stone and blade of grass.

A woman dressed in black sank into a curtsy the moment he joined them. The duke reached out to stop her and pull her gently upright. Nearby, five children huddled together.

He ordered five hundred pounds sent this afternoon.

And now he was here, standing out in the drizzle with his injuries doubtless paining him like the devil, clasping his hands in front of him while a priest spoke at the edge of the grave.

Millie watched through the coach window. A slow bead of moisture skidded down the outside of the pane. Next to the grave, the widow held a handkerchief to her face.

When he finally turned back toward the coach, Millie scooted away from the window and opened her medical bag, pretending to be preoccupied with the contents.

He climbed carefully back into the coach. Settled against the seat. Inhaled deeply. Exhaled. "Sodding, bloody state of affairs," he muttered as the coach rolled away.

"My condolences," she said.

"I didn't even know the man." He stared out at the passing streets as they clattered back toward the house. "He left a widow and five children." And that upset him. The distress was plain on his face.

"It was kind of you to think of them today," she said.

"Kind." The word shot from his lips, and his eyes shifted to her. "Kindness never raised the dead, Mr. Germain."

"Perhaps not, but it shows them respect, and it comforts the living." Which he already knew, or he would not have risked his own health to attend.

"He was an utter stranger. The entire debacle was complete happenstance—matter of timing. He died, I didn't." He said it flatly, matter-of-factly.

But a shiver touched her deep inside. "I see."

His hooded gaze said she could not possibly see. And his attention returned to the window.

The man seated across from her was not the man she'd met yesterday in his bedchamber, surrounded by highflyers.

"How are your injuries?" she asked.

"A man is dead, Mr. Germain. My injuries are nothing next to that."

"They will be if they fester and leave you dead, as well."

"Perhaps that would only be perverse justice."

It took a moment to credit his words. "Forgive me," she ventured slowly. "Of course your own death would put everything to rights."

"Mock me again," he said sharply, looking at her once more, "and you'll return to Lady Pennington minus your wages."

The coach hit an especially deep pothole, and he hissed, squeezing his eyes shut. For a moment she could almost imagine she felt his pain herself.

"Is there anything I can do that will help?" she said, more gently than she might have.

Those dark eyes opened, fixing on her with a shadow of pain that no compress could touch. "Are there any medicaments you can prescribe that will undo the past, Mr. Germain?"

IF THERE WERE any such medicaments, she would gladly take them herself.

After they returned to the house, Millie applied fresh dressings and compresses to his wounds and gave him a concoction to drink, and then there was nothing left to do for him except leave him to rest.

Downstairs in the library, she scoured the shelves for anything medical, and finally found a French volume about the nervous system that had been published in the past century, tucked in a row of books wedged between bookends formed like a woman's bottom and thighs.

She sighed and slipped the volume from the shelf. It was better than nothing.

For a moment she stared at those bookends, thinking of the man who owned them. If he'd been contemplating pleasures of the flesh this afternoon, he'd given no hint of it.

All around, the ornate library testified to his decadent mode of living. Here, as in the salon where she'd waited yesterday, the ceilings boasted vast paintings of colorful and illicit love affairs, edged by intricate plasterwork decorated with gold.

The furnishings were lush, befitting his rank, yet scattered about the room in an almost careless manner that seemed to perfectly reflect the man himself.

And yet…

Was it possible the accident truly had affected him? Could this afternoon have marked the first inkling of changes to come?

Her gaze landed on a Grecian plaque depicting a variety of ancient sex acts. *Of course not, Millicent. A man like that doesn't change.*

And yet, she couldn't shake the memory of his demeanor in the coach—his troubled eyes, his silence, as if perhaps he truly was grieving the death of a stranger.

There was no knowing, so she ordered tea, went upstairs and locked herself away in her dressing room to study until he awoke and required her attention again.

Within two hours' time, she began to hear noise through the wall. Five minutes more, ten, fifteen, and the noise and laughter coming from His Grace's suite of rooms had grown to a crescendo.

She stared at the bookcase. He had company again? So much for the inkling of changes to come.

She continued trying to read, but concentration became impossible. Plugging her ears only proved distracting. She caught herself clenching her teeth and finally stood up, glaring at the bookcase.

What she wouldn't give to march in there and evict the entire lot at pistol point.

Apparently all that business in the carriage this afternoon was nothing more than self-pity. And to think she'd begun to feel sympathy for him. Well, the sooner that debauched devil of a man recovered from his injuries, the better.

But not too soon. She needed all the money she could get from him.

A volley of laughter battered the wall.

She narrowed her eyes at the bookcase. Perhaps she *would* go over there. Make a big fuss about his health— more of a fuss than was strictly necessary—and if nothing else, give herself the satisfaction of interfering with his pleasure-seeking.

She grabbed her medical bag and went to her door, only to hear a knock. She opened it to find Sacks—

"His Grace is asking for you, Mr. Germain."

—summoning her.

"Now? Surely he can't be asking for medical attention."

Sacks grinned. "I believe it's more of an invitation, you fortunate cur."

"An *invitation*." That was a different situation entirely.

"Play your cards right, and you'll be readying for bed with company."

An invitation. She forced her lips into what she hoped was dry recognition of the possibilities. "You have a point."

"That's the spirit." Sacks laughed. "You'll learn the way of things 'round here."

Oh, the way of things around here was already perfectly clear. And suddenly she was angry—furious that he could pretend such distress and then, a few short hours later, act as if he hadn't a care in the world.

Invitation or no, she kept a firm grip on her medical bag and walked down the corridor and into the duke's apartment.

And there he was, on a sofa in his dressing room with a courtesan on either side of him, the afternoon's burial apparently forgotten.

"Ah, here is my new medic now," he announced when he saw her. The quality of his voice told her he was feeling his liquor—and the tilt of his smile told her he wasn't thinking of any widow and children now. The woman to his right wore an elaborate blue gown cut so that it concealed...very little. The duke had his arm around her, laughing, drinking deeply from a glass in his other hand.

Almost immediately a young Parisienne appeared at Millie's side. *"Bonsoir,"* she said, taking Millie's arm with one hand and resting her other palm flat against Millie's chest, smoothing it a little across Millie's lapel—dangerously close to a place Millie did not want her to touch for any number of reasons, the least of which being that the binding around her breasts was not completely effective, and she relied on the drape of her clothing to conceal what the binding could not.

Thank God her own breasts were not as generous as this woman's, or all would be revealed regardless of disguise.

"Bonsoir," Millie murmured, removing the woman's hand, too aware that she had the duke's full attention.

"Bring Mr. Germain a drink," the duke said, drawing lazy circles near the top of his companion's breasts.

The tormented man in the carriage was gone.

"No, thank you," Millie said firmly, approaching the sofa where he sat, lowering her voice. "I've only come to remind Your Grace that all this activity may not be wise."

"When did wisdom ever lead to entertainment?" And he might be laughing, but now she saw that his mouth was a bit strained and the laughter didn't quite reach his eyes.

"*Lack* of wisdom could easily lead to a sudden decline," she countered, and a servant placed a glass into her free hand while she spoke.

"Perhaps you'd care to join a game," he suggested.

"A medic and a gamer, eh?" an Englishman called over from one of several gaming tables. "Do, do! We've just finished and are about to begin another."

Across the room next to the duke's curio cabinet, a gentleman was tying a blindfold around a laughing woman wearing only her stays and petticoats.

Hmm. Perhaps joining a game could be advantageous—both for her purse and her desire to be rid of these revelers.

"I do believe I shall," she said, and Lord Winston grinned.

"Have a care with my medic, Perry," he called over to the card table. "I'll not have him taken advantage of."

Millie glanced at him as she seated herself at the card table and realized he found this entire thing amusing.

Her new female companion perched on the edge of Millie's chair, leaning so close that her bosom practically spilled into Millie's face.

One of the men at the table laughed, and too late Millie realized she had leaned away.

"Say, Winston—I daresay your medic here is only too ripe for an education, both at cards and at women." And then, to Millie, "But never fear, young lad. Mademoiselle Hélène will give you any experience you like."

Now Millie's face was inches from the woman's bosom, and she was staring directly into a deep cleavage that would have had a real man salivating like a hungry dog.

She moistened her lips and hoped it made her appear at least a little bit tempted.

"I'm feeling a bit…warm," the woman whispered suggestively in French. "Perhaps you can help me, *monsieur le médecin.*"

Little did she know. "Perhaps I can at that," she murmured, hoping she sounded genuinely interested. "Only let me collect some winnings first, hmm?"

"Oh, ho!" the man named Perry laughed. "Our young medic is more confident than he first appeared!"

The men at the table laughed, clearly believing they would fleece her of every last penny in short order.

They began the game, and Millie made a few mistakes on purpose, throwing the first round. And then, slowly, she began to change her tactics.

"Tiens, Monsieur Germain," one of the men said after a few rounds, by which time Millie had collected a sum about equal to that of everyone else at the table, "Perhaps I only imagine it, but Winston appears a trifle piqued."

Now the one named Perry glanced at the duke, who was engrossed in conversation while a woman nuzzled his neck. "Not as well as he'd like us all to believe, eh?"

"On the contrary," Millie said. "His injuries are progressing nicely."

And now, like a golden egg dropped in her lap, was the opportunity she'd been looking for.

"Wears on a man, that sort of thing," Perry said, shaking his head. "So difficult to imagine— Ho, Blanchet! Almost had her that time!"

Millie glanced over her shoulder and saw the object of Lord Perry's amusement—a man playing a game of undress-me-if-you-can with one of Winston's strumpets. "Exhausting," Perry said now, shaking his head, and she realized he was once again speaking of Winston.

"Mmm," she agreed, and played a card. "Especially with the— Well, he wouldn't want me to speak of that." She rearranged her hand and looked up to find Perry's attention torn between his own cards and her little "slip."

"Has he got something more than the injuries?"

"Forgive me. I spoke out of turn. His Grace's conditions are a confidential matter between him and me. You understand, of course."

"Of course."

"Le pauvre," the woman perched on the edge of Millie's chair said, looking at the duke. Poor thing? Hardly. "I think I shall go comfort him." How she would find room on the already crowded sofa was a mystery.

"That might not be…" Millie paused and shook her head. "No, I doubt he's contagious."

"Contagieux," one of the others said sharply under his breath. "How could it be that a few cuts and bruises are contagious?"

"Do forgive me," Millie said. "I should not have said anything. Please—let us not speak of it further."

As if divinely preplanned, the duke sipped his drink and coughed—twice, three times—and all eyes at the table shot in his direction.

Millie frowned thoughtfully at the Frenchman seated to her left. "I do believe it's your turn?"

His eyes dropped to his hand. *"Oui. Bien sûr."* He played a card.

Millie lowered her voice and murmured to the woman sitting beside her, "I suppose I would be wrong not to ask…none of you young women have been…" She trailed off again, shook her head once more. "Ah, well. In any case, what's done is done."

Worry tugged at the woman's carefully groomed brows. *"Quoi?"* she whispered urgently. *"Dites-moi."*

"I'm quite sure, as long as you don't plan on any further intimacies with him…"

"Mais, non," the woman assured her, eyes fixed on the duke. "Definitely not."

"I'm almost certain you needn't worry," Millie reassured her.

"I do believe," one of the players said to the others at the table, clearing his throat, "that the Comte d'Anterry had an entertainment planned for this evening."

Just then another of the duke's friends approached the table and leaned close to Perry. "You look disturbed. *Qu'est-ce que c'est?*"

"It's probably nothing." Lord Perry looked to Millie for confirmation. Mille only raised a brow.

The player to her left leaned across the table and spoke in a low voice. "We have just learned from Monsieur Germain that Winston is *contagieux*."

"Dieu." The man straightened sharply. Glanced over his shoulder.

"It's likely nothing," Millie told them. "I shouldn't have mentioned it. His Grace would be furious with me. Please—you mustn't say a word."

"Mais, non," the new man said, still looking surreptitiously at Winston. "Of course not."

One of the men at the table set down his cards and cleared his throat. "I do believe I never made proper excuses to d'Anterry. I'd best put in an appearance."

She watched the man walk over and make his excuses to the duke—from a safe distance, of course—and exit the chamber with two of the courtesans at his side.

Within fifteen minutes, fully half the room had emptied.

Within twenty-five, the room was unoccupied except for herself and the duke. He still sat on the sofa where he'd been since she arrived. She still sat at the card table, alone now with another—albeit much smaller—stack of winnings.

"Perhaps you would be so good as to tell me," Winston drawled, "what you've said to all my guests that has left me once again without company."

"I assure you, I am just as disappointed in the company's departure as you are. Just when I was holding out hope that the lovely Mademoiselle Hélène might be agreeable to a few moments of diversion."

"Were you?"

"Only with Your Grace's blessing, naturally."

"Naturally. Perhaps we could call her back. You could tell her you were mistaken about whatever you told them and have your entertainment, after all." He pinned her with that dark devil-gaze. "I hate to see you disappointed."

After what she'd just witnessed, she refused to be intimidated. "You are too kind. Unfortunately, my duties as your employed medic must come before my own pleasure. If I'm to ensure that Your Grace is in a proper condition to endure the strain of a journey to Greece, then moderation is in order."

"Did you tell them I had some kind of disease?"

"Good heavens, you don't have any disease."

"A mysterious fever?"

"You're not feverish, Your Grace."

"I'm well aware of that," he bit out. "A pox? Is that what you told them?"

She swept the coins from the table into her hand, then dumped them into her coat pocket. "Your Grace has already assured me no such condition is currently present."

"No such condition has *ever* been present, Mr. Germain."

"Well, I certainly didn't say anything about a pox. Or a rash."

"You told them I have a *rash?*"

"I said I *didn't* tell them that."

"I don't have a rash!" he exploded, just as Harris came through the door. Harris paused, hesitating.

"Mademoiselle Hélène is inquiring after her wrap," he said.

Millie spotted it on a chair in the corner and took it to Harris. "Please give Mademoiselle Hélène His Grace's assurances that her wrap has not been contaminated with any rash."

"Assure the woman of nothing except my continuing regard," the duke bit out sharply.

"Naturally, Your Grace." Harris bowed and left with the wrap.

He ought to dismiss her.

Winston stared at Miles Germain across his now-silent dressing room and contemplated his options—which, of course, were many.

"Let us have one thing very clear between us, Mr. Germain," he said now, not getting up from the sofa, but only because he didn't want to. Not because his leg hurt like the devil and the beginnings of a headache throbbed behind his eyes. "You are here to administer medical care, by which I mean compresses and bandages and the like."

"Which will do little good if you do not follow my advice."

"If I want medical *advice,* Mr. Germain, I will ask for it."

And there was that line above her lip.

Devil *take* it. He'd been doing perfectly well ten minutes ago. But now that everyone was gone, the day's events—his entire life's events—were returning to torment him with a vengeance.

Attending that burial was a mistake. Ordering her to accompany him doubly so.

"If I want to entertain guests, then I shall. Is that understood?"

"Perfectly."

"Without interference of any kind."

"As you wish."

"And that, Mr. Germain, is something you'd best remember. As *I* wish. Not as *you* wish." Yet even now he doubted her capacity to comprehend that basic reality.

The question now was how best to undo the damage she'd done. By now the news of his rash—or whatever the bloody hell she'd told them—would have made its way to half the salons in Paris.

He *should* dismiss her. And if her ministrations weren't having an effect already, despite his disregarding her advice, he *would* dismiss her. But even a man as stubborn and reckless as he could tell that the switch from turpentine to whatever she was mixing was helping.

He would have to hire a reputable physician to give him a clean report and then not so discreetly let it be known that the young Mr. Germain's assessment had been mistaken.

He rubbed his forehead, pinched the bridge of his nose.

"Perhaps you ought to return to your bed," she said now. And then, quickly—sarcastically?— "Forgive me. You'll need to define 'advice' so that I understand very clearly what recommendations I am allowed and which I am not."

"Any recommendations pertaining to my choice of entertainment," he ground out, "are strictly forbidden."

"Then advice to take to your bed, depending on the circumstances, may or may not…" She trailed off, furrowing her brows even as a spark of triumph in her eyes made it clear she was toying with him. Still. Now.

Standing there in her bagwig and breeches, she probably fancied herself immune to seduction.

If he were willing to show her his hand and reveal that he had seen through her disguise, it would take all of five minutes to prove to her she was mistaken. And then they would see about that advice to take to his bed.

If he were willing to seduce a virgin. Which he was not.

The reason why not snuck in like a cold draft on a winter day, carrying his vow with it, and now he pushed himself off the sofa, keeping a hand on its back for balance against a sudden light-headedness.

"There's been a change of plans," he told her now, hearing himself as if listening to someone else.

Consider your ways, Winston. It was the only thing Edward had ever asked in the face of Winston's sin against him so many years ago.

"We shan't be traveling to Greece, but to my estate."

"Your *estate*." Her words shot across the room.

It was a ridiculous notion that wouldn't change anything. The past was as immutable as the names on the headstones in that cemetery this morning. His sin against Edward—against Cara—could never be repaired.

Denying himself would not change that.

Keeping that ridiculous vow would not change it, either. And yet...

"Yes."

"But the understanding was we would be traveling to Greece," she said sharply.

Her eyes shot daggers at him. And...fear? "Indeed, it was. But circumstances compel me to return to my estate instead. I will still require your services for the journey."

"But I can't go to England."

"No?" he asked irritably. "Are you in exile?"

She inhaled visibly. "What I meant to say was that I did not expect to go to England and I do not wish to go to England."

"Much, perhaps, as I did not expect or wish for my medic to drive away my acquaintances by implying I am a threat to their health."

She took a few anxious steps forward. "I shall tell them all I was mistaken. That I lied, even."

Her sudden turn toward desperation was fascinating. "I haven't changed my plans because of that, Mr. Germain."

"Then why?"

Why, indeed. In those moments on the street, when a piece of that building could have fallen and smashed his own skull, he hadn't actually made a promise to Edward. Hadn't made a promise to anyone. They were just words, uttered in a moment of terror.

By God, I'll do it!

It was more an oath than a promise, anyway. But he'd made a decision about Greece, and he would probably regret it, but it bloody well wasn't Miles Germain's place to question him. By withdrawing to his estate, removing himself from temptation, perhaps he would miraculously become the man Edward wanted him to be.

"Was there a reason you had hoped to go to Greece?" he asked.

"Not at all," she said quickly. It was obviously a lie. He watched her thinking, contemplating the change of events, weighing her options—which, if he didn't miss his guess, were few.

He already knew she was hungry for the wages from his employment. But her counting on Greece, as well...

Mattered not one whit to him.

"The journey to Greece would have been much longer than a simple jaunt to England," she pointed out now. "The change will have an effect on my wages."

"You needn't fear for your wages," he told her. "I intend to keep you in my employ at my estate until I make a full recovery, at which time you will be free to travel anywhere you like."

And by which time he would doubtless have proved once and for all his own folly and the imprudence of reading too much into a single, random incident.

CHAPTER FIVE

THEY ARRIVED AT the estate in the moonlight, amid the loud clang and clatter of carriages and the shouts of footmen as they pulled to a stop in front of a palatial house ablaze with whale oil and candles. Outside lanterns around the grand entrance cast V-shaped spills of light against the smooth facade, and already the main doors were being opened, and through them Millie could see servants crossing this way and that in a glittering entrance hall with red-and-white marble floors, preparing for His Grace's midnight arrival.

"I think the wound on my thigh is bleeding again," Winston said as he prepared to get up.

Of course it was. They *should* have stayed in Paris, where they *should* have been making leisurely preparations for Greece.

"Fysiká," she said under her breath. Instead, they'd made a reckless and hasty journey here. To England.

He looked at her sharply. "Pardon me?"

"Naturally," she repeated in English, and much more deferentially. "I shall inspect it the moment you're settled."

"Did you just speak to me in *Greek?*"

"I'm sure I don't know what you mean. We are in England, Your Grace."

Those devil eyes narrowed at her. His humor had deteriorated steadily the closer they'd come to his estate— a ridiculously hard push of travel aided by a full moon and perfect weather in the channel, which had put them here in less than two days.

He had required her presence in his coach in case he needed her, but had spent most of the time trying to sleep, and she had spent most of the time trying to read. Harris and Sacks and a few others came in the carriages behind.

A footman opened the coach door. Winston stepped out, and Millie followed without being handed down, as any man in service would.

The house seemed to extend as far as the eye could see in both directions, the farther reaches of it covered by the shadows of night. Beyond loomed great murky masses of trees. It seemed to have hundreds of windows, all framed by carved stone, many flickering with light. Nobody was counting candles here. Above, silhouetted against the sky, dozens of chimneys testified to an enormous number of rooms.

Only imagine how many nude statues a building of this size could hold. The wild debauches that must take place here and that would no doubt begin immediately now that His Grace had returned.

Indeed, Millie thought as she was swept through the grand entrance on a wave of activity in His Grace's wake, Lord Winston's country estate was everything a ducal residence should be.

There was only one thing it wasn't.

Greece.

Inside, Harris began giving instructions to half-a-dozen servants, and footmen carried trunks up a massive red marble staircase that curved in two directions. Winston exchanged a few words with Sacks, and then with a woman who looked like she must be in charge of the house.

The entrance hall alone was so vast one could probably build a ship inside it.

The walls were deep red, the ceiling covered with murals and edged with gold plasterwork. Five chandeliers blazed with candles.

And that was when Millie realized there wasn't a nude to be seen save for the paintings on the ceiling. There was hardly any artwork at all. Few statues—a bronze horseman in a corner of the entrance hall, and through a doorway she could see the bust of a man on one side of a hall that looked as if it was made of gold and extended for a mile.

There were no paintings, few sculptures.

After what she'd seen in Paris, it didn't seem possible.

And then Winston was climbing the stairs, and Harris came to tell her that she would be taking a room on the same floor and in the same wing as Winston's so that she could properly attend him, and soon Millie was shown to another apartment, this one twice as grand as the one she'd been given in Paris, and ten times larger.

Footmen brought her trunk plus another that held all the medical supplies she'd collected in Paris and carried for the trip.

And still the question remained: What were they *doing* here? She never should have said a word to his guests that night. If only she hadn't opened her bloody mouth and sent everyone away, giving him the opportunity to think. With all that distraction, he would never have considered returning to his estate.

If she'd known it was a choice between his ribald entertainments or this monumental setback...

She'd barely unlatched her trunk when the duke's sharp bark shot faintly down the corridor.

"Mr. Germain!"

Devil take the man, anyway. She'd never known a person to change their mind as erratically as he did. And now here she was. In England.

She went down the hallway to the duke's bedchamber and found him seated on the edge of a chair with his breeches around his knees and blood seeping through the bandage on his thigh.

"Oh, for God's sake," she muttered.

"You say that as if it's my fault."

"It *is* your fault. This never would have happened if we'd gone to Greece." It was the kind of statement that could get her dismissed, but after crossing the channel and riding nonstop over rutted roads deep into the night, she was too aggravated to care.

"I don't want to hear another word about Greece," he said as she crouched in front of him and began unwinding the bandage. "Do I make myself clear?"

"Polú."

"And I do not want to be spoken to in Greek."

"Bene."

"Or Italian. Or *any* foreign tongue."

She tucked the bandage back in place for the moment. "I'll have to bring more lint and fresh bandages.

Lie down and elevate the leg on a pillow, and I shall return momentarily."

There was no reason he could not have continued to recover in Paris. No reason at all.

Within a quarter of an hour, she'd stopped the bleeding, applied fresh dressings and bandages, and the duke was resting comfortably.

Except that he wasn't.

"Devil *take* this blasted sling." He shifted, reaching behind his shoulder, tugging on the strap. "I can't quite seem to…"

"Stop fussing and let me do it," she said, and leaned across him.

"I'm not fussing." His voice feathered her jaw as if he spoke against her skin, even though he was inches away.

The front of her coat grazed his chest as she adjusted the sling.

Her hip pressed against his arm.

And it didn't matter how many times she'd done this for him… Little sensations shot through her, tickling her lungs and tripping through her belly.

He stopped struggling—seemed to stop everything, even breathing, while she worked at the strap.

And then it was finished, and she stepped back. "Better?"

"Yes."

She turned to her medical supplies even though there was nothing she needed.

"What in God's name am I supposed to do now?" he muttered behind her, as if it wasn't the wee hours of the morning.

"May I suggest *sleeping?*"

"That's not what I meant."

She turned back to find his gaze shifting about the room as if he'd never seen the place before. "I'm sure there will be no need for that question once your company arrives," she said.

"There isn't going to be any company."

She looked at him. "No company?"

"Rest and solitude," he said shortly. "That is your prescription, is it not?"

"Yes. Yes, it is." And that was why he was here? For rest and solitude? "Although I seem to recall Your Grace referred to it as my strict regimen of boredom and frustration."

He grunted an unhappy acknowledgment.

She clenched her jaw. *Now* he wanted to follow her advice? Now that her entire plan was in tatters? Bloody nobles and their whims—and she was the one to pay the price. Greece or England…what could it possibly matter to him?

And now, looking around, she saw that his apartment was just as free from lewd knickknacks as the entrance hall had been. There wasn't a breast or phallus to be seen. "Is this where you always come to withdraw from entertainment?"

He looked at her. "Quite," he drawled, and his lip curved a little in that semi-amused smile that made him look impossibly wicked. "I've always liked to think of Winston as my refuge from all things carnal."

MOMENTS LATER, OUTSIDE Winston's apartment, Millie found Harris and Sacks conferring tight-lipped at the top of the stairs.

"Everything's been put away," Harris told her in an alarming tone when she joined them. He took a pinch of snuff and scowled down the staircase. "The paintings, the sculptures...I'm told a letter arrived from Paris only this morning, instructing that everything of a certain nature be put away in the attic."

Everything of a certain nature?

"Even the portrait in 'is bedroom is gone," Sacks grumbled. "Princess What's-'er-Name from Prussia. I'll miss that portrait," he said, irritated. "She was a damned ripe one."

Refuge from all things carnal, indeed. And yet... "He *instructed* them put away?" Millie asked.

Sacks took his turn at the snuff, sniffed, rubbed his nose and nodded. "The whole lot of it."

"When he decided to return to Winston," Harris said, "I was convinced that all was finally becoming as it should be. After all..." He gestured lamely toward the staircase.

"After all," Sacks said, "there's never any lack of sporting activities 'round here."

There wasn't, was there?

"So I am to understand," Millie said slowly, "that His Grace normally entertains while he is in residence."

"Entertains!" Harris barked, then hushed his voice. "This house has seen routs that would redden a harlot's cheeks."

Of course it had. Millie stared down the corridor toward the duke's apartment. Rest and solitude. Apparently he had gone to great lengths to achieve it. Because of his health?

If she'd realized *that,* she would have taken special care to emphasize the benefits of a warm climate.

"It can't be permanent, can it?" Harris asked her. "His Grace's lack of interest?"

"He seemed interested enough in Paris, didn't he?" Millie snipped.

"That?" Sacks lowered his voice. "He hasn't *interested* himself with a single one—not since the accident." Suddenly his monstrous dark brows knitted completely together. "The accident didn't—" he gestured in front of his crotch "—damage his vitals…?"

Oh, for heaven's sake. "No."

"He spoke of nothing but Grecian orgies for weeks before we left for Paris," Harris told her. "He spoke of little else in Paris, as well."

"Well, now he says he doesn't want anything to do with Greece," Millie said. "He says he wants rest and solitude."

"Rest and solitude."

She didn't believe it for a minute. He was being flighty, making more out of his injuries than he needed to, and costing her the price of travel from England to the Mediterranean in the process.

If he'd just gone to Greece, the trip would have cost her nothing, *and* she would have been collecting wages the entire time.

"We ought to bring the whole bloody lot down from the attic while he's sleeping," Sacks grumbled. "Let 'im wake to that magnificent pair of Prussian breasts and see if it doesn't restore 'im to full operation."

Millie looked at him.

Sacks shifted his gaze to Harris, who frowned.

"We couldn't simply…" The idea hung in the air. "Couldn't we?"

"Indeed," Millie said slowly, considering the possibilities. "In fact, I might even recommend it. As a restorative measure for his health."

As changeable as the duke clearly was, a bit of encouragement could be all it would take for him to abandon this plan and set out once more for Greece.

"That is to say," she went on, "it's never a good sign when a person loses interest in his usual activities." That much was true. And it wasn't as if the duke weren't capable of enjoying himself—hadn't Paris proved that?

It had.

Now Sacks was nodding. Harris raised a considering brow. And Millie could not believe she was suggesting this, but if it would work…

"A dose of his usual *mode of living*," she said authoritatively, "could be just the curative he needs."

WINSTON STOOD IN his library the next morning, staring at the empty spot above the fireplace where a carved wood panel from India used to hang, and contemplated ordering his bags packed for Greece, after all. Or at least Paris.

What the devil was he *doing* here?

He needed company. Women. In his bed, on top of his desk, against his bloody *wall,* and he needed them now.

This was folly. Changing his entire existence because of a freak accident…

Because it could have been you.

But it wasn't.

And because of Cara and Edward.

Devil take it. One incident fifteen years ago— something that couldn't be changed—had no bearing on the present.

He treaded lightly toward the windows, careful not to disturb his freshly bandaged leg. The empty house felt like a tomb. Looked like a bloody monastery. At the very least he could order all the adornments taken from the attic put back in place.

He didn't even know what to do with himself.

One very particular activity leaped to mind, and God's blood, *this* was what it had come to? Fantasizing about pleasuring *himself*?

Reading, Miles had suggested. But all his favorite books had been stored away in the attic with the rest.

He paced a few feet to the nearest bookcase, built between two windows, and pulled a book from the shelf. Flipped through its pages. Slammed it shut.

He didn't want to read. He wanted to do something very, very different from reading.

His hands tightened around the book.

He breathed deeply. Forced himself to remember the accident. The burial. The widow and her five children, standing in the gray drizzle while the priest tossed clumps of mud into the grave. The way those clumps had hit the coffin with a soft splat.

He would do this. He would sit his arse down and read this goddamned book and he would not think about any of the things he *wasn't* doing, because the man in that coffin wasn't doing them, either.

He sat. Opened the book cover. *Fauna of the Tidal Flats of Devon.*

Perfect.

He leafed through the pages, found a plate illustrating a clam digging through mud. And damnation if the clam's extended foot didn't look exactly like a man's—

"Excuse me, Your Grace. I thought I should see if you require anything for your comfort."

Miles's voice cut into his thoughts and nearly startled him. She stood there looking…younger than he might have liked. His comfort? Oh, indeed—but not at all in the manner she meant. "Thank you, Mr. Germain. I'm doing well enough at the moment. Are you settling in?"

"Yes."

"And everything is to your satisfaction?"

"Not at all, Your Grace."

Somehow that was no longer a surprise. He watched her wander into the library and wondered if she realized how much her face gave away as she stared at the vast shelves.

She had a hunger for these books that he could scarcely fathom.

Her lips were parted a little, and he studied them, only now realizing that he knew their curve and color by heart.

He returned his attention to the book. "There are some who find my estate quite comfortable, believe it or not," he said, feeling unaccountably grouchy.

"No doubt they do." From the corner of his eye, he saw her move closer. He shifted his eyes, watching her legs as she moved. "What are you reading?"

His gaze snapped back to the page. "A treatise about tidal flats."

"Have you a particular interest in tidal flats?"

"Yes." He'd never thought about tidal flats in his life. "I find them fascinating."

"Indeed? I never would have guessed." She didn't sound pleased.

"I can hardly keep my eyes from the page." He started to read aloud. "'The lugworm is a creature that buries itself in the soft, wet sands,'" he began, then wished he hadn't, because the concept of being buried in anything soft and wet was not helpful. He skimmed ahead. Ah, yes. "'It feeds on detritus left behind by other creatures, such as the fecal matter of clams and other burrowing mollusks.'" He looked up at Miles and smiled. "Fascinating."

That line appeared above her lip. "Such a marked change from your interests in Paris, which as I recall, were—"

"I am quite aware of what they were." He looked up now, straight into her eyes—good God, he knew those by heart now, too, with their deep brown streaks set in rich walnut—and held her gaze on purpose, but she refused to look away. "As I've said, this house is my retreat from the world." Starting yesterday, anyhow. "When I'm here, I indulge all of my quieter interests."

"Such as reading." She said it doubtfully, as if she wondered whether he could read at all.

"Among other things, yes."

"What other things?"

Oh, for God's sake. "Any number of things. Was there something you wanted, Mr. Germain?"

Because the longer she stood there, the more there was something *he* wanted, and he could *not* start down that road or there would be no end to the torment. He was alone in this blasted house, and the only women here now were the servants, whom he refused to turn to because he wasn't running a brothel…

And her.

She smiled tightly. "Not at all, Your Grace. I shall leave you. Happy reading."

Oh, indeed. He let his eyes follow her as she walked out—her legs, anyhow, encased in their breeches—and thought of something that would make him incredibly happy, and it had nothing to do with reading.

CHAPTER SIX

"READING," HARRIS SCOWLED, then narrowed one eye. "Well, if it's reading he wants, then I know just the thing."

Ten minutes later, Millie stood with Harris in an attic room packed with erotic art. "He ordered it all stored away up here," Harris said, and led her through the statues and paintings to a set of trunks, which he opened to reveal a large collection of books. "If he wants to read, let him read these."

And so as evening fell, and His Grace was safely upstairs resting, Millie snuck into the library. Tidal flats, indeed. If he was going to change his mind about Greece, he would not change it because of any feces-eating lugworm.

Millie finished slipping the seventeenth potential motivation onto the bookshelves in His Grace's library—thank you, Harris and Sacks—and stepped back. In a library this size, he might not even find these books. Perhaps...

She glanced at the desk, where three books sat together in a stack. If it wouldn't be too obvious, she would plant one there. But he had certainly set those books aside himself, and he would know immediately if someone had added a title—especially a title as eye catching as *A Widow's Adventures, being the Story of a False Virgin Unmasked.*

She narrowed her eyes at a shelf near the floor by the window, where a book had fallen over. Hmm. She glanced over her shoulder, went to the bookcase, crouched down. Added *A Widow's Adventures* on its side next to the other fallen book—*A Beekeeper's Guide*—and stood up. Nudged the widow's adventures a bit to the right with her toe.

There. That stood a good chance of catching his attention. Except...

She frowned at a space on the next shelf up. Would he ever notice a book lying so close to the floor?

She picked it up. Spent a moment second-guessing the new location—

"Looking for any book in particular, Mr. Germain?"

Devil *take* it.

The book felt coal-hot in her hands. She didn't dare put it down, didn't dare keep it—

"Not I, Your Grace," she said accusingly, turning, holding the book out, "but I see that *you* have been doing a bit of reading—and exactly the sort you should *not* be doing. This is precisely the kind of thing I advised you against," she preached, tapping the book's cover. "And here I find it within easy reach of your desk. How do you expect to make any sort of quick recovery when you're exciting the senses with—" she leafed quickly through the book and stopped at the first image she came to "—with *this.*"

Which turned out to be—dear God—an engraving of a man fondling the merry widow's breasts.

The duke glanced at it, at her, and raised a brow. "How indeed."

"I can't think why you hired me if you didn't plan to follow my recommendations." Millie's cheeks flamed hot. She pretended it was indignation.

"You needn't be embarrassed in front of me," he said. "I am all too sympathetic to a man's weaknesses." He reached for the book, took it from her hands. "Let us see what you've been entertaining yourself with, shall we, Mr. Germain?"

"Your Grace, I assure you—" *That I was not entertaining myself.*

"Mmm, yes," he murmured, paging through it, glancing at the images, skimming. He looked up. Offered a little grin that she felt in her knees. "Do let us peruse it together, shall we? Perhaps with a bit of snuff and some brandy?"

Because that, apparently, was what men did?

"There's nothing healthful about snuff," she said. *And I don't wish to peruse that book with you.* Except there could be no assurance that he would peruse it on his own if she made her excuses.

"Just the brandy, then. Ah—here's a fun one." He turned the book around and held it out so she could see the image.

She nearly choked, and he had yet to call for the brandy. "Exceedingly fun," she said. If you enjoyed images of a man's exposed organ taking aim at a woman's exposed—

"Read to me while I pour, will you?" He handed her the book.

"Your Grace, you misunderstand the situation. I suppose it's time for me to admit that I cannot stop you from such pursuits with any amount of healthful reasoning." She put the book down—open, of course, to the plate he'd found, and facing his direction—and gave him what she hoped was a look of resignation. "Perhaps there *is* something healthful about a man's happiness, even if it comes from…"

He returned with two glasses and glanced down at the book. "From the wheelbarrow position?"

"Precisely."

He held out a glass, and she took it, and her fingertips brushed his—warm, thick, solid.

A quiet tingle found its way down her throat to her belly, and she swallowed before even raising the glass to her lips.

"Let me assure you," he said, "that I instructed every form of entertainment in the house to be locked away in the attic before our arrival. I have the utmost respect for your medical opinion, Mr. Germain."

Indeed. Now that he'd brought her to England. "You will tell me if you start to feel any adverse effects from the deprivation," she said.

His lips curved. "Consider yourself told. I have been feeling any number of…*adverse effects* since we left Paris."

"Well, then. That certainly explains why you couldn't resist the need to…" She gestured toward the book. "Indulge."

Now he laughed, coming around the table and standing much too close to her—or he probably only seemed too close because the wicked light in his eyes was making her very, very uncomfortable. Her gaze fixed on his mouth, and suddenly she wondered what it might feel like to have a man's lips—his lips—pressed against hers. What it might feel like to be kissed. By him.

She pushed the thought away as quickly as it came.

"Mr. Germain," he said in a confidential tone, "surely, as a man, you understand all too well—and believe it that I confide in you only as my medical advisor and for no other reason—that my idea of *indulging* includes a great deal more than simply viewing a crude sketch of such a pleasurable activity."

"Indeed. All too well." His scent filled the air around her, aristocratic and sensual, and if only she were taller she could look him more directly in the eye instead of having to look up at him. "But perhaps, until the opportunity presents itself, you will have to satisfy yourself with the sketches."

The corners of his mouth curved up, and his eyes brightened with a kind of pained amusement, and she watched him tip his head back and drain his glass.

"Perhaps I will, at that. Enjoy your time in the library, Mr. Germain. I shall leave the *Widow's Adventures* here for you—perhaps it will aid you in the study of anatomy."

HIS OWN ANATOMY was bursting to conduct a study of its own, and three hours later when he lay on his stomach during her now-routine late-afternoon check of his injuries, he decided that it was a damned good thing his wounds were on his back and not his front.

Her competent hands moved over him, arousing him in a way that suddenly presented a much bigger problem than it had seemed to in Paris.

Especially if she was going to start calling his attention to erotic books.

Perhaps—*perhaps*—a single book had been overlooked as the rest were being packed away, but for her to have found one straggler among an entire library full of tedious volumes...

It defied the laws of probability.

And it savored strongly of Harris's and Sacks's handiwork. He hadn't missed the looks of alarm passing between his butler and valet when he'd ordered the company away in Paris. That was no surprise. But Miles...

She was trying to divert his interest toward sex, and there could be only one possible reason: she imagined it would cause him to decide to go to Greece.

And what in God's name a young woman wanted in Greece, he didn't know. Clearly she spoke Greek...a lover she left behind? No, she was too obviously a virgin. A lust for adventure?

He turned his head and found himself face-to-face with her crotch. If he peeled away those breeches, what would he find?

"Did I hurt you?"

Her voice nearly startled him. "Pardon?"

"You made a noise. I thought I hurt you."

"Not at all."

"Good." She sounded relieved. She may have been playing a game with him in the library, but whenever she attended to him medically she turned deadly serious. "Your wounds appear to be healing nicely... I feared there might be a festering I couldn't see."

Oh, there was a festering all right, digging hard into the mattress beneath him.

Devil take it. He should have slammed that book shut the moment he realized what she'd held. This was never going to work if he couldn't stop goading her.

This was what it had come to: fantasizing about a woman who was dressed as a man. And who wasn't even the caliber he preferred.

But right now, *female* was the only caliber he preferred.

"HE NEEDS COMPANY, that's what he needs," Harris said as they sat around the card table in her dressing room late that evening.

Oh, certainly. A debauched house party. That was all the unwanted return to England needed to make it truly perfect, Millie thought.

"I've never seen him do without it in all my years of service," Harris added, genuine concern in his eyes.

"Has he said anything about invitations?" Sacks asked.

"Not a word." Harris took a drink. Grimaced. "And Mrs. Coombs said there's been no orders given below stairs to prepare for visitors."

Sacks looked at Millie. "He didn't take an interest in the book at all?"

"No." To his credit—his very small credit.

"Wouldn't even take a quick peek?"

"Oh, certainly. He peeked. But it had no effect." Not that Millie was completely sure how the effect might have manifested itself. Perhaps some sort of anguished crisis in which Winston declared that he was afflicted with a terrible desire and that something catastrophic would happen if he could not indulge himself with a woman immediately. "I told you, he wasn't interested in 'viewing pictures.'"

"I suppose it shouldn't come as a surprise," Harris sighed. "He's a man given to touching, not viewing. I only thought, with his being injured…"

"Well, he isn't going to be viewing *or* touching, is he," Sacks grumbled, shooting a look at Millie. "Not at this rate."

A quick memory—Lord Winston's fingers touching hers as he passed her the glass—ignited something physical inside her that she immediately tried to snuff out. "I can't stop him from shutting a book," she snapped. And it had certainly stayed open long enough to make the afternoon's examination of his injuries very…uncomfortable.

She shoved that thought away and latched onto another idea. "Is there nobody here, no chambermaid whose favors he already…?"

Sacks was shaking his head. "He never touches the 'elp."

Harris made a noise. "If *I* had an entire household at *my* disposal…"

"You do have an entire 'ousehold at your disposal," Sacks grunted. "Don't tell me Paris blinded you to Bethie's charms."

Harris grinned a little.

Sacks put his elbows on the table, rubbed the back of his neck. "He needs something he can't shut. He needs that damned portrait of the princess returned to 'is bedchamber."

"And company," Harris insisted. "A good debauch.

That'll be the cure, seeing as how he's missing all that he would have had in Athens."

And she couldn't believe she was saying this, but, "I agree," she told them. "It was the company in Paris that did the most to lift his spirits." It was the last thing she wanted, but if she'd managed there, she could manage here. If it worked, it would be worth it.

"Very well," Harris said. "It's settled. I'll send out a dozen invitations first thing tomorrow morning."

"I want you to prescribe me a regimen for healthful living," Winston told her the next morning, startling her at the edge of the herb garden. She glanced up with a sprig of sage in her fingers and found him bathed in sunshine. It glowed richly over his black embroidered jacket and breeches, glinted off the hilt of the smallsword peeking out at his hip. Except for the white sling cradling his arm, he looked impeccable. And exceedingly... aggravated.

"Down to the minute," he went on. "Not a single second unaccounted for. I'm at a complete loss for how to proceed, but I have little doubt that you can help me."

"Healthful living?" Millie straightened. Hopefully his definition included taking full advantage of company.

"Surely I don't need to explain that to *you*," he said irritably.

"Well, given Your Grace's idea of healthful, I should think—"

"A *medical* idea of healthful."

"Oh, I see," she said slowly, twirling the sprig of sage between her fingers. "In that case, a warm climate is always excellent for one's general health." The look he gave her made her decide that line of reasoning would avail nothing.

"I want a healthful regimen that can be carried out *here*," he said. "At my estate." She could almost hear him adding, *Not in Greece, Mr. Germain.*

"Hmm."

He narrowed his eyes. "In Paris, you were full of suggestions for how I might change my mode of living." A dark brow lifted. "Has something changed, Mr. Germain?"

Indeed, and he knew damned well what it was. "*Why* do you want such a strict regimen?"

"I did not retain you to question why."

"I ask strictly in the interest of Your Grace's health. If I can understand what you hope to achieve, it will help me recommend the most suitable regimen." And determine the best way to turn his interests back toward Greece.

He only looked at her.

"Very well," she said. "It would probably benefit you to begin each day by walking. Nothing terribly vigorous, perhaps a thirty-minute turn about the gardens."

"I need something *distracting*."

"Distracting from what?"

"Something that will absorb my entire attention."

"Such as lugworms?"

He glared at her.

She considered reminding him that he'd been very distracted by his company in Paris, but that was clearly not what he wanted to hear. So finally she said, "There must be *some* activity beside fornication that you've engaged in at some point in your life that you could now resume. How did you spend your time as a child?"

"For God's sake, a grown man can't spend his time catching insects and watching the waterwheel at the mill."

No, she certainly could not imagine him doing either of those things.

"I don't know how I am to devise a regimen when I have no idea what you might possibly find distracting. I suggest you consider the things you enjoy. The things that give you the most pleasure." With any luck, the invitations would bear fruit and he would soon have company that would remind him very clearly of what those things were.

He watched her for a long, unsettling moment.

"I've got an idea," he said slowly, glancing around at the herb garden. "I shall look to you as my guide. I shall carefully observe your daily activities and model myself after your example."

"That is no solution, as you and I have very different—"

"Oh, Mr. Germain," he said, smiling at her, "I think it will be the perfect solution."

FOLLOWING MILES GERMAIN everywhere was not the perfect solution. She was too much of an unhelpful distraction herself. But it couldn't hurt to see what more he could learn about his medic-turned-antagonist.

He observed her that afternoon from a window in the south wing as she made her way meticulously through the herb garden—so meticulously that he gave up after ten minutes.

Conducting a thorough examination of each and every plant in the garden was not an activity he ever planned to engage in.

Later he saw her heading toward the conservatory, and good God, only imagine how long it would take her to inspect every plant in *there*.

The next day he found her nosing through books in the library. From just beyond the doorway, he watched her study the shelves with the kind of intensity he could only aspire to.

She was deadly serious about...everything.

He wondered whether his library, vast as it was, included any medical volumes. If it did, there was little doubt she would find them. If he had half the resolution she clearly possessed, he bloody well wouldn't be prowling around his estate like a caged animal.

What he really needed to do was visit Edward. And he would. He just needed a bit more time, a bit more to show for his efforts, so that when he did face Edward he could feel some measure of success.

That night, he turned to the stack of correspondence waiting for him. There was always politics. National affairs. But a man had to have some kind of pleasure in his life. He'd be damned if he was going to become one of those men who caused people to doze off at parties by theorizing about taxes.

He tossed a letter aside and wondered what Miles had been doing in the conservatory. Perhaps there was something of interest in there he was unaware of.

"Harris!"

Moments later, Harris appeared in the doorway.

"Ask Mr. Germain to come to the library, will you?"

"I would, Your Grace, but he has ordered a bath, and I believe it has only just been prepared. But of course, if you would like me to interrupt…"

"That won't be necessary. I'll speak to him tomorrow."

"Very good, Your Grace."

She'd ordered a bath.

The news and all of its implications lodged in Winston's mind like a slow-moving pistol shot.

Waistcoat, shirt, breeches, stockings…all stripped away. Bagwig, gone.

He reached for another correspondence that had arrived while he'd been in Paris. Nothing urgent—something about the niece of a cousin getting married. He tossed it aside.

And his thoughts immediately took him upstairs, where surely by now Miss Miles Germain was preparing to step fully naked into a tub full of water. His imagination was only too ready with possibilities.

The reality would likely pale in comparison to the fantasy.

He returned his attention to the letters.

And imagined a pair of breasts, full and ripe and unbound from whatever concealed them beneath that waistcoat and jacket.

Oh, for God's sake. He was acting as if seeing his medic in the altogether was the most erotic prospect he'd ever encountered, which was very decidedly not the case. He didn't even have to witness it to be certain.

His gaze slid to the doorway, and he narrowed his eyes, contemplating a new possibility.

No. He shouldn't do it.

He had more respect for her than that. And she deserved at least a modicum of privacy. And in any case, he wasn't the kind of man who had to resort to peeping in on women.

He reached for another weeks-old correspondence.

She would never have to know.

But *he* would know.

You'd only be satisfying your curiosity. It's not as if you'd walk in and offer to assist.

No, he certainly wouldn't do that.

You're paying her, after all.

But she wasn't a harlot, for Christ's sake. She was his medic. His brown-eyed, sharp-tongued, Greek-speaking temptation of a medic who was becoming more of a problem by the day—precisely *because* he'd never seen her nude.

In a very plausible way, that was the whole issue.

He needed to see her in her natural state. Once his curiosity was foiled, she would no longer be a distraction.

He looked at the doorway.

Pushed his chair back from his desk.

It wasn't as if she was the kind of woman he preferred, anyhow. This wouldn't be some kind of deviant titillation. It was necessary for business. His imagination would be quelled, and there would be no more episodes like this afternoon. She would truly be his medic, not his forbidden fantasy, and he could get on with becoming the kind of man Edward expected him to be.

CHAPTER SEVEN

MINUTES LATER, WINSTON let himself silently into the room on the other side of the dressing room Miles occupied. He shut the door behind him—slowly, quietly—and crossed the room.

Faced the bookcase, and smiled.

She'd had the right idea in Paris…only the wrong house.

The panel opened silently on well-oiled casters, and he slipped into the tiny room he occasionally used to escape obnoxious guests, leaving his candle behind. Only the faintest rays followed him inside, preventing his stumbling over a favorite old chair.

He put his hands on the opposite panel. Hesitated.

Applied just enough pressure to crack it open a fraction of an inch.

Her dressing room glowed with the light from a candelabra, flickering over the walls, the furnishings…

Over *her*.

She rested with her arms on the edge of the tub—head back, eyes closed…breasts, two perfect handfuls of them, peaked with rosebud nipples. The water lapped at their curves. Glistened on her pale skin.

His mouth went dry.

A shimmer of thick, mink-colored hair cascaded over the back of the tub, stopping short a foot off the floor.

Her knees were bent, rising out of the water smooth and sleek. And then she moved, and his breath froze in his lungs, and he watched her raise one shapely leg into the air…stretching…and slip it back into the water.

She reached for something—a towel—and he stepped back. Slid the panel shut. Listened to the sound of the water through the panel while his cock strained inside his breeches and guilt assaulted him and the truth pounded through his blood that he'd been wrong, that this wasn't going to solve any problem, but that every-thing had just gotten worse.

No waistcoat and jacket were going to make him forget those breasts.

She was every bit as forbidden as before, but now she was ten times the fantasy. He wanted to catch the beads of water on her nipples with his tongue. Run his mouth along those legs. Discover what the water had concealed and taste it—taste *her*.

His curiosity was satisfied—oh, indeed, it was—but that was the extent of it.

No other part of him was satisfied. Not by a bloody mile.

MILLIE HAD JUST reached for her towel when she caught a movement out of the corner of her eye. She snapped her gaze to the left and clutched her towel, holding her breath, but—

She exhaled. It must have been the movement of her own arm.

She dried herself, stepped out of the bath, double-checked the lock on the door. Turned abruptly, stared at the wall again, with its bookcases and paneling.

And thought of Paris.

Padding barefoot across the floor, she peered at the wall, but it was difficult to see much detail in the low light. She moved to one of the panels that separated the bookcases. Tapped.

Moved to another. Tapped.

She was being ridiculous. If anyone in this household suspected her—including the duke—she would already know about it, because there wasn't a soul under this roof who would keep his hands to himself if they knew the truth.

He never touches the help.

Millie went to the dressing table and paused. A man like Winston almost certainly availed himself of his servants. Didn't he? Didn't they all?

Healthful regimen, indeed.

She pursed her lips and brushed out her hair, running her fingers through it to help it dry. Why on earth would Winston suddenly be interested in healthful living when he so obviously had never been interested in it before?

He wouldn't really start observing her. Would he?

She set the brush down, looked at herself in the glass and fluffed her fingers through her hair. It would have to be cut the rest of the way. It fell just below her shoulders now—barely short enough to stuff inside her wig, and even now it made the wig sit too far from her scalp. But she hadn't been able to bear cutting it all off.

She pushed it back from her face, loving how thick and soft it felt.

But Miles Germain would not have thick, soft hair.

For now she let the towel fall away and pinned it up, reaching for her jar of salve, turning, straining to see her back over her shoulder. Scars. Great, pink weals—five of them—crisscrossed her back in long, ugly lashes. The weals were a few months old now, and healed, but the new skin was raw and pink and raised. The scars would last forever.

She thought of William. It was impossible to look at the scars and not think of him. But no matter how many times she relived the events in her mind, she could not change what she'd done—nor the punishment he'd meted out.

She dipped her fingers in the salve, stretching awkwardly to reach her bare back. She nearly had a method now—behind her left shoulder with her right hand, behind her right shoulder with her left hand, an extra stretch to reach between the shoulder blades…

She craned her neck to see in the glass. Hers was one nude figure that would send His Grace reeling backward with revulsion. But that was the least of her concerns. No man would ever see these scars, least of all Winston.

Every day she was proving that Miles Germain could hold his own in the world, undetected. Soon Millicent would be a figment of the past.

"WHAT THE DEVIL is this painting doing here?" The duke's voice thundered from his bedchamber the next morning, carried through his anteroom and into the corridor, where Millie was just approaching his apartment for her routine check of his bandages.

She paused.

They'd done it. Harris and Sacks had returned the painting.

But the duke did not sound like a man overcome by a pair of magnificent breasts.

She considered whether to delay the examination a few minutes. Imagined him ordering the painting removed without anyone to reason him toward a different course of action, and continued forward.

"Good morning, Your Grace," she said evenly as she entered the room to find him glaring up at a portrait of—

Well, yes. Harris had been right about the size of the princess's breasts.

"I see you've added to your decor," she said, setting down her medical bag, pretending she hadn't heard his outburst. "An excellent sign that you're feeling a bit more like yourself."

"I'd ordered this removed," he said sharply. "And now I've just returned from the library to find it hanging once again."

"There must have been a misunderstanding," she offered. "Someone must have thought you'd ordered it returned."

"I haven't said a word about it since we arrived." And now he turned away from the painting, which wasn't good at all. An image like that was supposed to snare his attention with hypnotic force.

"She's a great beauty," Millie said, to draw the duke's attention back to the painting. "Who is she?"

"An acquaintance," he said, still not turning. "Sacks!" he barked.

"You *know* her?" Millie asked, because it seemed

reasonable that Miles Germain would be in awe of a beauty so far out of reach. "For God's sake, man, why do you not have her here at your disposal?" Perhaps, if she could get him to talk about the princess, he would begin to remember how much he'd enjoyed the liberties she had so obviously allowed him.

Perhaps he would even invite her for a visit.

"Princess Katja is at no man's disposal," he said.

She looked like a woman who was at *every* man's disposal—and exactly the kind of woman His Grace needed.

"If *I* had a painting like that..." she started. "If I *knew* a woman like that—"

"You'd what, Miles?" he demanded, facing her now—much closer than he'd been a moment before—and suddenly she didn't feel like Miles at all, but some breathless creature, humming inside from his nearness. "What would you do?"

She moistened her lips, squared her shoulders. "I wouldn't be spending my afternoons here alone, Your Grace."

"No?"

"But I shan't dishonor Your Grace's acquaintance by specifying any particulars," she said. "I'm sure your own experience can fill in the details."

Her imagination was already filling in those very details, and an uncomfortable feeling tightened in her gut at the thought of him lavishing attention on the princess's magnificent breasts.

And *still* he wasn't looking at the painting—he was looking at *her,* angry, perhaps, at Miles Germain's insolence. But it was making her think of the fact that she herself had lain nude, last night, only steps away from this very room.

"Your Grace," came Sacks's gravelly voice from the doorway. "You called?"

The duke backed away from her. "I ordered this painting removed," he said, still looking at Millie as if she'd been the one to replace the painting. "I expect it to *stay* removed."

"As you wish," Sacks said.

The duke snatched a book off the table. "As I wish," he muttered, and stalked out of the room.

MILLIE DIDN'T REALIZE how hard her pulse was racing until he'd gone.

"D'you see now?" Sacks asked in a low voice, approaching her. "What kind of man wants to remove *that?*" He gestured toward the portrait. "A man who's lost his faculties, that's who."

He turned on his heel and returned to the antechamber, where she heard him calling for a footman.

She looked up at the princess, at those sly lips and huge, aristocratic eyes. Those breasts. She was everything a man should want.

So why had the duke ordered the portrait put away?

She picked up her medical bag and returned to the antechamber. "Perhaps he and the countess are at odds," she said to Sacks, who was arranging the duke's toiletries on his dressing table.

"Would you be at odds with bubs like that?" he said, yanking open a drawer. "Me, I'd be frigging 'er 'til my prick fell off."

Millie made a noncommittal noise of agreement and

left Sacks to his duties, skirting past a pair of footmen who had likely come to return the princess to the attic.

Winston was setting her nerves on edge following her about. As if he was really going to take up a serious study in the library? Or spend any amount of time in the conservatory?

He wasn't finding himself a distraction. All he was doing was distracting her.

She snuck out a quiet door in the farthest reaches of the house carrying a small basket borrowed from Mrs. Coombs and made her way to the woods on the other side of the drive, beyond the parklands. Just an hour or two without him... An hour or two to collect a few herbs and simply be herself.

She'd nearly reached the edge of the woods when his voice rang out behind her.

"Mr. Germain!"

Damnation.

"Ho, Mr. Germain!"

She stopped. Turned. Felt a quick little catch just below her ribs, because he *was* handsome. There was no denying it.

He caught up to her and offered a smile that made her very uncomfortable. "For a moment, I thought you were going to sneak away and deny me the opportunity to observe your activities," he said, and looked past her to the woods. "What are you doing?"

"Just a short walk to look for herbs," she said. "There won't be anything to interest you here."

"On the contrary," he said again, still smiling. "What interests you, interests me."

CHAPTER EIGHT

SHE WANTED TO *play games?* Winston thought as he followed her into the woods. He could play games.

Frustration roiled inside him—irritation about the
portrait of Katja that he'd explicitly ordered put away,
aggravation at Miles's attempts to arouse his interest in
it. Wouldn't she be shocked to know that her untutored
attempts had only succeeded in making him think of
something very different from what she had in mind?

Her. And he wouldn't have any trouble specifying
the particulars.

She wanted to discuss sex? He could discuss sex.

The trees' canopy and the overcast sky shrouded
the woods with gray gloom as she walked a few paces
ahead, basket in hand. He watched the back of her slim
shoulders, feeling more than a little satisfied at the look
of consternation on her face a moment ago. "In any
case," he said now, conversationally, as they picked their
way through the woods along the stream, "you did suggest I should not spend the afternoon alone."

"Surely Your Grace can find more interesting company than this."

"I very much enjoy your company, Mr. Germain."

She paused to survey the stream bank in both directions, shifting her basket from one hand to the other.

And now her cheeks were flushed, and she looked more innocent than ever, and suddenly all he could see was her sitting in that blasted tub, candlelight bathing her breasts while he spied on her like the most depraved lecher....

He started to reach for her basket, remembered she was supposed to be Mr. Germain and stopped. A man didn't carry another man's basket.

And there was the answer: stop thinking about that bath and continue treating her like a man. Pretend she *was* a man.

"It occurred to me that perhaps you could use your expertise to help me combat my latest affliction," he said now.

She's a man. He made himself look at her nondescript jacket, breeches, shoes. *Miles Germain. A man.*

If anyone could read his thoughts, he'd be committed to an asylum.

"And what affliction is that?"

"I find myself suddenly accosted by thoughts of a highly erotic nature."

"Only suddenly? You've never had these kinds of thoughts before?"

"Not while I was attempting to follow a healthful regimen." Which was perfectly true. "But now—since this morning, in fact—I find myself contemplating, shall we say, the fields of Venus."

"Vastly more interesting than the woods, I daresay." She continued along the stream, unperturbed, skirting around a pair of tree trunks.

Winston surveyed her legs, remembering how they'd looked in the bath, gleaming wet and bare—

"Oh, there," she said suddenly, spotting something on the other side of the stream. She turned back, held out the basket. "Hold this, will you?"

Just forget about that blasted bath.

He should already have forgotten it. For Christ's sake, how many women had he seen in his lifetime? And he could scarcely remember any of them.

But the image of *her* was engraved in his mind.

He reached for the basket, and at the last moment a devil made him grasp the handle where their hands would touch in the exchange. The brush of her fingers sent heat snaking up his arm.

"It's comforting to have a man about that I can speak to frankly about these matters," he told her while she picked her way across the stream on three small stones.

"Would you not find it more comforting to act on them?"

Oh, indeed. He considered what he might say that would be truly shocking. Ruffle her feathers a bit, make her think twice next time before trying to ruffle his.

He watched her crouch down, pick a handful of stems and return to place them in the basket, looking nothing at all like a man, but rather a young woman pleased with her find.

Pink touched her cheeks, and her eyes lit with satisfaction. "Fresh water mint will be just the thing for your evening tea. Not too strong, good for the digestive system."

His evening tea could go to the devil.

He wanted *her*.

"I feel as if I could recover much more quickly if I could only put my hands on a fine pair of breasts," he said now, and immediately imagined what hers might feel like. Taste like.

"Then I'm not sure what you're doing out here with me, Your Grace."

He ignored that. "It's been nearly two weeks since I've spent myself between a woman's welcoming thighs. That can't be healthful, can it? After all, I can hardly spend the rest of my life without ever enjoying a woman again."

"Rather a leap between a fortnight and a lifetime, isn't it? But if that is your definition of healthful living, a surgical procedure would do the most good—not a regimen." She looked up at the treetops. "What an aggravation…it looks as if it could rain at any moment." Her gaze fell back on him. "You'd better turn back. It wouldn't do for your bandages to be soaked in a downpour."

It would be so easy to seduce her. He imagined pulling her with him to the ground, making love to her right here, right now on the grass. And now he wondered what it might be like, pushing inside her virgin body. Watching those eyes widen while he breached her maidenhead, feeling the grasp of her channel as he opened it.

It would be impossibly tight. He'd probably need something to smooth the way, help things along.

"No," he said roughly. "Wouldn't do at all." He imagined having her beneath him. Kissing those pink lips while he thrust inside her.

Are you going to do this again, after what happened with Cara?

"Is something paining you?" she asked, genuinely frowning now. "I should have insisted that you turn around the moment you saw me. It isn't a good idea for you to be walking about like this."

And no, this wasn't a good idea. Hadn't been from the moment he'd decided to follow her into the woods for no better reason than to goad her.

"It's fine," he murmured. "I can hardly feel a thing." Except for screaming need in his breeches and the pounding thrum of blood in his veins.

She still frowned at him, slender brows in a vee. "I'll check everything very thoroughly this evening."

"Perhaps…" *Perhaps you ought to check everything very thoroughly now.*

That day with Cara reared up in his thoughts—an innocent ride through the woods. That was all either of them had intended. All it was ever meant to be.

All it should have been.

"Perhaps?" Miles prompted.

He stepped back, with his heart thudding so hard he could feel it against his chest.

"Perhaps this evening, indeed," he said, clearing his throat. "There's someone I need to call on in the village this afternoon."

"Then, by all means, don't let me keep you a moment longer."

He needed to go. Now. Because if he did remain a moment longer, he was going to touch her, and then there would be no question between them that she was not a man and they both knew it.

And because doing that would violate the one standard he'd held for himself all these years, would destroy the one thing he'd done to make up for his sin against Cara and Edward.

"Very well." He was not going to seduce Miles Germain on any grass—wasn't going to seduce her at all, ever. "Until this evening, Mr. Germain."

By which time he intended to have himself firmly under control.

SOMEONE IN THE VILLAGE, Millie wondered after he left, with a fine pair of breasts and a welcoming pair of thighs?

The possibility shouldn't have bothered her even a little bit.

She gathered some ground ivy into her basket and told herself it was a good sign that he was having... erotic thoughts. Apparently the painting had affected him more than it seemed to.

She shouldn't be wishing he hadn't left. She did, but she shouldn't.

She found a patch of dead-nettle away from the stream and collected a few stalks, and told herself she was not going to develop an attraction for the duke. She was intelligent. Sensible. She knew her place and was all too aware of his. More than that, she had her eyes open—wide-open—to his ways.

So she simply would not develop an attraction.

The important thing was to encourage him in the right direction and hope he realized how very much he really did want to visit Greece.

But when she returned to the house, she learned that Winston had not gone to the village at all, but had been in the library again. And now she wondered whether he might have been covering up his pain in the woods.

An examination that evening revealed no discernible changes.

By early afternoon the next day, he still hadn't gone to the village or done anything even remotely erotic that Millie was aware of, so she decided to speak with him again and press him to find out whether he was, in fact, in more pain that she realized.

He was nowhere to be found.

Someone said they'd seen him walking outside, and she finally found him at the far end of the gardens in a corner where two hedges came together, grabbing for something one-handed while a small net hung limply in his slung hand. She watched for a moment, but it was impossible to tell what he was after.

"What are you doing?" she called, close enough now to hear him cursing.

He whipped the net from his idle hand and slapped it against the top of the hedge, digging it into the leaves. Cursed again.

She stood beside him, frowning into the bush.

"Almost had the little bugger," the duke growled. She saw that a book lay open atop the hedge nearby. A page flipped in the breeze, and he reached to flip it back. "'*Leptophyes punctatissima*,'" he read from the page. "There's no doubt in my mind that's what it was."

Millie stepped closer and saw a drawing of a cricket-looking creature with long legs. She looked at him. "You're collecting insects?"

"I can't think why you sound surprised."

First tidal flats, now insects… What next, a study of fungi?

"I didn't realize you had an interest in insects," she said carefully.

"Entomology is a valid aspect of natural history."

"So it is. I just didn't realize you had any interest in it."

"I have a great many interests," he said, snatching up the insect net from the hedge where it rested.

Indeed—if one counted all the various parts of the female body. "How *long* have you been interested in insects?"

"An exceedingly long time, Mr. Germain."

Bollocks. "I do hope this isn't a sign of malaise." She plunked her medical bag on the ground next to the hedge and sighed loudly. "I suppose this is as good a time as any to warn against the dangers of sudden changes of interest. They can signal any number of mental difficulties. Malaise, for example, which could significantly retard your recovery." She was improvising now, but it wasn't irresponsible advice. It was perfectly reasonable, in fact.

He peered into the shrubbery once more, net in hand. "I do not have—" whack "—malaise." He grabbed for the net, inspected it closely. "Bloody hell."

Empty.

This was the furthest possible thing from erotic thoughts. Yesterday's discussion in the woods had seemed somewhat productive toward her goal of getting him to Greece. And now this.

"I've long wondered how one determines the sex of an insect," she said now, frowning at the drawing. "Can one tell by looking?"

He looked at her. "The sex of an insect?"

"Indeed. Certainly the female must have…distinguishing characteristics."

His attention returned to the shrub. "I don't know."

"Mmm." And after a moment, "Do they not have privy parts, then?"

He turned on her. "Privy parts?"

"Yes."

He studied her rather too long, and his brows ticked downward. "Precisely which privy parts might those be, Mr. Germain? I'm not at all sure I understand what you mean."

"Well…"

"No, do—describe them to me in detail."

"I'm quite sure there's no need to describe privy parts to you, Your Grace. In any case, I only came here to find out whether you were indeed in pain yesterday in the woods, and if perhaps you haven't been truthful with me your condition."

"I assure you, I've been entirely truthful."

"You mustn't undo your progress," she lectured sternly, both relieved and frustrated that her attempt to turn his thoughts toward eroticism had gone nowhere.

"My thoughts exactly," he said, still looking at her too intently.

She swallowed. "You aren't entirely out of danger. If I've given you the impression that you are—"

"Not at all, Miles. I'm quite aware of the danger."

And so was she, suddenly—but of a very different kind. And the fact was, it was too late. Despite her protestations to the contrary, she realized suddenly that she'd already developed an attraction for him. Sensations coursed through her veins, pulsed in her nerves, spread hotly across her skin.

She.

Millicent Germain.

Feeling…desire? It couldn't be.

The breeze flipped the page in the book, and something caught her eye. "Look." She turned away from him, feeling her pulse in her throat. "There's writing on the back side of the plate." She held the page down and read aloud. "'Discovered in hedges at far end of garden, past third pond.' It's in a child's script."

He slid the book from her grasp and closed it. "And in the hedges is exactly where the little devils will stay. I've had enough of this."

Past the third pond…

"Is that your writing?" It was. She could tell by the way he was avoiding looking at her as he collected his net and turned away from the shrubs. And hadn't he mentioned insect collecting when she'd asked him what he enjoyed as a child?

She tried to imagine him at age ten or eleven but honestly couldn't.

"I really can't recall," he said.

HE MANAGED TO avoid his medic for the rest of the day.

Endured her evening examination by pretending to be utterly exhausted.

By bedtime, it was obvious that what he'd told Miles was true: he was taking things too far. Considering his ways could not mean adjusting to a life of abstinence and boredom. Two weeks of monasticism certainly proved the depth of his sincerity. Perhaps, now, a quick trip to London was in order. It could be a discreet trip. Just a few days, just enough to take the edge off.

There was plenty in London to make him forget what he'd seen through the crack in that panel.

Yet he didn't call for his carriage. This was his home, for God's sake—there must be some source of entertainment here that would be acceptable.

Yet the best source of entertainment—Miles—was also the most dangerous. The amount of effort it was taking to keep from touching her was stretching the limits of his endurance.

This morning, he would try again to do something constructive. He'd remembered overnight that Finchley was always talking about hours of satisfaction spent in his conservatory studying plants—and he knew Finchley well enough to know that was not an innuendo for anything.

Winston went to the library, searched until he found a suitable book. *Plants and their Parts, Explain'd.* It sounded about as enthralling as the tidal flats of Devon.

Hopefully the title wasn't referring to privy parts.

Inside the conservatory, two paths made from paving stones extended in either direction, with plants growing along the glass and in the wide middle section. Trees and shrubs grew so tall and thick it was impossible to see to the ends of the conservatory.

What in God's name did Finchley do in a place like this?

Miles would probably know. There were times when she seemed to know just about everything.

Well, not everything.

But he didn't dare think about that.

Without the least idea where to begin, Winston made his way along one of the paths, looking for a plant that seemed suitable for a beginner—how the devil could a person tell?—pausing to consult his book, when up ahead he saw Miles.

He stopped. She hadn't noticed him. She was seated on a bench, book at her side, with her elbows on her knees and her face in her hands.

He felt something in his chest at the sight of her. Was she that unhappy about being here?

Of course she was. She'd thought her employment would take her a stone's throw from her ultimate destination, and instead he'd brought her even farther away.

There was a moment of indecision—did he try to leave before she noticed him, or did he say something?—but it seemed worse if she noticed him while he was walking away, so he walked a little closer.

"Mr. Ger—"

He didn't get the entire word out before she bolted off the bench, whirled toward him and whipped her small-sword from its sheath, ready in a heartbeat for battle—until recognition lit her eyes, and her posture eased.

Her reaction had his own hand shifting to the hilt of his sword, but now he let it fall. "Forgive me," he said. "I didn't mean to startle you." He knew only one other woman with a sword arm like that, and she'd nearly cut off his vitals once.

She sheathed her sword with no more than a glance at the scabbard. "I didn't hear you."

"Obviously."

"Is everything all right? Do you require attention?" Her eyes dropped to his shoulder, and she frowned.

"No…no. Nothing like that." Perhaps she hadn't fabricated the story about serving aboard a ship. It would certainly explain how she possessed such facility with a sword that he wondered who would have come out the victor had she tried to engage him.

"Was there something else you wanted?" she asked now.

Something very particular leaped to mind— something he had no business wanting from her—and he tried to shove it away.

"I thought I'd have a look around the conservatory. It seemed like a healthful pastime— Of course, I didn't realize I would end up at sword point." He raised a brow. "At least I don't have to wonder if you can defend yourself should the need arise."

"I am as capable of looking after myself as the next man, Your Grace," she said with a bit of indignation. "Despite my stature."

"Rather more capable than the next man, I might venture." He smiled a little.

And damnation, there was that response—that flicker of desire in her eyes that was so clearly unintended. He needed no other clue to determine that her romantic expertise lay at the opposite end of the scale from her expertise with a sword.

Good. Excellent. Only let her inexperience be on display at every moment, and these licks of desire that attacked him while she looked after him would cool, because nothing could be more tedious and uninspiring than the thought of an inexperienced miss who assumed he wanted to have his way with her.

Give him a woman who would demand her way with him. That was the kind he liked.

"Tell me, Mr. Germain…why do you want to go to Greece?"

MILLIE LOOKED AT him and decided there was no reason not to tell him the truth. "Not Greece, Your Grace. Malta."

"Malta. What in God's name would a—a young medic want there? Good God, tell me you don't have fantasies of joining the order of Knights."

"I have plans to attend the surgical school there."

"The surgical school." His brows furrowed.

"It is an excellent school," she said stiffly. "Renowned for its teaching."

"Yes, I've heard of it."

He had?

"And you plan to…obtain a degree?" he asked, still observing her with knitted brows.

There was no reason the question should make her flush, but it did—sudden, hot blushes on the apples of her cheeks. She imagined the surgical school. She'd seen it plenty of times from the outside. Had seen the professors in their robes, students walking together deep in discussion.

The yearning to be a part of that drove so deeply it hurt.

"There's nothing foolish about wanting a degree." At least, not for Miles Germain.

"No, I suppose not."

He supposed? "I may be young, but I have a great

deal of experience. It's education I lack, and that's a deficit I plan to remedy at the first opportunity."

"I see. And your father…is he a surgeon?"

"An apothecary." Here, too, she could afford truthfulness.

"And so you learned your skills…"

"From my father. And my brother. And from reading, of course. I don't have as many books as I'd like—" just the one now, or two counting the old volume she'd brought here from his Paris library "—but the few I have are excellent, and I've memorized every word."

"I see," the duke said. "And the reason you didn't apprentice as an apothecary?"

"My older brother."

"Of course."

"He has my father's shop now." And the last time she'd seen him, he'd beaten her nearly to death for shaming the family with her world travels. "I was planning to ask whether, when my employment with you is ended, you might be so kind as to prepare me a letter of introduction that would help me when I reach Malta."

He smiled a little, and she felt it in her knees. "I rather thought you might say you hoped I would personally enroll you. Malta is in the general vicinity of Greece, after all."

"Whatever Your Grace thinks best."

"Unfortunately, you'll have to settle for a letter, Mr. Germain, assuming I recover successfully—" he leaned close "—because I am not. Going. To Greece."

CHAPTER NINE

EVEN IF HE *were* going to take her to Greece, Winston thought in the carriage on his way to finally see Edward, he would go mad long before he arrived.

She was intelligent.

And driven—more so than most men he knew. Certainly more so than himself.

And she had the most beautiful breasts he'd ever seen.

Which was obviously an exaggeration, and a testament to his new monastic mode of living, because he'd seen a great many breasts. Larger ones, certainly. Katja's, for example, and what the *devil* her portrait was doing in his bedchamber this morning he didn't know, but there bloody well would not be a repeat or someone would find himself transferred to the kitchens.

Malta's School of Anatomy and Surgery. Yes, he'd heard of it. It was highly acclaimed, just as she'd said. And it was obvious that her desire to attend was not just a story made up as part of her disguise.

She—whoever she really was—wanted to attend for herself. And she likely planned to do it as Mr. Miles Germain.

Could it be possible that she planned to spend the rest of her life disguised as a man? Certainly difficult, but admirable in its commitment. Winston's coach pulled up in front of the cottage next to the church and he got out, only to see Edward on the road some distance away, apparently walking home from somewhere.

They'd gone fishing mere weeks earlier, a few days before Winston had left for Paris.

Edward was his best friend. They'd grown up together—the heir to Winston and the son of the parish vicar, riding hell-bent across the countryside, hunting small game, climbing trees and walls and just about anything else that appeared scalable. He, Edward and Cara, the daughter of the village solicitor.

He stood watching the familiar, easy gait of his childhood friend and hated that part of him wanted to make a hasty excuse and climb back into the coach. At the same time, he didn't want that at all. It was good to see Edward again.

Edward approached now, smiling quizzically. "You're not in Greece."

"No." He was starting to wish Greece did not exist.

"It's good to see you, my friend," Edward said, and then just noticing, "Your shoulder— You've been injured? Is that why you've returned?"

"A minor accident in Paris."

"I'm sorry to hear it. But you're not too badly injured, it would seem."

"A few cuts and bruises. Nothing too serious." He hadn't had trouble looking Edward in the eye—not in fifteen years. But now, suddenly, it seemed easier to survey the shrubbery near the church doors.

"Walk with me," Edward said. "I just promised Mrs. Marsh I would pay respects to her husband."

They went around the side of the church to the grave-yard, and then it was either continue with Edward or admit that graveyards made him uneasy these days, so he stepped through the gate and onto the spongy grass.

He shouldn't have come. He was doing just fine on his own. He was here at the estate, wasn't he? Considering his ways while half of the decor in the house sat covered with linens in the attic.

Considering how to seduce your medic, more like.

"Mrs. Marsh has been having trouble walking these past months, else she'd be here every day herself," Edward was saying, and Winston knew him well enough to know when he was making conversation simply to bide the time until Winston decided to tell him what was the matter.

Unburdening himself was not something Winston was particularly fond of.

He tried not to think of those who rested beneath their feet, and especially tried not to think of that man in Paris and how easily it could have been himself rotting away beneath the soil. How it probably should have been him, and not a man who left behind a wife and five children.

"Here we are." Edward stopped in front of a stone with neat, clean carving: Peter Marsh, b. 1697 d. 1765. The soil mounded above the grave but had settled already, and a soft green fuzz covered it. Edward stepped forward and placed his hand on the stone, gripping it the way one might grip a friend's shoulder, then stepped back and folded his hands in front of him.

Winston waited, thinking Edward might be saying a silent prayer.

A moment went by. Another. And another.

And Winston realized Edward wasn't praying anymore, but was waiting. For him.

"The accident in Paris," Winston finally said. "A man died."

"No." Edward turned his head to look at him—equal height, but entirely different coloring. Gray eyes, sandy blond wig that matched his own hair. "What a terrible thing."

Winston told him about the crumbling facade, the pure chance of his having been walking a few feet farther from the building than the other man.

He didn't tell Edward about the vow.

"What horror," Edward said. "And praise God you weren't killed, as well."

Winston stared at Peter Marsh's headstone, searching for a way to query Edward about which of his ways in particular Winston should consider. Edward knew him—knew what Winston could reasonably expect of himself, where the line between excess and sense could be drawn.

But now Winston wasn't sure exactly how to frame the question without earning himself one of Edward's damning looks of reproof, which cut all the more deeply because they were so bloody sincere.

"And so you've returned here to recover from your injuries."

"Yes." Better, perhaps, that Edward believe it to be true. "How is Cara?"

Edward smiled. "Lovely as ever." The smile dimmed a little. "But she's seemed different lately, and I fear she's unwell and hasn't been telling me. When I ask her about it, she says she feels perfectly well. Says she doesn't need to see Dr. Brunt."

"Has she been ill?"

"No…nothing obvious. No fever, coughing… I suppose it's been more in her demeanor."

The obvious possibility hung between them unsaid, and Winston's gut knotted a little.

Cara could be with child again. But he didn't dare mention it—not when he was the reason Edward and Cara had remained childless all these years. And Edward didn't suggest it, and the silence stretched uncomfortably long while Winston wondered if it were possible for a woman of Cara's age to finally carry a child to term after so many miscarriages.

Each and every one of which was his fault.

"Perhaps you ought to insist that she let Brunt examine her," Winston said.

Edward shook his head, smiling a little. "I don't need to tell you the response I would get if I tried that."

Edward always talked about Cara. It was only natural for a man to discuss his wife with his closest friend. Before Paris, Winston had scarcely given it a thought.

Now, suddenly, it felt profane.

For years Winston had shoved away the things he didn't want to remember, but now all he could think of was that long-ago afternoon. His memories of it were hazy. He and Cara had gone riding. Had stopped in the woods—he couldn't recall why. He'd been drinking, basking in a few weeks' freedom from university and the power of the horse beneath him. Had known Cara fancied him, had known his rank prevented him offering her anything—hadn't *wanted* to offer her anything.

And he'd known Edward loved her. But that afternoon none of that had mattered. She'd flirted, he'd flirted, and somehow they'd ended up on the ground in the grass with her skirts up to her hips.

And he couldn't even remember, now, what it had felt like.

"I hired a medic when I was in Paris," Winston said now, through a throat that suddenly felt dry and scratchy. "Was supposed to accompany me to Greece. I've an idea Cara might prefer my Mr. Germain a good deal more than Brunt." The doctor was at least sixty and had watery eyes and a permanent frown and, despite his good intentions, could be off-putting. "I could send him down."

"I doubt Cara will let him examine her. And she'd be furious that I told you."

"But if it would help…"

Edward sighed, considering that, while Winston recalled the expression on Edward's face when he'd learned what Winston and Cara had done.

They'd had too much respect for Edward to try to hide their mistake from him.

And Edward, studying to follow his father as the parish vicar, had forgiven them. Forgiven Winston and married Cara, selflessly protecting Cara and her reputation, as well as that of the child that resulted.

A child who had not survived birth and who had nearly drained Cara's lifeblood in the process.

And yet Edward never spoke of it. Nor did Cara.

Fifteen years in the past, it was as if none of it had ever happened, and the three of them were exactly as they would have been if that day in the woods had never taken place.

Before Paris, Winston had been happy to let it stay there. But now...

Now, HE TOLD himself in his coach an hour later, it could be a mistake to disturb the status quo.

Several times during their walk it had been on the tip of his tongue to tell Edward about the vow, but he couldn't bring himself to do it. The moment he told Edward what he was about, there would be no going back. He would be committed.

And perhaps he didn't want to be committed.

Things were fine the way they were between himself and Edward. And really, things were fine with Winston's life. He wasn't some grievous wrongdoer.

He simply enjoyed a good time.

And it wasn't as if he couldn't recognize boundaries that were not to be crossed. He knew any number of desirable women he had no intention of seducing. Friends' wives, for example. Hadn't he extricated himself from a delicate situation with Lady Rhys not two months ago for that very reason?

It wasn't as if the sight of a desirable woman sent him on a mindless rampage. He wasn't going to attack Miles just because she aroused him, for Christ's sake. Men who pressed the issue—*they* were the ones who needed reforming.

The coach stopped in front of his house. Yes, he might have come damned close to doing something he shouldn't have when he'd walked with her in the woods, but that was a situation that would not be repeated.

He climbed out of the carriage. He had barely touched a foot to the ground when another coach was spotted coming down the drive at a fast clip.

Who the devil—

In a matter of moments, the coach was close enough to answer the question: It was his friend Urslane, almost certainly come from London, and where Urslane went, Pendergast always followed—and they rarely traveled alone.

Especially not when they came here. Which they did, regularly, and not to stand around toeing the grass in a cemetery searching for moral ground.

Winston met Urslane as he emerged from his coach, followed by Pendergast and two women Winston would have been mightily glad to see a month ago. Already a third carriage was coming down the drive.

"Winston!" Urslane called, slapping him heartily on his good shoulder. "Heard the terrible news—a narrow escape, eh? But all's well that ends well."

"Indeed," Winston said, although so far nothing had ended well at all. "To what do I owe the visit?"

"To what—" He looked at the others and laughed. "Listen to Winston, pretending surprise. Is that to be part of the game this time, then?"

"Just out for the country air," Pendergast said exaggeratedly. "With our friends." He winked at the two women that had ridden with them, then looked at the carriage behind them, from which were emerging four women Winston recognized from a dancing troupe whose entertainment he had procured on several occasions. "Lo, there—more city folk with a hankering to *take the air*."

"There'll be more coming," Urslane said, already heading toward the door as his footmen were taking down an alarming amount of baggage from the top of Urslane's coach. "That is to say, I shan't be a'tall surprised if we aren't the only ones with country notions today. Hensley, for one. And our titillating trio shouldn't be far behind," Urslane told him now, as if imparting confidential state secrets. Winston conjured up an instant mental image of the trio in question: dark-haired Spanish beauties, all, with lusty bodies that were available for much more than just the dancing exhibitions that made them so sought after in certain circles.

He greeted the theater women, bowing and kissing each one's hand as if he greeted the king's daughters. He recognized one of them—artful blond hair, sly blue eyes, crests of pink barely peeking from her décolletage.

"Your Grace," she said, curtsying in a manner carefully designed to afford him a clear view of her assets.

She was beautiful. Uncomplicated. And most definitely no innocent miss. The kind of woman who would as soon throw her skirts up as smile at a man.

The kind of woman who was meant to be enjoyed.

The kind who could distract him from Miles.

The other carriages slowed, stopped, and out came the very Spanish trio Urslane had predicted. Already some of his visitors were making their way toward the entrance, their loud conversation punctuated by laughter and bawdy remarks.

A few hours earlier, his house had been a mausoleum.

But, suddenly, things had shifted back to normal. And perhaps it all made perfect sense.

He couldn't have known it at the time of the accident, but fate had known—that he would employ a desirable young innocent, and that he would need the strength to resist her.

Perhaps Miles was the true test. A young—if a bit worldly—virgin who roused his desire the way no virgin normally did. All he had to do was resist the temptation. Not touch her—not even to see whether she would respond.

Because he already knew she would.

This, then, would be his new vow: he simply would not touch Miles.

Surely he could manage that for as long as it took him to recover from his injuries—especially with his usual company to distract him.

Indeed, it seemed fate had intervened just in time.

CHAPTER TEN

"THEY'RE HERE," SACKS said, charging across Millie's dressing room, where she was studying, going to the window to look out.

And then, moments later, Harris ducked in just long enough for a happy "They've arrived! I can't think when I've been so relieved," and left to carry out his duties.

Millie looked up from her desk toward Sacks, who stood at the window looking down approvingly.

"It's those Spanish doxies," Sacks almost groaned, as if the ecstasy had begun already.

Millie closed the book on her finger to mark the page and finally joined him at the window, hugging the book to her chest as she peered down. Below, a crowd of colorful, magnificent people emerged from half-a-dozen carriages—ladies in elaborate gowns, gentlemen in colorful embroidered coats, all talking and laughing.

Her eyes found the duke immediately, already with a bevy of women around him.

Sacks made a noise of appreciation. "Miss Tensie," he said. "All will be right very soon, mark my words."

Millie peered below. "Which one is she?"

"The one on 'is arm, of course. He always enjoys 'er the best."

A quick and visceral objection knotted behind Millie's ribs. The book clamped harder around her finger.

But…good. This was good.

It was.

Whatever had him reading about lugworms and trying to catch insects and ordering nude portraits stored away was clearly fading. Perhaps it had something to do with whomever he'd visited this afternoon.

Perhaps he had a mistress in the village, and he'd gone for—

"A good, fast frig," Sacks said now in a low voice, gaze intent on the scene below. "That's what we all need after this past week's ordeal."

"Indeed," she made herself murmur, and told herself it was true—for the duke, at least.

And perhaps she'd experienced a few dangerous moments of breathlessness in the woods, and perhaps for a second or two she'd imagined what it would feel like if he kissed her, but that was very different from actually *wanting* him to kiss her.

This is perfect. Only let him enjoy himself with these women and remember what he planned for Greece.

"The Spanish ones know a thing or two," Sacks told her, "and they're not fussy about who they lift their skirts for. See 'er with the long curls?" He pointed. Chuckled. "Knows how to give as good as she gets, that one. Here—follow me."

They left her room and went to a spot near the top of the grand staircase where they could discreetly observe the entrance hall as the group entered. A crescendo of voices filled the hall. There were peals of feminine laughter—and not laughter of quality. Very, very common laughter.

She heard the duke's laughter, too, and it struck a vibration inside her like a mellow note on a harpsichord. She inhaled deeply, exhaled slowly.

Do not *be ridiculous.* It was *this* kind of women that dissolved into fits of silliness in his presence—not her.

By all means, let him have his fun.

A voice boomed up from below—an awful voice from the past that she recognized too well. "Where's that delicious little marble that used to stand in that corner? God's sake, Winston, you've practically emptied the place."

A chill ran across her skin, and revulsion soured her stomach.

Lord Hensley. Here.

"Just making a few changes," she heard Winston say evenly. "How are things in the Lords?"

"The Lords! Good God, man, I didn't come here to talk about that."

She breathed deeply. Of course Lord Hensley would be here, at a place like this, for this kind of reason. She was trembling a little, and she told herself to be calm. She was in disguise, and she would scarcely see him, and he wouldn't recognize or remember her anyhow. And unlike before, this time she wore a sword.

They all disappeared into the grand salon, and she saw Winston give some quick orders to Harris, which must have been favorable because Harris glanced up then, spotted her and Sacks, and smiled.

"There'll be entertainments aplenty tonight," Sacks said.

"WE CAN'T REPLACE *EVERYTHING*," Millie hissed hours later as she and Harris and Sacks wrestled with a marble nude in the attic. "And we'll need at least three more men for this one."

"It's too plain anyhow," Sacks grunted, trying to shift it without success.

"It's His Grace's favorite."

Millie wasn't sure how that could be possible, considering it was a simple statue of a woman leaning against a pillar—lips parted, modest breasts, one knee slightly bent. Eyes closed, head back, as if being carried away by some invisible ecstasy.

"Never mind about that," Sacks said irritably. "Let's find some of the others."

Which would be moved to the main ballroom while the guests were enjoying a late-evening meal, and if the duke asked about it, the change would be blamed on one of the guests whose name would be conveniently forgotten.

Harris held up his candle, peering through the crowded attic full of draped sculptures. It looked like a roomful of ghosts.

"Oh, for God's sake," Sacks muttered, and pushed past him, checking beneath one sheet after the next.

"See if you can find those nymphs Lord Hensley was talking about," Harris said. "We could blame it all on him."

"It's 'ere," Sacks called a moment later. "Let's take it and those two."

Harris peeked at the first choice and smiled. "I'd gladly be turned to stone if it could be *me* doing that for all eternity."

They gathered around the statue, lifted on a count of three and dragged the sculpture to the door.

What could be so enthralling about a handful of sculptures when there were a dozen real women at hand, Millie didn't know. But if the duke was returning to his ways, she'd count her blessings and plan for Malta.

BY NIGHTFALL, the entertainments were in full swing. Winston stood in his salon, surrounded by the sights and sounds of pleasure, and couldn't stop thinking about his visit with Edward.

Couldn't stop feeling like a bloody coward for slinking away without confessing all, couldn't stop wondering what might be the matter with Cara.

At the far end of the salon, where the floor was raised for musicians, Urslane's merry band of harlots was putting on a fascinating rendition of a Greek tragedy.

One of the Spanish women was whispering suggestive things in Winston's ear, and two others Winston had never seen before were eyeing her venomously even as they allowed Pendergast and two of his London friends to laugh and tug at their bodices.

A young brunette squealed in mock outrage when her nipple popped free.

Winston raised his glass to his lips and made himself enjoy the view. Perhaps he would take all three women to his bed later. He wasn't dead, for God's sake.

That was the entire point. He *wasn't* dead.

If anything, he should show his gratitude by living all the more fully.

On the stage, one of the harlots "accidentally" gave the audience a peek between her thighs. Urslane called

out something obscene. Kerwood pulled a willing companion toward the curtains at the side of the room.

And Winston's thoughts shifted to Miles, who even
now was upstairs probably mixing up his ghastly nighttime tea.

Would she order another bath?

He imagined those shapely, perfect legs.

Those small, tender nipples no man had pinched and
pulled the way Pendergast was doing to that brunette right
now as the little strumpet laughed and grabbed for him.

And God help him, Miles's nipples were exactly what
he shouldn't be thinking of.

What he would *not* think of, even though the mere
memory of them was having an effect on him that a
quick look at a harlot's quim hadn't done.

Miles was no harlot. She was a skilled medic, stu-
dious, with more gumption than he would have in her
position—or foolishness, perhaps. But she would likely
know exactly how to convince Cara to submit to an examination, during which she would doubtless figure out
exactly what the problem was.

The theatrical women grew more daring with their
antics, and his guests grew more ribald, and two of them
were moving in on his favorites—something he should
put a stop to, if he planned to enjoy them later himself.

Which he should. That was the plan, after all…enjoy
himself so thoroughly that no thought for Miles would
remain.

He shifted his attention to the beauty at his side and
earned a suggestive smile from full stained lips. Generous round breasts pushed against him, his for the taking.

But the greater temptation was upstairs bundled in men's clothes, which made absolutely no sense at all.

One of the harlots tripped and fell, and three or four men rushed to help her, and suddenly he was worrying about Cara again, about whether Miles would agree to see her, and now the harlot was on her feet once more complaining of a bruised hip, and God's *blood* this was nothing like these parties used to be.

He should send them all back to London. Throw them out like he'd done in Paris.

Only to change your mind the moment everyone has gone?

This was intolerable.

He disentangled himself from the woman clinging to him, made a quick excuse and a hasty exit and took refuge in the library—but not for long, because anyone could find him here. He poured himself a quick slosh of brandy, knocked it back in two swallows.

A large book on a side chair caught his eye—or rather, the title caught his eye.

Wartime Injuries Examined.

There was only one person who could have been reading this. He picked it up, felt its weight in his hands as if they held Miles herself and quickly set it down.

A roar of laughter drifted from the salon.

He ought to be in there laughing with them instead. He headed upstairs, too frustrated now to care whether his guests noticed him missing.

BUT MILES WASN'T in her rooms.

Sacks was nowhere to be found, either, nor Harris. He scoured the rooms, went up a floor and did the same. Nothing.

And then, a thud. A hard one, drifting faintly from somewhere above. He narrowed his eyes at the ceiling, listening. Headed up a flight of servants' stairs and then another, all the way to the attic floor, where he heard the unmistakable murmur of voices.

What the devil was anyone doing in the attic rooms at this hour?

He followed the sound, pausing when he located the room it came from.

"Careful, now—" There was a clatter of objects hitting the floor. An oath. "For God's sake, we shan't need *all* of them!"

"Then 'ow many?"

Harris. And Sacks.

"I *told* you we should leave well enough alone." And *Miles?*

He pushed open the door and went inside. Found the three of them amid a forest of draped statuary, crouched next to an open trunk, picking up erotic playthings that were scattered on the floor. "What the devil is going on here?"

CHAPTER ELEVEN

THE DUKE'S VOICE shot through the room. Millie's attention snapped to the doorway, and her fingers tightened around a wooden phallus.

"Your Grace," Harris said calmly, placing the objects he held back in the trunk and then reaching to adjust the sheet on a statue they never should have attempted to move. He bowed. "Forgive me for being away from my post. Do you require attention?"

Her hand seemed permanently clamped around the phallus while her mind screamed at her to put it down.

"I'd hoped for a sedative tea," Winston drawled, and his eyes shifted to her. "But I couldn't find my medic."

Her cheeks flamed, but there was nothing to be done except brazen it out. She stood and deposited the disgusting toy calmly into the trunk as Harris had. "Forgive me, Your Grace," she said. "But we—"

"Learned that your artifacts had been very hastily stored away," Harris explained, "and given the extraordinary value of some of the pieces, we thought it imperative to ensure everything is as it should be. Would you believe it, at least half of these sculptures had not been properly covered."

Sacks shook his head as if to comment on the disgrace of it all.

"I intend to have a talk with Mrs. Coombs immediately," Harris said.

Sacks said, "Is Your Grace finished for the evening already? Right, then," he went on without waiting for an answer, "I'll go lay out your bedclothes while Mr. Germain prepares that tea."

"I'm not ready for my bedclothes," the duke said irritably. "And Mr. Germain will stay here. The two of you are excused."

Stay here!

"Your Grace," Harris said evenly, "the sooner the tea can begin steeping—"

"I understand the workings of tea, Harris."

"Very well, Your Grace." Harris bowed, casting a furtive and apologetic glance at Millie. And then Harris and Sacks were gone, and only the duke and her own candle remained, its solitary light flickering over his impossibly handsome face and the open trunk full of disgusting playthings.

She pursed her lips and bowed. "I am at your service, Your Grace."

"Indeed you are, Mr. Germain. And what a fascinating pastime I find you engaged in. I'm well aware of Harris and Sacks's proclivities, but I had no idea you were interested in such things. Tell me, what did the three of you intend with all of these?"

"We only meant to ensure that your guests have access to…whatever they might need."

"Or perhaps you were choosing something for yourself, hmm?" He reached into the trunk and picked up the same wooden phallus she'd held seconds ago. His teeth flashed wickedly. "This, perhaps?"

Her face flamed. "Your Grace is well aware there was a mishap and we were only picking things up from the floor," she snapped.

He tossed the object back into the trunk. "You've turned quite red, Mr. Germain. One might almost suspect you are uncomfortable with the male organ. Rather odd for a medic, isn't it?"

"A box full of disgraceful *objects* has nothing to do with medicine."

"You're quite right. All the same, you do seem remarkably off put."

This line of conversation could not continue. "I've been giving your situation a great deal of thought," Millie told him now, firmly, "and I've been thinking that perhaps you ought to enjoy some company, after all."

"Have you."

"I never expected you to be this out of sorts," she explained. "Your situation has led me to develop a theory that rest and solitude may not be the best regimen for every person."

"A theory, you say."

"Yes. And I've found my theories quite sound in the past."

"Mmm." The corner of his mouth might have moved, or she might have imagined it. "I have a theory, too, Mr. Germain."

She didn't like the way he was looking at her.

"My theory is that you will stop at nothing to convince me to pack my bags and set off for Greece. My only point of uncertainty is how you imagine a book full of erotic sketches or an insect's *privy parts* could possibly accomplish that."

"Your Grace, now you are talking nonsense. Perhaps just a quick rest before you rejoin your company—a half hour's lie-down in your bed, for example—"

"Where I might gaze upon my friend the princess? Or do I have my trusted butler and valet to thank for that? I daresay they've appreciated that portrait more than anyone...except perhaps you."

"You misunderstand entirely, Your Grace."

He scratched his chin. "I think not. In fact, I have another theory, Mr. Germain. Although it isn't so much a theory as it is a fact."

No, she definitely did not like the way he was looking at her.

"My theory, *Mr.* Germain," he said, coming closer, "is that the reason for your embarrassment a moment ago is because you have little to no experience with the male organ at all." He stopped in front of her, much too close. "And the reason for *that,* factually speaking—" he took her chin in his hand and glanced over her face "—is because, quite simply, you are a woman."

The vast attic room swallowed up the words into silence.

Blood rushed in her ears, pounded in her throat, paralyzing her tongue.

"You must admit," he went on reasonably, dropping his hand, raking his gaze critically over her body, "it would account for your small stature."

No. *No.* This would ruin everything.

There was a split second, a hasty and half-coherent decision, and she glared at him. Drew herself up to her full height. "I take *great* offense, Your Grace. I may be small, but not every man is blessed with as...*athletic* a figure as Your Grace's. Being less well-endowed is hardly grounds to call a man's gender into question."

"I am quite certain you are not *endowed* at all...*Miss Germain*, is it?"

But she was not going to tell him anything. "If I dared to suggest anything so outrageous about Your Grace's *endowment*—"

"Did it occur to you that I might prefer if you were a woman?"

"Oh, yes—I have no doubt Your Grace would *greatly* prefer it." He knew. He *knew*. "I can only imagine the fate of a female medic in your employ, as if such a thing could even—"

"The *fate* of a female medic in my employ?" he interrupted sharply. "Pray, do tell me what you imagine that fate might be."

"One would only have to make a quick appearance in Your Grace's salon at this very moment to answer that question."

"Those women are whores."

"Forgive me if I haven't met any men of your station who comprehend the difference—"

"You have now!"

"—which is neither here nor there to *me*, of course. Quite honestly, I'd been contemplating taking advantage of the entertainments myself, since you made it clear in Paris you have no objection to my indulging. Perhaps have a go at one of those bits of Spanish tail—"

"Good *God*." He stared at her in apparent frustration.

Clearly he hadn't expected her to deny his allegation. Had expected, apparently, that she would... What? Simply confess? *Ah, you've discovered me, Your Grace.*

Absolutely not. He had no right to expose her—none at all.

"Is this your plan, then?" he demanded. "To remain in disguise indefinitely? For the rest of your life, even?"

"I have no idea what you could possibly be talking about." All the times she'd touched him, changed his bandages, put her hands against his bare flesh mere inches from his sex...

Every time she'd done those things, he'd known.

"Oh, for Christ's sake," he said. "Good. Excellent, in fact. Perhaps it's better this way." He turned to go. "Enjoy your attic discoveries, Mr. Germain. I have no doubt they're proving every enlightening."

THE MOMENT HE was gone, Millie replaced everything and fled back to her rooms.

This was a disaster.

What was he going to do now? Would he tell anyone else his suspicions? Would he tell *everyone*—including Lord Hensley?

She never should have accepted this employment with Winston. None of this should be happening. It wasn't fair.

If it weren't for Philomena, who must have known the duke would see through Millie's disguise...

Before that, though, if it weren't for William, hunting down Millie and India like dogs and leaving Millie with no resources, she'd never have had to rely on Phil's connections.

But really, if it weren't for Katherine returning to England and thus ending Millie's position aboard the

Possession, she'd never have resorted to stealing the ship and running away.

She sank into the chair at the writing table.

Truly, if it weren't for *herself* and the terrible things she'd done, she wouldn't be in this position.

She and India were the ones who'd stolen the *Possession* from Katherine. William had only retrieved it. And without Katherine, Millie never would have had the opportunity to sail aboard the *Possession* in the first place. Likely she would still be in Lord Hensley's employ, and by now he certainly would have demanded more than he'd taken back then.

But now she was trapped, and Winston knew about her, and it was only a matter of time before...

Before what?

Before he stripped away her disguise entirely. She could be unmasked at any moment, humiliated, her options taken from her.

Suddenly she reached for the quill, dipped it, slid a piece of paper closer.

Dear Katherine,

An apology hummed in her fingertips, hovering unwritten over the page.

Faded. What good could it possibly do now? Katherine would never accept it. An apology would change nothing. She could write the words, but she couldn't rewrite the past. She couldn't unsteal the ship from her dear former captain and friend.

A wave of grief swelled up and she sat for a moment, thinking of times gone by—times that would never be again. All of them sailing aboard the *Possession* with Katherine at its helm…India somewhere up in the rigging, Philomena adorning the upper deck, William conferring with the boatswain or barking orders to the crew. Millie helping the crew when the infirmary was empty.

Back then, she'd had a place. People. A future in which her skills were needed, and she was protected and had the means to protect herself, and the surgical school at Malta was within her reach.

Now she had none of that.

She pushed the paper away and stood up. There was nothing she could say to Katherine anyhow that would make a difference. Millie's betrayal was too complete. She'd lost Katherine's friendship—all of their friendships—forever.

A knock at the door startled her from her reverie.

It was Winston, which startled her even more. "What do you want?" she asked him, forgetting her deference for a moment, wondering if he could have decided to press his advantage this quickly.

"There's something I need you to do, the reason I was looking for you in the first place," he said, making no move to enter her room. "There's a friend I would like you to see in the village. The vicar's wife, Mrs. Edward Cady."

Millie's knees went weak with relief. "The vicar's wife," she repeated. "Is she ill?"

"I don't know. That is to say, Edward—the vicar, and a very great friend—doesn't know. He says Cara's been acting strangely and refuses to see the physician in the village."

"Then she'll hardly be willing to see *me*."

"Not if you tell her the truth."

She narrowed her eyes. "There is no truth to be told."

"Mr. Germain." His expression hardened. "Deny the facts as much as you wish in my household, continue to hide in your bagwig and suit, but Cara *must* be seen." The violence of his concern took her by surprise. "If that requires you to reveal yourself to her, then as a person in my employ, I expect you will do it." He looked her up and down. "Even if you refuse to admit it to me."

SHE WAS NOT going to tell the vicar's wife a bloody thing.

It was early afternoon the next day when Millie trundled alone toward the village in the duke's coach while His Grace and all of the guests still lay abed after a night of excess.

She would perform the examination just as she did for Winston himself or anyone else, for that matter, and that would be that.

Except that she couldn't keep examining him now, could she? Not and touch him the way she'd been doing, knowing that he would be watching her and feeling her touch and knowing she was not *Mr.* Germain but *Miss* Germain.

Miss Germain, who took more pleasure than she should from touching him and required far too much effort to keep from staring at him and ridiculously daydreamed about what it might be like to kiss him.

None of which he could possibly know. Could he? What if he'd somehow guessed all that, as well? Surely there would have been some hint of that. Wouldn't there?

What kind of hint? A declaration of passion? Good God.

There was a reason he'd agreed to go on pretending. Compared to the women he favored, she may as well be Miles Germain—plain, mousy, dressed in men's clothes.

He may have seen through her disguise in one respect, but in another, it was working exactly as intended.

The coach stopped in front of a cozy stone cottage next to the church but set back from the street. A tidy flower garden bloomed in front. Before she reached the door, she could hear the Reverend and Mrs. Cady arguing inside through a pair of open windows on the far right side of the cottage—the vicar pleading with her to let Mr. Germain examine her, his wife insisting she did not need to be seen.

"I'll not brook a refusal, Cara. Not this time."

"It isn't for you to refuse or not refuse," his wife said angrily. "I don't need a physician."

"I say you do," the vicar said firmly. "And this is Winston's own medic. He's bound to be one of the best."

"I still can't believe you discussed this with him."

But judging from the expression on Winston's face last night, Millie could believe it. He cared about these people. She'd seen it in his eyes when he made this demand—genuine concern.

"Cara, I'm worried about you," the vicar said. "That even Winston could see something was bothering me ought to convince you of that, at least. See this medic when he comes. Satisfy my mind if nothing else—and promise me you won't be rude to him."

"And if Mr. Germain examines me and says I am well?"

"Then that will be the end of it."

There was a pause. "Very well."

Millie knocked and was admitted to a salon, where the vicar and his wife were standing in the middle of the room waiting.

"Mr. Germain," the vicar said with a bow. "Thank you so much for coming. This is my wife—we are both very appreciative of your time and attention."

Mrs. Cady looked anything but appreciative and offered only a perfunctory curtsy. She was a beautiful woman, but not by Winston's standards—she was earthy, with thick, honey-blond hair pulled up into an informal chignon. Her nose was dusted with freckles, likely from working in the flower garden. Rich brown eyes watched Millie with...

Fear.

And Millie knew, suddenly, that the woman had lied to her husband.

"Shall we go upstairs?" the vicar asked in a firm tone that left no question but that they *would* go upstairs. His wife led the way up a narrow staircase with Millie in her wake and the vicar following behind, and they went into a spacious sitting room done in light blue with windows that faced the churchyard cemetery to the south. Sunlight streamed in, warming the room if not the chill of Mrs. Cady's objections.

"I will be fine with Mr. Germain," she told her husband in the same firm tone he'd used downstairs, while Millie set her bag on a small table and opened it.

In the looking glass she saw the vicar press a kiss to his wife's temple, and she heard him murmur, "Thank you."

The moment he'd gone, Mrs. Cady strode to the table where Millie was getting out her instruments. "I do not need an examination," she said in a low voice. "My husband is overreacting. I want you to tell him you looked at me and concluded nothing is amiss."

"If nothing is amiss," Millie countered reasonably, "then why not consent to an examination?"

"That is just the very thing a man would say," Mrs. Cady whispered crossly. "Because I do not *want* an examination, and I did not *ask* for an examination, and as much as I appreciate Winston and Edward's good intentions, I will not *have* an examination."

Millie could not have admired her more.

"You find this amusing?" Mrs. Cady hissed when a smiled tugged at Millie's lips. "Of course you do. You are in cahoots with them."

"I am not in cahoots with anyone, Mrs. Cady." Millie turned away from her medical bag and faced her. "You're afraid to be examined. Why?"

Mrs. Cady crossed her arms. "I'm not afraid."

"What are the symptoms that caused your husband to insist on this visit?"

"They are nothing serious. Fatigue, that's all. One can't be summoning a physician every time one feels a bit tired."

"That can't be all."

"Mr. Germain, if I wished to discuss this with you, I would submit to an examination."

"Have you had pain anywhere? Stomach? Chest?"

"No."

"Are you certain? Even any tenderness, perhaps in your breasts or belly?"

"No." The answer was breathier this time. Tighter. Mrs. Cady let her arms fall and turned away, going to the window, resting her fingertips on the sill.

"Because if you truly are ill…"

"I am not ill, Dr. Germain. Not in the least. It's nothing. I already know it won't be— It isn't—" She cut off and pressed the back of her hand to her mouth, still facing out the window. Millie heard a sniffle and a muffled "Damn Winston and Edward, anyway."

Millie's heart squeezed. Something was very wrong—there was no doubt.

"Mrs. Cady, if you'll only allow me a brief examination—"

"I said I don't *want* one."

Millie watched her for a moment. Glanced at herself in the glass across the room—her suit and bagwig, her unsmiling mouth.

She reached up.

Hesitated. Glanced at Mrs. Cady, saw the woman's shoulders shaking with silent tears.

And Millie grasped the wig, pulling it back and away, revealing her pinned-up hair. She returned to the table and set the wig next to her bag. Pulled out the pins and set them there, too.

"Mrs. Cady…" She used her own voice, softer than Mr. Germain's voice.

"Please leave. Tell my husband whatever you wish."

"I'm not going to tell him anything," Millie said, joining her at the window, touching her arm. "I only hope you'll be kind enough to do the same."

Mrs. Cady turned her head. Her brown eyes widened when she saw Millie's hair, and then—

"Oh." A sob ripped from her throat, and she threw her arms around Millie, crying in great sobs that seemed to rip from her deepest soul.

Emotion clogged Millie's chest, and unshed tears burned her eyes even though she wasn't sure why— but she was sure that something was terribly wrong, and so finally, when Mrs. Cady pulled away, Millie gripped her arms.

"*Please* tell me what is the matter so I may help."

Mrs. Cady shook her head. "There is nothing you can do."

"You can't know that."

"Yes, yes I can. And you mustn't—you mustn't breathe a word to Edward. Not a word! Nor to Winston, either."

"I've already told you I won't, and doubly so for Winston. It's hardly *his* business, is it?" Even though he clearly thought everything was his business. "Are you pregnant?"

Mrs. Cady closed her eyes. Nodded.

"He does not want the child?"

"No— Oh, heavens, it isn't that. Edward would love a child more than anything in the world. But I can't… Every time a child takes root, it lives for two months, sometimes nearly three, and then…" Fresh tears flooded her eyes, and she shook her head mutely. "There's nothing to be done. And this time I can't bear for him to know. The pain in his eyes is too much… I can't bear to see it again."

"How long has it been this time?" Millie asked.

"That's just the thing." The fear returned to Mrs. Cady's eyes now. "It's been four months. I've never carried a babe this long—not since the first time."

"How long the first time?"

"The full term. But something went wrong in the delivery… The child died, and I nearly did, as well. Ever since then…"

Ever since then, there had been nothing but miscarriages. And now, she obviously expected one any day.

"Oh, Mrs. Cady. I am so very sorry."

"Please." The woman reached for Millie's hands and squeezed them. "Please call me Cara. I've thought of going to my sister's…making some kind of excuse to Edward, and staying with Ruth until…" She shook her head. "But somehow I can't bring myself to do it. As if it wouldn't be fair to him. And then I keep thinking, what if this time…" Another head shake, as if she couldn't bring herself to express even the smallest hope.

"Will you let me examine you?" Millie asked quietly.

This time, Cara nodded.

CHAPTER TWELVE

HE'D MADE A bloody mess of things, and there was no undoing it.

Winston prowled his upstairs library alone, fully aware that his guests were downstairs making merry in the late afternoon and that he should join them—*wanted* to join them—yet here he was, doing absolutely nothing.

A packet of papers had arrived this morning—some information from DeLille about a new enclosure bill—and he'd skimmed through them, but now the papers lay scattered on the table.

Miles should have returned by now, shouldn't she?

He went over to the window, looked out at the brilliant day and suddenly wondered if she might never return, after what he'd done last night. Sacks had told him she'd gone to the village to see Cara, but—

He left his small library, strode down the hall to Miles's rooms, opened the door...

And sighed with relief to see that all of her things were still there.

Well, of course they were. Hadn't she made it clear enough that she needed the wages from this employment? She would stay for that reason if for no other.

And it wasn't as if her gender could have remained a secret forever.

Of course it could bloody well have remained a secret. She could have finished her service, collected her wages and left without ever knowing he suspected a thing.

That wouldn't happen now. Instead, the next time he saw her, she would know that he knew, and he would know that he knew, and the only thing standing between them would be her suit and that god-awful bagwig—and his self-control.

He briefly considered looking through her trunk to see if it contained anything that would shed light on her background but decided he knew enough already.

Knowing more would only make things worse.

What things?

His attraction for her, he admitted with no small amount of aggravation as he returned to his private library. Voilà, there it was. He was attracted to her.

It was hardly news.

He entered the library and had taken two steps when he realized it was occupied.

"There you are," purred a familiar figure waiting in the middle of the room.

"Miss Tensie," he murmured. Good *God,* she was the last person he wanted to see.

She came toward him. "I haven't seen you nearly as much as I'd hoped this time. We've had such fun before."

From much farther down the corridor, he heard voices. A door open and shut. Guests were returning upstairs for a late-afternoon...rest.

"Indeed," he said as she pressed herself against him,

which wasn't striking him as *fun* at all, even though it should—it certainly should.

He set her away, but she only dimpled at him.

"Are we in a foul mood this afternoon?"

"Not at all. I simply—"

"I daresay I know how to change that," Tensie said, and slipped two fingers into her stays, giving a gentle tug that exposed two plump, pale nipples to his view. "Mmm? Better?"

He tried to grin, but it felt more like an awkward twist of his lips. "Quite."

No, it wasn't better. It should be, but it wasn't.

Why not? It's Miles you've vowed not to touch.

He cleared his throat. "Unfortunately, there's some business I must see to…" He went to his table, gathered up the paperwork DeLille had sent.

Tensie followed. "Surely it can wait…" she pouted, drawing a finger up the length of his thigh to his—

"It can't." He smoothly backed away, already feeling a stirring that Tensie could easily satisfy. It could be fast. Simple.

"I shan't let you spend the afternoon with the doldrums," Tensie declared, with those nipples jutting brazenly out at him. "If you have business…I can help."

MILLIE RETURNED LATER than she'd meant to, after enjoying a long tea with Cara in the upstairs drawing room at the vicarage. It was an enlightening visit. Too enlightening, really. Cara, the vicar and Winston had been the closest of friends since they were children, and Cara was only too willing to discuss her childhood friend.

The childhood walk by the river when Winston and

Edward had collected an entire bucket of frogs—and dumped it over Cara's head.

The private dinner at Cara and Edward's table after Winston's father's death, where he had broken down and wept.

The generous sums sent to any woman on the estate who lost a husband.

"He isn't as shallow as he likes to pretend," Cara had said, right before she'd asked, "Can it be true that he has no idea of your gender?"

That was when Millie had spouted a lie, offered an oh-how-time-has-flown excuse and made a hasty retreat.

And now she was back in her rooms, and any minute now she would have to face him. He'd never called for his morning examination, and she'd left for the village without ever seeing him.

But he would need his injuries examined this evening whether he called for her or not. She would have to go to him. See him undressed. Lean close and touch his bare skin, breathe his intoxicating scent—dear God, it was as if she could smell him just by remembering— and know that he knew. There was no safety left in her disguise, at least not with him.

And yet he'd known all this time, and he hadn't done anything.

She leaned toward the glass and adjusted her wig. It hadn't been sitting right since she'd removed it this afternoon, even though she and Cara had both tried to put it to rights.

Of course he hasn't done anything. Just look at you.

It was true. She stood back from the glass, realized

that things weren't as bad as they seemed. Disguise or no, she wasn't the kind of woman that Winston would take an interest in. So really, it didn't matter that he'd figured out the truth. She was perfectly safe either way.

Just then, there was a knock at the door. It was Sacks, brows furrowed, mouth tight. "Have you seen 'is Grace?"

"No. I only just returned from the village."

Sacks exhaled and glanced back at the door. "He hasn't left 'is rooms all afternoon, so we finally sent up Miss Tensie to entertain 'im. Now they're both gone."

They'd sent up one of the whores. She didn't have to wonder what that meant. A sudden pain caught her in the gut. "Perhaps they've rejoined the party."

Sacks shook his head. "Harris said Miss Tensie never returned downstairs. Nor 'as His Grace."

"Then they've gone off together, obviously." The pain in her gut twisted hard. "Which is precisely what you wanted, is it not?"

And it was precisely what *she* wanted. He would never change his mind about Greece if he refused to join his company and engage in his usual sport. The man she'd first met in Paris needed to be restored. And if that involved intimacies with a whore...

"I've looked everywhere," Sacks said with frustration. "If he's gone off with 'er, they've gone to the bloody moon."

Just then Harris walked in, lips tight. "I've found Miss Tensie—in a back stairwell with one of the guests. I've no idea where His Grace could have got to."

"Bloody hell," Sacks muttered.

The sharp twist in her gut released itself suddenly,

but then, "He could have found other company," she suggested.

Harris was shaking his head. "All the ladies are accounted for downstairs."

"We'd best start looking," Sacks grouched.

Except it seemed that the duke did not wish to be found, and *she* certainly didn't want to be the one to find him—or them, if he wasn't alone—but Harris and Sacks expected her to help, so she made a cursory search that turned up nothing. Forty-five minutes later, she was checking the rooms nearest to hers and his and was about to exit the room adjacent to hers when she heard a noise behind her.

She turned just in time to see a panel slide open and the duke emerge with a sheaf of papers in his hand. He stopped when he saw her. Cursed under his breath.

"You have a secret hiding place, after all, I see," she said sourly, crossing her arms, remembering her search in Paris. "We've been looking everywhere for you. I was beginning to fear you might have fallen somewhere and injured yourself." *Or gone off with a woman.*

The bite of jealousy was so very, very irrational.

"An unwanted visitor found her way up to my rooms," he said, looking at her…more closely than usual?

Nonsense.

"Given your present company, I'm not sure how that could be possible." Miss Tensie, unwanted? "Unless it was one of the gentlemen," she added for good measure.

"I'm not in a frame of mind for company." Annoyance colored his tone. "In fact, I've been toying with the idea of having you work your magic again as you did in Paris. I'm not even sure I care what you tell them, as long as everyone leaves."

That was alarming news, which didn't explain the surge of relief that left her suddenly hopeful. "Surely you don't mean that."

"I don't know *what* I mean."

And what could *that* signify? "What a vexation, unplanned revelry and merrymaking," she said a bit sarcastically.

"Oh, it was planned," he said, slipping something from his pocket. "Only not by me." He unfolded a piece of paper and held it out to her.

His Grace the Duke of Winston invites you to a...

"It would seem Harris and Sacks have been looking out for my interests," he said wryly.

She handed the invitation back. "They've been very concerned. They meant no harm."

"Don't you mean *we* meant no harm?"

Her cheeks grew warm. Now he *was* looking at her more closely, more intently.

"Why can you not send them away yourself? You did that in Paris," she said to distract him.

"It was one thing to evict friends when I was mere hours out of a fever. But this time— Bloody hell. Someone's coming."

The door was open, and there were voices outside. Laughter, a lewd comment—

"It's Hensley." The duke moved forward, taking her by the arm before she realized what was happening, pulling her into the secret closet and quickly sliding the panel shut behind them.

There was the scrape and flare of a match, a dim

glow as he brushed against her, reaching to light a candle in a small holder resting on a shelf.

The room was barely big enough for two people. An old chair with worn velvet took up most of the space. And now they stood there, pressed together, listening to murmurs and laughter from the room they'd left just in time.

His scent filled every breath, sending heady yearnings deep into her most secret places.

He'd been in here, hiding from Miss Tensie.

And more the fool her, she was glad.

Through the wall, Millie could hear the murmur of Hensley's voice, and she shivered. "Is there another way out?" she asked, turning to the opposite wall, which was made of panels like the one they'd just come through.

"No," he whispered quickly. "I fear we're trapped here for the duration."

She put her hands flat against the panels. Realized, suddenly, what was on the other side.

Her dressing room.

The other night, when she'd thought she'd seen something move…

"These panels *do* open."

"Stop." His hand covered hers, pressing firmly. "Hensley will hear. Even Harris and Sacks don't know about this closet," he hissed in her ear. "God help me if that cad Hensley discovers it."

His hand was large. Warm. Sensations from his touch raced through her arm, spread through her body all the way to her knees. His breath feathered her ear, and she felt it low in her belly.

Felt him right behind her, felt his body pressed up against hers, even if only lightly.

And awareness of him boiled together with awareness of something else. "You were in here," she hissed back. "The other night."

"I don't know what you're talking about."

She wrenched her hand free, dug her fingers at the edge of the panel, only to have him stop her more firmly with both arms around her, grasping her wrists, pulling her hands away.

"You watched me in the bath!"

"Be *quiet*."

She struggled against him, whispering furiously. "There *is* another way out, and you bloody well know it, and you used it to peep—"

"I did no such thing."

"You *spied* on me." In the nude. She'd been in the *nude!* "Let go of me. I'm leaving this closet at once, through *this* panel," she said, fighting him to keep her hands on it and pull, "because I know bloody well that it—"

The panel slid open.

Opens. I know bloody well that it opens.

The struggle suddenly ceased, and she stared into her dressing room with Winston still holding her arms, the rise and fall of his chest against her back and his breath against her ear.

The panel really did open. And there was no doubt, none at all now, of what had happened.

"How *dare* you." Her words were a breathy hiss as she fixed on the spot where the tub had sat.

"The temptation was too great," he murmured, and

his voice traveled across her skin to all the places he would have seen that night.

She tore away, turning to face him, throwing her pointing finger toward the door. "Leave," she ordered. "Immediately. I don't want you in here—nor in *there*," she snapped, glancing toward the open panel. "That panel will be nailed shut tonight, even if I must do it myself, and it will *not* open again."

"Miss Germain—"

"*Mister.*" She stalked to the door, jerked it open, raised her chin at him.

"You have my sincerest apologies." He exhaled, mouth grim. "And my solemn promise that none of this will happen again."

This being assessing her nude body, comparing her to the kind of women he was used to, violating her privacy in the most humiliating way imaginable.

"You're bloody right, it won't." She looked pointedly at him and pulled the door fully open. "Good night, Your Grace."

CHAPTER THIRTEEN

MILLIE'S HEART STILL raced after he'd gone, and she glared at the door—at the gaping panel—cursing him.

Devil take him, he was no better than Lord Hensley. Which should come as no surprise.

But her skin still tingled with the memory of his nearness, and each breath still carried his scent. She turned her face, pressing it into her shoulder, sniffing...

And yes, the scent of his cologne lingered there on her clothes, even though they'd been pressed together for a matter of seconds, and now the merest whiff did things to her on the inside—warm, heady things she wanted no part of.

She unbuttoned her coat, tearing it from her shoulders and tossing it over a chair, but it was as if the smell of him had penetrated her skin. She went to the panel and studied its fitting, making a mental list of the materials required to nail it shut. Serving aboard a ship taught a person about more than just sails and wind.

Bloody bastard. At least now, she wasn't afraid to tell him exactly what she thought of his lewd behavior.

Years ago, when Lord Hensley had unfastened his breeches and made her touch him, she hadn't dared object. And unlike Winston, he'd made no promises that it would never happen again.

It *always* happened again. She'd hated the feel of Hensley's member. The sounds he'd made, and the mess afterward. She thought of him in Winston's room next door, probably availing himself of those whores even now, and felt a little sick.

But she reminded herself of all the reasons it didn't matter that Lord Hensley was staying in this very house. She was safely hidden in her disguise, and it seemed Winston would not unmask her.

What *did* matter was the fact that Winston was not responding to any of the temptations presented to him, yet somehow found it irresistible to spy on *her,* damn him.

A few minutes later, wearing a fresh coat with a short materials list tucked into the pocket, Millie found Harris and Sacks at the top of the staircase. "I found him," she told them irritably. "He's in his rooms now."

"Where was he?"

"*Hiding.* In—" It would serve Winston right if she told them. "In one of the spare rooms." She didn't need them spying on her, as well.

"I *checked* all the bloody rooms," Sacks said.

"He was hiding from Miss Tensie," she practically snapped. "He didn't *want* her company. Doesn't want *any* of this. Bloody sod—there's plenty here to entertain him. He wants for *nothing.*"

They looked at her.

Sacks's dark brows knitted together, and Harris frowned a little. "It isn't His Grace's fault if he's feeling out of sorts," Harris said.

"He can be a bloody aggravation, but he deserves no disrespect," Sacks added disapprovingly.

She inhaled deeply. Silently. "Forgive me. I meant no disrespect, naturally. I'm merely frustrated that he presents such a…a stubborn case. I could not convince him to join his company, and I fear he's thinking of throwing them all out. I can't think what else can possibly be done."

But it was easy to imagine how much money it was going to cost to travel to the Mediterranean on her own.

"We may have a solution," Harris said tentatively, "but it cannot be guaranteed. I heard from one of the guests that Princess Katja—" he looked pointedly from Millie to Sacks "—is in London. I sent her an invitation yesterday. If the princess answers the invite, I think it'll do the trick."

Princess Katja. The one in the portrait. They'd invited *her.*

"I can't think how," Millie said, "when he didn't even want to look at her portrait. If he wasn't tempted by that, and he's not tempted by any the women downstairs, he'll hardly be tempted by one more." And he wasn't interested in Tensie or the other whores, who were every bit as voluptuous as the princess.

Harris smiled at her as if she was a dull-witted fool. "The princess is hardly *one more* woman."

Sacks snorted. "Right, that. She'd do the trick for a dead man."

TEMPTATION, THY NAME is Miles.

Winston took a swallow of brandy and swirled the liquid in his glass, staring at his empty bed, pondering the possibilities downstairs but wanting only one thing:

Miles, fully unclothed, in his bed and open to him for the rest of the day. Hell, the rest of the week.

But that was not going to happen. He'd found a vow that meant something, a manner of *considering his ways* that he could fully comprehend, and that was the end of it.

He'd meant what he'd said. It would not happen again. Nothing. There would be no touching her, no spying on her, no bloody *fantasizing* about her, which was easier said than done because she grew more tempting by the hour.

He knew better than to call her in for his evening's examination.

He was about finished with examinations, anyhow. His wounds were scabbed over now, healing nicely, she'd said, and all he needed her for were the ones he couldn't reach on his back. Those had been the deepest, the most in danger of festering.

But even they were healing now. And he had a good mind to rid himself of this sling.

It was probably time to rid himself of Miles, as well.

He needed to stop this nonsensical hiding away in his rooms and rejoin the entertainment downstairs. Get a bit foxed and take advantage of those Spanish vixens, whose lusty thighs would willingly part for him. He could spend himself there and forget all about Miles. Or close his eyes and pretend it *was* Miles—nothing wrong with that.

He could only imagine what Edward would say to that, and devil take it, this was no time to be thinking of Edward.

Consider your ways.

He was considering his bloody ways. What more could possibly be asked of him?

He drained his glass and went downstairs.

ONE MORE AVAILABLE female was not going to do the trick for anything, Millie thought as she tapped the last tack into place as quietly as possible. She left the secret compartment through the other panel into the study on the other side, with Lord Hensley and his companion long gone.

After a quick test from her side of the panel and finding it secure, she turned her attention to another of the musty old volumes from the duke's library, leafing briskly through pages filled mostly with superstition and wives' tales.

She'd barely settled in the chair when Sacks poked his head in the room to report that Winston had joined the company in the grand salon.

Had he.

After Sacks left, Millie stared blankly at the page in front of her while her mind conjured up graphic images of Winston...*joining the company.* Her chest squeezed, and her throat tightened up.

She flipped a page, shoving the thoughts away. This was a hopeful sign. Even now, he could be—

Never mind about that. He was finally turning his attention in the proper direction, the direction that would take them both to Greece.

Until Sacks poked his head in again, an hour later, to complain that Winston had already returned to his rooms, having done nothing more than play a round of cards, watch a bit of dancing, and oblige a pair of

Spanish breasts that had been presented for his entertainment.

"It's more than he's done yet," Sacks said hopefully. "Perhaps he's on the mend, after all."

Millie tried not to imagine what was involved in *obliging* a pair of breasts and quietly disagreed.

Except the next morning, when she went to Winston's bedchamber, she was met by a startling sight.

"What are you doing?" she snapped the moment she entered. "It's too soon for that."

He stood by the window, tentatively flexing his arm, while his sling lay draped over a nearby chair. He wore his blue banyan over his breeches and waistcoat. Without his wig, his own dark hair curled up at the base of his neck. A thought flitted through her—a fleeting desire to touch it.

She did *not* want to touch Winston. She didn't. It was just…

Nothing. It was nothing.

"I disagree," he said, and continued flexing his elbow, moving his arm in slow circles from the shoulder. "It's feeling a good deal better."

"So you've told me, but—"

"If it worsens, I shall put the sling back on."

He glanced at her, and their eyes held just long enough for a shiver of memory to cut through her— his whisper against her ear, her back against his chest, his arms practically around her…

Only because he was trying to stop you from discovering what he'd done.

"Very well." She plunked her medical bag on the table and yanked it open.

"I'd like to take my horse out—"

"Your *horse!*"

"You did say my wounds were healing," he said irritably.

They wouldn't be for long if he began racing across the countryside on horseback. "I can't stop you," she said shortly. Because, as she well knew, the duke did as he pleased. "But riding horseback is not advisable at this time."

She felt him looking at her, but she only continued setting out the light bandages she would need now that his wounds were scabbed over and, indeed, healing. Just a bit of protection to keep them clean and prevent chafing against his clothing.

"I understand you went to visit Cara yesterday," he said now. "How did the examination proceed?"

Was he thinking about last night at all? About his complete and utter violation of her privacy? "As well as any." The examination had revealed nothing abnormal. Nothing Millie would not have expected to see in any woman four months pregnant. She wasn't sure when she'd felt so relieved after a patient visit.

"What does *that* mean?"

"It means that my examinations are confidential, and if you wish to know anything about Cara, you'll have to ask her yourself."

"Cara is my friend. I demand to know what you've discovered."

"You certainly are interested in everyone's private business, aren't you?" Millie snapped, and looked up.

His eyes narrowed.

"In fact, you seem interested in everything except that which is freely available to you."

"Is that so?"

"Healthful regimen," she scoffed. "You order a princess's portrait returned to the attic, you store away all your nude sculptures—yet you couldn't resist peeking at *me* in the bath?" She tossed the bandage aside and faced him. "Perhaps I ought to remove myself to the attic and drape myself with a sheet."

"Mr. Germain—"

"Oh, yes, and what fun you've had with *that,* haven't you? *Mr. Germain,* you said, as if you believed it to be perfectly true, giving no hint that you saw through my disguise, making sure I suspected nothing, all the while you were anticipating your first opportunity to peep at me like a boy outside a privy house."

"I seem to recall you refusing to admit the truth even when I told you I knew it."

"Well, I can hardly deny it now, can I?" she shot back. "And were you titillated, skulking in your darkened peep-chamber? Were you amused? Of course, I already know the answer to *that.* And now you refuse to entertain yourself with your company—your *very willing* company, I might add."

"I have my reasons," he said tightly.

"Indeed—reasons known only to yourself. This *never* would have happened if we'd gone to Greece, unless you have secret closets in every coaching inn on the continent and aboard every ship in the Mediterranean. And perhaps you do," she said, making a show of looking at the walls. "Perhaps you have them everywhere. Do your guests know you spy on them? Or perhaps they enjoy that sort of thing."

"I do *not* spy on my guests."

"Only your medics, then?"

"I gave you my apology," he ground out.

"Which does me little good now. All has been revealed—nothing is left to the imagination, and it cannot be undone. It's past time for you to get on with your business here, whatever that might be. So far you have me at a loss."

"Perhaps it would help if I were free from distractions," he said darkly.

"You've kept yourself closeted away for days." She gestured toward the empty bedchamber. "You can't be any less distracted than this."

He stared at her. The look in his eyes made a nerve pulse in her belly. And suddenly—

Dear God, he was saying that *she* was a distraction.

"There's no earthly reason for us to be here," she said now, thickly. "You could have healed just as well in Paris. Found ten times the number of activities. What you need now, Your Grace, is—"

"Do you want to know what I need, Miles?" he asked darkly, advancing on her. "Do you really?"

And there wasn't time to think before he reached for her and pulled her to him, bringing his mouth down on hers, forcing her lips apart.

Fire raced hotly, startlingly to her most intimate places. He possessed her mouth completely, finding her tongue, mating with it.

He tasted of sin and excess.

The devil duke. His lesson was immediate and thorough. He parried with her tongue and she parried back, learned quickly how to devour him the way he devoured her—madly, recklessly.

And the world shrank until nothing existed but him and the sensations he was igniting in her body that were impossible to resist.

She splayed her hands across his chest.

Felt his hands slip down, curl around her bottom as he pushed her backward, backward, until she bumped into something—a table. He half urged, half lifted her onto it, and stood between her parted legs, brought her snugly against his erection.

Nerves flamed to life in her breasts, belly, thighs, taunting her to press herself closer.

She wrapped her arms around his neck, dug her fingers into the curls at his nape. Writhed at the startling pleasure where he rocked against her. He reached beneath her waistcoat and yanked her shirt from her breeches. And then—

His hands, hot and demanding against her bare skin. He groaned with frustration into her mouth when her clothes hindered his exploration, but yanked them higher and now she felt his fingers at the edge of her binding.

Skimming over top of it.

Finding the peaks of her breasts that strained hard against the binding. Circling them.

She clung to him harder, pressed closer, cried out a little into their kiss.

And ignored the voice telling her this needed to stop. That she knew better.

Because his fingers were pushing at the tight binding. Shoving it up, and now his hands covered her bare breasts, and the flesh between her legs was on fire. And she didn't know what to do—how or where to touch him—but she ran her hands over him impetuously, crazily, the way no medic would ever do, closing over his firm buttocks the way he'd done to her, pulling him closer—

And then, suddenly, he tore away.

Snatched his hands from beneath her clothes as if she were on fire.

"Damnation." He backed up, breathing hard.

The separation stunned her, left her sitting there with her legs still spread and her heart pounding a deafening pulse through her veins, in her ears, and her breath coming too fast through lips that still throbbed from the ferocity of his kiss.

He shoved his hand through his hair. Cursed again. "I promised I wouldn't do that. I *vowed* I wouldn't."

He'd vowed? Not to...*kiss* her?

She closed her thighs, slipped onto legs that trembled so strongly she wasn't sure she could stand. Everything they'd just done burned into her skin, her lips, her hands.

She opened her mouth to speak, but nothing came out.

"Miles— Oh, for Christ's sake, whatever your name is— What *is* your real name?" But, "Never mind," he went on sharply. "I don't want to know. And let me make one thing perfectly clear— There will be no journey to Greece."

Greece? "I didn't say anything about—"

"I shall be staying right here, at my estate, for the rest of eternity if that's what it takes to—" He broke off.

She waited. To what?

He watched her through eyes that burned with something she'd never seen directed at her before.

Raw desire.

White-hot yearning.

Even as they stood there, he wanted to kiss her again. She could see that, too.

And she may still be bundled up inside breeches, waistcoat, jacket and bagwig, but her disguise was in tatters.

"Harris will make sure you receive your wages," he said in a low voice, barely audible. "My carriage will take you to London, and you shall have a letter of credit to see you to Greece or Malta or wherever it is you wish to go."

It took a moment to grasp what he'd said. "You're *dismissing* me? Because of *this*?" Outrage reared up inside her, comforting and familiar.

"I'm not dismissing you. I am anticipating your resignation."

Her insides were spinning out of control, swept up in feelings she'd never had for any man in her life, feelings she wanted no part of—especially not with him.

She made a desperate grab for control. "I've endured worse from an employer," she said, sounding not nearly outraged enough to her own ears. "You shall have to do more than that to be rid of me—"

"Which employer?" he demanded.

"—and I assure you that if you try to do more than that, you'll be sorry."

"Which employer?"

"Not one of any significance." Shame burned through her at the thought of him finding out about her employment as governess to Lord Hensley's children—how he'd taken advantage of her, how she had complied because she'd thought she had no choice, how being a governess did not always mean only looking after the children.

Lord Hensley, Winston's friend. Which was all the more reason she needed to be furious. Repulsed. Sick, even.

Instead, her nipples still peaked sensitively against her shirt with the lingering effects of his touch searing into them, sending warm yearnings down through her belly to her most intimate places and beyond, making her yearn for his touch again. Making her yearn to touch *him*.

And now her binding was stuck awkwardly above her breasts, and there was no way to reach beneath her clothing without calling attention to all the places he'd just touched.

"Perhaps I *should* speak with Harris about my wages," she said, but just then something caught his attention outside, and he went to the window.

She took advantage of the moment to quickly stuff her shirt back into her breeches, but there was no doing it properly, and the shirttails bunched and bulged beneath the fabric, so she pulled her jacket tightly around her, quickly fastening the buttons—

"Who in God's name... Bloody *hell*." Winston was already heading for the door before Millie could get to the window to see what was happening. "I've got to find Urslane immediately. Sacks!" And then he was ripping the banyan back off, striding into his dressing room, yanking open his armoire and pulling out a jacket without bothering to wait for Sacks. Stuffing his arms through, he practically ran from the room.

And now, looking down, Millie saw why: An ornate coach had arrived at the front of the house, and emerging gracefully from its interior was...

One of the most beautiful women Millie had ever seen.

CHAPTER FOURTEEN

PRINCESS KATJA. This was the last straw. And it could ruin so many things.

Winston raced down the stairs, his body still hot and tight and pulsing with something that never, ever should have happened.

There wasn't time to consider it now. He strode through the entrance hall, through the empty ballroom and into the dining room, where he found everyone just finishing a leisurely breakfast.

He walked straight up to Urslane and murmured in his ear.

Urslane bolted from his chair. So did Pendergast.

"It's Princess Katja," Winston said under his breath, and Pendergast paled.

"Who in God's name—"

"Never mind about that." He already had a good idea who had invited her. "You know what needs to be done."

Urslane nodded once. "Of course, of course…"

"The back courtyard…"

"Consider it done."

If Katja thought Winston had invited her to participate in *this*… Bloody devil.

"I shall see you all in London," Winston said, even though he had no intention of going there—no thought for anything except the impending disaster that was Princess Katja.

"Indeed, indeed," Pendergast said. "London." He turned to Hensley. "There's no time...Princess Katja of Prussia..."

Winston returned to the entrance hall, pausing to instruct Harris to order all the harlots' things packed away immediately and taken out the back, and made it to the front door just in time to greet Katja.

As always, she was done to perfection. Beautiful, with a small upturned nose, high cheekbones and blue eyes. Her blond hair spilled over one shoulder, over a velvet cape lined with ermine. She stood perfectly straight—a porcelain doll surrounded by the marble and gilt of his entrance hall. But he knew full well she was no fragile untouchable, and that beneath the robe and gown waited the lush body of a young widow with strong desires.

A body he'd enjoyed even in her absence, since she had gifted him with that sensuous portrait. The princess was a woman who nodded to society but did as she pleased.

She never would have come to his bed otherwise.

"It was so very kind of you to invite me," Katja said when he bowed and kissed her hand. "I have missed you."

"And I you." Which wasn't true at all, but perhaps it should have been, and even now his hands still hummed with the softness of another woman's breasts—breasts he ought to be hanged for touching.

"I confess, I almost did not come," Katja said, gently scolding him with a sweep of her lashes. "But when I heard you had injured yourself…well, I thought there must be something I could do to help."

And even though her tone was elegantly innocent, he knew exactly what she meant.

"The rumors of my injuries have been somewhat overstated, as you can see," he told her. "You may well have made the journey for nothing."

"That cannot possibly be true." She smiled at him in a small, mysterious way that was no mystery to him. "I confess I was finding London rather boring."

"Now that cannot possibly be true." He made himself smile, but it only made him too aware of his lips, and the taste of Miles lingering on his tongue, and the way her kiss had shot straight to his cock—her *first* kiss, and he didn't need to have seduced any virgins to determine *that,* and good *God.*

He guided Katja toward the small salon, where none of the past days' entertainments had taken place, and called for tea.

Katja put a hand on his arm. "If you please, I would adore some wine."

Of course she would. He canceled the tea and ordered wine instead. He had to keep her here at least as long as it would take for the harlots and all of their baggage to be loaded into his guests' carriages and taken away.

And then his house would be empty except for one woman whose body was available for the taking, and another whose body was strictly forbidden and who, if there was any mercy in the world, was even now packing her bags to leave.

He inhaled deeply, grateful when the wine arrived

almost immediately, taking a large swallow to wash away the taste of innocence.

"Such a lonely place for you," Katja said, sipping her wine and casting her deep blue eyes around the empty salon over the rim of her glass. "I would not have expected it, after we last saw each other."

On his last visit to Prussia, Katja had been made aware that Winston had been frequenting a well-known brothel that catered to Prussia's elite. His fiery lover had very quickly iced over—and exerted her influence over an important negotiation that had been taking place, which had been saved only thanks to Urslane's stellar diplomacy.

Yet, now, here she was, as if fate had known he would end up giving in to his impulses and could never resist temptation on his own.

Princess Katja would require his constant attention. She came with expectations. And, he already knew, hopes for an exclusive and enduring affair.

They drank their wine and talked of London, of Prussian politics, of all the small annoyances Katja had endured since arriving in England. And at last, Harris appeared in the doorway and gave Winston a discreet nod.

Everyone had left, and the guest wing was clear.

"No doubt you'd like to rest awhile after your journey from London," Winston said smoothly, standing.

She looked up at him, cocking her head a little to the side, a question in her eyes. "Oh, I do not know. Perhaps."

He felt a stirring—a response purely physical and

not entirely unwelcome. He could join her in her guest chamber. Ease his tension between her sensuous thighs.

"I have some business I can attend to while you rest," he said instead, because now he was thinking of the way he'd pressed himself between Miles's thighs, and God help him, he would send her off with an extra hundred for that—but *not* as any kind of payment for his pleasure.

Disappointment touched Katja's eyes and was gone. "Actually," she said, reaching to set down her empty glass, "I feel quite rested already. Perhaps you would take me for a turn in your gardens. They looked so lovely from my carriage."

The gardens. When he had another apology to issue to Miles. But he didn't want to apologize. He wanted to kiss her again, and this time he wanted to touch all of her.

"An excellent idea," he said, and meant it. Now was no time to be alone with Miles.

In fact, he should never be alone with Miles. But he could do it once more—just long enough to finish their business and see her off.

And then there would only be Katja, who would not be staying in the guest wing, after all.

MILLIE WATCHED FROM the window as Winston and Princess Katja strolled through the garden on the other side of the drive. The garden seemed to stretch for an eternity, marked with small hedges and geometric plantings and three oval ponds stretching end to end the entire length of the garden.

Princess Katja walked with her hand tucked into

Winston's arm. She held herself perfectly straight, with her skirts flaring out fashionably from her hips, her light blond hair arranged elegantly with three fat curls falling to the front over one shoulder.

And thanks to that portrait, there was no mystery in what Winston would find once that beautiful gown was removed.

And it would be removed. There was no doubt of that.

Whatever Winston's trouble was, clearly he was coming back to himself. *He never touches the help.* Indeed?

It was those very touches that burned into her skin even now. Into her breasts, once more secured beneath their binding, yet she was more aware of them than she'd ever been.

He'd touched her *breasts*. And she'd *let* him, like any one of those strumpets downstairs.

"The estate is becoming a bloody madhouse," came Sacks's voice from behind her. "Never saw a hastier exit, and all because of 'er." He joined Millie at the window.

"Exit?"

"All of 'em. Gone back to London at the drop of a hat."

"Everyone?"

"I said all of 'em, didn't I?"

Which meant Lord Hensley was gone. That, at least, was something to be grateful for.

"And just look at that," Sacks went on approvingly, watching Winston and the princess. "He won't be turning 'is back on 'er, no sir."

Sacks was right. Winston may have hidden from Tensie, but he would not be hiding from Princess Katja.

"I'd better go see if anything's been overlooked in 'er rooms," Sacks said now. And then, turning back in the doorway, he grinned. "Perhaps she'll fall sick while she's 'ere and need *your* services."

"I should be so fortunate," she said, offering the expected grin back but letting her smile fall the moment Sacks walked away.

The window drew her like a siren's call. And she shouldn't look, had no *reason* to look, but…

Oh.

There, between the first and second ponds, Princess Katja had her face upturned, her hands resting on his chest…and he was kissing her.

It was impossible to look away. He had his hands on her wrists, holding her delicately the way one *would* hold a princess. Not searching beneath her clothing, the way one apparently touched…

A distraction.

And still her body taunted her, burning with new desires that would not be cooled.

Her, Millicent Germain.

Who knew better.

Who had always, always been sensible.

Out in the garden, the kiss ended. The princess tucked her hand into Winston's arm, and they continued slowly past the pond.

Millie finally turned away from the window, breathing past a tightness in her chest, feeling…

She wasn't sure what she felt. But it didn't matter,

because Winston was finally succumbing to distraction, and that was exactly what she'd hoped for.

SEVERAL HOURS LATER, alone in the vast and wondrous library without fear of revelers seeking a place for a quick tryst, Millie was deep in the solace of a newly discovered treasure—a treatise about medicinal plants of Africa and the Barbary Coast—when Winston entered at the far end.

Everything inside her stilled.

He hadn't seen her. And watching him was the last thing she should be doing, but he was just so... fascinating.

She studied the angle of his nose. The pure sculpture of it.

The slash of cheekbone and jaw.

He was a devil indeed.

And then he spotted her and started in her direction.

Every coherent thought fled, and blast it all, she was more intelligent than this. But with every step of his approach, her body came alive in places that needed to stay dormant. A deep breath, another, and thoughts returned, though not helpful ones.

Thoughts of touching him. Of tangling her tongue with his, of his hands cupping her breasts, of the hardness in his breeches rocking against the softness in hers.

She stood up quickly, facing him, because otherwise she might not ever be able to tear her gaze from the page and look him in the eye.

"We need to finish our conversation," he said, stopping a few feet away.

"I'm not resigning," she told him now.

"You should," he said flatly.

"Yes. I should. But I won't." She called up her outrage—at herself as well as him. "And I expect that nothing like *what happened* will ever happen again."

What happened.

Him kissing her, reaching beneath her clothes, touching her bare skin. She could still taste him. Her lips still felt raw. She felt like someone else—someone languid and sensuous. Reckless.

She couldn't afford to be reckless, not with her livelihood on the line.

"Forgive me." His voice was low. Rough. His mouth was tight.

He was…*apologizing?*

"A vow, it seems," he went on, "is only as good as the character of the man who makes it."

The vow that made no sense. "I don't understand. What vow?"

After a moment he said, "Edward's been telling me for years that I should devote myself to a quieter and more moral mode of living."

But there was a heat in his eyes that betrayed thoughts that were anything but quiet and moral.

"And…you've vowed to do that?" It didn't seem possible.

"Amusing, isn't it?" One corner of his mouth quirked up, and he wandered a few steps away, pulled a book randomly from a shelf. Leafed through it ten or twenty pages at a time. "It wasn't a conscious decision. It was more of a semiconscious impulse, brought on by large chunks of masonry crashing dangerously close to my skull." He shoved the book back into its place. Looked at her over his shoulder. "I'm not even certain that counts as a vow. Do you think?"

The accident. His brush with death. Those moments must have been terrifying, and rightly so.

She thought of the man whose burial Winston had attended. The torment in his eyes that day. *Are there any medicaments you can prescribe that will undo the past, Mr. Germain?*

She'd assumed he was talking about the accident. But now…

"Did you…vow to change?" she asked, incredulous. "Is that why you came here?" She thought of his reading. His insect-collecting.

His lips were still turned upward in self-mockery. "I can't say I've fully committed to it."

And now, suddenly, things made sense: his throwing everyone out in Paris—and inviting them back again. His storing away all those erotic statues, storing away the princess's portrait. Allowing his uninvited guests to stay—yet refusing to join them. Or resisting, at least.

The decision to come to the estate instead of proceeding with his planned debauch in Greece.

"And that's why you were hiding from Tensie," she said now.

"I wasn't *hiding,*" he said irritably, as the amusement fell away from his mouth.

"Avoiding, then."

The only thing that still didn't make sense was why he'd spied on her in the bath. And why he'd kissed her.

Improvising to distract himself from the real temptations, probably. Or erupting frustrations after denying himself what he wanted so badly.

And even though she knew better, she asked, "And what about the princess? Will you avoid her, as well?" Hope rose frighteningly in her chest.

"I *can't* avoid her."

The hope shriveled and sank.

"There are political implications," he explained.

"And she is your lover."

"Was."

"And hopes to be again, else she would not have come." That kiss in the gardens had not happened in the past tense.

"It's not as if a man can truly change, not after so many years," he said, picking up a polished stone obelisk that sat between two rows of books. "But then, you've already discovered the truth of that."

"There must be a reason you think you should, or else the thought would never have occurred to you in the first place."

"Reasons hardly matter, as one cannot undo the past." He turned the obelisk in his hands, set it back in place and looked at her. "I shan't make you any more promises if you stay on in your employment. I shall only say that I will do my best to conduct myself in a moral fashion where you are concerned."

He wasn't going to tell her the reason, not even now.

"Thank you." With the princess here, there wasn't any risk that he would repeat what he'd done this afternoon.

He bowed, excused himself, and she stood watching him walk to the other end of the library, her fingers still gripping the edge of the table behind her bottom, hating that she wanted him to repeat it.

All the while he was trying to live a more moral life, she was slipping into a sensual quicksand.

CHAPTER FIFTEEN

AN HOUR LATER, while Winston and Princess Katja ate in the great dining room, Millie sat down at the writing desk in her dressing room. Slipped out a sheet of paper that already had writing at the top.

Dear Katherine,

That was the problem. The address was far too presumptuous under the circumstances.

She set that sheet aside, took out another. Dipped her pen.

Dear Captain,

And then she sat there, ink drying on the nib of her pen while no words came.

It shouldn't be so difficult. She'd written to India weeks ago, from Paris, just before her employment with Winston. Had somehow found the words to apologize for aiding India's marriage to a man India hated. For accepting money from that same man in exchange for her betrayal.

India had trusted her.

As had Katherine, who had offered Millie a new life,

only to have Millie steal her ship when circumstances changed. And Philomena, India's aunt and Katherine's closest friend.

And William.

Her crime against William was the most unforgivable of all. Knocking him unconscious, taking over his ship… And all he'd done was whip her, when he'd had every right to hang her from the yards and toss her body overboard. She knew better than to imagine, even for a moment, writing an apology to him.

She set down the pen and rested her face in her hands. If only.

She thought of Winston and his efforts to change. The uselessness of it all. Because, as he'd pointed out, one could not undo the past.

Being here was her own fault.

Millie raised her head and sat back in the chair. The only point of hope was her new life as Miles Germain. Certainly she'd masqueraded as a man occasionally. Aboard the ship, she'd worn breeches. But now she'd become Miles Germain, and she was making her way in the world alone. As a man.

No, there was nothing princesslike about her at all.

And Winston would not be touching her again with Princess Katja here, she could be certain of that. Yet even now, the memory touched her skin, parted her lips, ignited a fire on the inside—a slow burn that needed more of what he'd begun this morning.

She pushed back from the desk, grabbed up a book that had turned out to be not so useful, after all, and headed toward the library.

Into the corridor, past the door that led into Winston's

dressing room, through which she caught a glimpse of his bedchamber, where only a short while ago she'd experienced a man in a way she never dreamed.

She hugged herself against a nonexistent chill, rubbing her upper arms. *Stop. Just stop!*

There would be no more of that. She was Miles Germain. *Needed* to be Miles Germain. The best thing she could do toward that end was admit that Winston could easily find someone to replace her, and then collect her wages and leave.

Except that wasn't the best thing at all.

As Miles Germain, she could hire on to a ship's crew bound for the Mediterranean—unless someone saw through her disguise as Winston had, in the cramped quarters belowdecks where little could remain secret among sailors.

But if she spent the money to book passage, it would leave her too little on the other end.

In the library, she stared blankly at the enormous cavern of books. What were the chances, really, that she would ever have enough money to support her studies? Even if she worked weeks more for the duke, even if she somehow managed to find the *Possession* and sneak aboard and retrieve her hidden stash of money...

Students did not scrap by on a modest sum they'd saved. They had patrons. Or family wealth.

She would have a tiny rented room somewhere in Valetta and a fast-dwindling reserve.

But what was the alternative? There wasn't one. Staying and collecting as many wages as possible from Winston was the only option—except for prevailing upon

the very people she had betrayed and who would laugh
at her for imagining that they would help her now.

Choices, she'd learned, were a luxury. For a woman,
life tossed you about like a dying fish in the surf until
a merciless, foraging gull devoured you.

But she was Miles Germain now, and she *was* making a choice—the choice to stay with Winston a little
while longer.

HE DIDN'T GO to Katja that night, even though he'd installed her in the same wing as himself for the sake
of convenience. Instead, he lay in his bed thinking of
Miles. *Miss Germain,* if Germain was even her true
surname.

Miss Germain, who refused to resign.

Miss Germain, whose kiss raced through him like
fire.

Miss Germain, whose breasts were gently curved,
with silken skin and firm, peaked crests.

His cock strained beneath the covers, demanding
more of what he had tasted this morning. And how in
God's name he was supposed to exist under the same
roof with her without giving into temptation again, he
didn't know.

He probably should have terminated her employment this afternoon in the library. It would have been
the wise thing to do. The moral thing.

He told himself he hadn't because the wounds on his
back still presented a risk.

He knew Katja to be a midday riser, and so he rose
early and went to the stables. Pulled himself delicately
into the saddle once his horse was readied and felt an

immediate sense of relief. He put his weight in the stirrups and shifted to take the pressure off the wounds on the backs of his legs, which turned out to be impossible, but he didn't care.

He needed to ride.

And he needed to speak with Edward.

He took it slow and easy at first, walking. Found a trot unbearable, and slowed. Reached an open field and urged his horse into a gallop—full weight in the stirrups, horse thundering beneath him, every thought except this very moment taken by the wind.

It ended too soon, but he felt a good deal better by the time he rode into the village. And then everything turned for the worse.

The church stood up ahead, and the vicarage. He would go in, bare his soul to Edward. Tell him about the vow and how he'd broken it, how he had failed at considering his ways.

He stopped his horse in the middle of the road in front of Cara and Edward's home.

He couldn't do it.

He looked the other way, toward the river and the old mill. He urged the horse forward, away from the vicarage now and through a small meadow to the river. Stopped by a stand of trees.

Stared at the waterwheel, turning, turning, turning. Splash-splash-splash.

The reins lay slack in his hands, but his fingers were tight around them. He needed to turn around. Edward would have the answers he needed.

Instead, he dismounted, looped the reins around a low limb and walked closer to the waterwheel, still fascinated by its motion. Perhaps a man *could* spend his life like this.

He'd only stood there a moment when he saw Edward walking toward him from the road.

And the spell was broken, and watching Edward approach, he knew he wasn't made for a life of quiet goodness and contemplation.

"Don't tell me you're thinking of replacing this with some new kind of machine," Edward said as he joined Winston, assessing the mill with his hands on his waist. "Old Kane would never stand for it."

"Not at all," Winston said, laughing a little. "I wouldn't dare."

They exchanged a few more pleasantries, a few more observations about the mill, and then Winston couldn't stand it anymore.

"Edward—" He broke off, suddenly unsure how to say what he wanted to say. His friend merely waited for him to gather his thoughts.

"Suppose one makes a promise," Winston began slowly. "During a moment of grave danger." Of course, Edward would know Winston was talking about himself.

"A promise to whom?"

And he wasn't going to tell Edward that he was the object of Winston's vow, so he said, "I don't know. To whomever might be listening."

Edward smiled a little. "'Lord, only save my life, and I shall never sin again'?"

"Something along those lines." Winston shifted his attention back to the waterwheel. Thought of Miles, and how badly he burned for her. "Does such a promise count?"

"Count against what?"

"Is it valid? As a promise?"

Edward thought for a moment. "I'm not sure that's precisely the right question. I rather think one would ask whether the action promised is reasonable—nay, even humanly possible, for we *are* human, after all, and prone to failings despite our best intentions."

Indeed. Edward knew all about Winston's failings. And now Winston was teetering on the edge of failure again, and he needed Edward to pull him back.

"And then," Edward went on, "I should think one would consider the origins of the promise. Whether it has its roots in one's conscience, perhaps in some defect of character one is already aware of. And whether the promise, if attempted but not fulfilled, would nonetheless tend to elevate one's spirit."

Attempted but not fulfilled. He'd bloody well *attempted* to keep from touching Miles. Perhaps that was enough.

"Tell me about the promise you made," Edward said quietly.

There was pressure in Winston's chest, in his throat, in his head behind his eyes. But he made himself look at Edward. "I vowed to consider my ways."

Comprehension settled instantly in Edward's eyes. "And what have you determined?"

"That celibacy is killing me."

Edward laughed. "Please don't tell me that is what's meant by 'considering one's ways.' I couldn't survive it, either."

The difference being, Edward cleaved only to Cara, while Winston had always cleaved to whichever pair of thighs he fancied at the moment—or pairs, as the case may be—and there didn't seem to be a reason to do anything differently.

"Forgive me, my friend," Edward said now, and turned to face him squarely. "When I've suggested in the past that you consider your ways, I meant your motives. The effects of your actions on others. The activities that occupy your time, and whether they feed your soul or eat away at it."

And there was the issue. The effect on Miles if he gave in to his desire and seduced her. It would take nothing—he knew that for certain now. And he would leave her ruined, possibly pregnant, and then there would be another irreparable harm eating away at his soul, just as Edward said.

He preferred his sins to be of the mutually beneficial variety.

"Still no thought of marriage?" Edward asked.

"Good God, no." It was out of the question. "The estate is vast enough as it is—I don't need anyone else's fortune."

"Fair enough."

Imperative, more like. Being content with the excess he already possessed gave him freedom. He would not be bought and yoked to the daughter of any Spanish prince or Italian noble—or even Princess Katja, if that was what she secretly had in mind. His nephew Theodore was a perfectly sensible heir, with a large estate of his own and five children.

"Is that what's required, then?" Winston demanded. "Marriage?"

Edward put a hand on the back of Winston's shoulder and looked him in the eye. "*I* don't require anything of you, my friend. I've only ever hoped you might consider what you require of yourself."

AND THAT, WINSTON thought as he rode home a while later, was exactly why he would go to Katja tonight.

Edward might not require anything, but Winston owed him everything. He would become the man Edward wanted him to be—*that* was what Winston required of himself.

And Katja was the answer.

Monogamy. He would stop the ribald activities Edward disapproved of and limit himself to one woman. Princess Katja, his most logical alliance if he were to choose one.

He could make Katja his mistress. Not that the princess needed to be under any man's protection, but it was clear what kind of relationship she wanted from him. He could limit himself to her, perhaps for a period of three months.

He exhaled, guided his horse over a stone bridge. Three months. And then what?

Perhaps by then Katja would have tired of him anyhow, and he could get another mistress. One woman at a time certainly seemed reasonable.

A thought of Miles crept in, but he snuffed it out with thoughts of Katja: shapely legs, round hips, bountiful breasts. Curves he could hang on to when he sank inside her, which by this time tomorrow he would have.

He had a choice to make, and it was only too clear which one was right and which was very, very wrong.

CHAPTER SIXTEEN

PRINCESS KATJA.

Millie paused on the walkway, halfway to the conservatory, her path blocked by the princess herself coming the other direction.

She was the last person Millie expected to see this far from the house, but apparently the princess was not averse to walking.

"Mr. Germain," the princess said, seeing Millie approach. "Winston's medic?"

Millie bowed. "I am, Your Highness."

Up close, the princess was…stunning. Delicate, perfectly formed features. Exquisite gown in the very latest fashion, decked with ribbons and lace, like the ones Philomena wore—and so unlike anything Millie would ever own.

Or *wish* to own, she reminded herself.

"Winston says that you have worked miracles," the princess said, "but he is not himself at all. I believe he has been dishonest about his recovery."

"A man never wishes to appear compromised in front of a lady." Especially not one like this.

But Millie already knew from Harris and Sacks that Winston and the princess had not been together last night. And she hated that it gave her even the small-est hope of…anything. There was nothing to hope *for*.

The princess smiled. "No, a man certainly does not." She looked at the book Millie carried. "What have you there?"

"This?" It took a moment to credit that she was in-terested in the book. "It's a reference. A compilation of medicinal plants native to North Africa and the Bar-bary Coast."

"How fascinating." The princess turned a little, and her perfectly arched brows dove and she studied the frontispiece Millie showed her. "I have been to the Bar-bary Coast," she said, straightening. "With my husband, years ago. Such a fascinating and exotic place."

The closest Millie had come was miles offshore, aboard the *Possession* on the Mediterranean.

"I cannot say that I spent any time studying the flora, however," Princess Katja added. "Perhaps I should have."

"The conservatory has an entire collection of African plants," Millie told her. "I had planned to see whether it includes any mentioned in this book."

"I thought Winston would be available this morning, but I am told he has gone to the village." The princess frowned in the direction of the house. "It would seem I am left to my own devices. Perhaps you would not ob-ject if I accompany you?"

THE PRINCESS WAS beautiful and intelligent. Inquisitive. And, as the portrait in Winston's attic attested, open to adventure.

She was everything a man like Winston would need if he was to truly change his ways.

Late that night, fool that she was, Millie listened for any sign that the princess had gone to the duke's bedchamber—or vice versa. But all was quiet. Millie cracked her door open, peered out into the blackened hallway. Listened.

Nothing.

And then—a sound.

A door being opened. The glow of a small candle, the whisper of fabric as the princess let herself into the hallway and went to Winston's door.

Not a woman to be put off for long, but then Millie could have guessed that after their time together today. Princess Katja did not hesitate to offer her opinions, to speak when she had an idea, to say what she wanted.

And there was no doubt that the princess wanted Winston.

Millie watched through the most slender crack in her door as the princess silently raised the latch and let herself into Winston's dressing room without knocking.

Millie shut her door and leaned against it, closing her eyes, trying not to imagine what would come next.

This was what was supposed to happen.

She *wanted* this to happen.

She returned to her writing desk. Tried to read, her eyes skimming over the words without really seeing them. And all the while, inside, the screws turned. Tighter, tighter.

It was for the best. He would be happier. Less tormented.

Cinching, cinching, until it felt like her ribs caged

nothing but tense muscle, and breathing became impossible.

She stood up.

Don't be a fool.

Went to the door.

It's inevitable anyhow.

She left her room, walked to his and knocked—three times, loudly—with no idea at all what she was about, what she would possibly do if he answered, what she hoped to accomplish. They could have started already. He could be kissing her, working his way beneath her nightdress, touching—

The door opened and Winston stood there in his red banyan. Beneath it she glimpsed his waistcoat and breeches. Beyond, the room was well lit and the princess sat on a love seat in a cloud of lace.

Millie swallowed. "My deepest apologies for disturbing you, Your Grace," she said. "I was concerned that you might have forgotten to take your medicine, and I promised that I would see to the bandage on your lower back."

He looked down at her. Of course, she'd promised no such thing, and now he would send her away with instructions to return in the morning.

"So you did," he said after a moment, and opened the door wider. "Do come in."

He wasn't sending her away. She hesitated, too surprised to believe it.

She stepped inside.

"Mr. Germain," the princess said. "We were just speaking of you."

They were?

"Indeed?" Millie said, and swallowed.

"Winston was recounting the many ways in which you have improved his health since his accident in Paris. I have been treated to the entire story." Princess Katja offered a pleasant smile that might have been a bit strained. "But of course, I might have guessed, from our time together this morning, how skilled you would be. After tonight's conversation, I feel as if I know you intimately."

"Such flattery," Millie managed. "Your Highness is too kind." And then, in a sterner tone, "Your Grace, I do not see your medicaments anywhere about. You have forgotten them, haven't you?" Certainly now he would tell her that all was in order, and he would speak with her further in the morning.

But he was looking about, frowning a little. "I wonder if they weren't carried off with my tray." He looked at her. "Perhaps you'd better bring some more. In fact, this is excellent timing, as I believe the princess was growing weary of my company anyhow."

He didn't want the princess here, Millie realized. It didn't seem possible.

Princess Katja stood up and came to him, her hand lighting on his chest. "Not weary at all. But surely your medicaments can wait until morning...?"

"I'm afraid not," he said, sounding for all the world as if his nighttime medical routine was a complicated and time-consuming procedure that could be fatal if missed. "Missing even a single dose leaves me in a good deal of discomfort, and I was beginning to feel a pain in my lower back—but how indelicate of me to describe the details. Please accept my apologies," he murmured, and stepped away from her.

The princess looked at him, and Millie knew she was far too intelligent to be completely fooled. She could tell that—for some reason unfathomable to Millie—Winston wanted her to leave.

"I shall see you in the morning, then," the princess said smoothly, reaching up to kiss his cheek. "Good night."

The countess left, the door latched behind her, and Winston turned. Stared at Millie with eyes gone frighteningly savage. He stalked past her, snatching the wig from his head, tossing it on the dressing table and roughing his fingers through his hair. Staring into the looking glass.

At her.

"What excellent timing you have," he said, and turned, going to his armoire, yanking his greatcoat out, shrugging into it without bothering to call for Sacks. "Come with me." He grabbed Millie's hand and led her out the door and left, not right, down the servants' stairs, through another hallway and outside into the darkness.

In the shelter of the doorway, he reached for her wig. "Off with this."

"Wait! I need that!"

He tossed it atop a box hedge. "It will be here when we return."

Return? "Where are we going?"

Instead of answering, he led her toward the stables. He didn't bother to wake any help there, either, but saddled a horse himself—a great bay gelding that seemed as restless in the night as Winston himself.

And then he reached out his arm, beckoning her. "Ride with me."

There was a moment suspended when she realized what he intended—that she would take his hand and mount the horse, and the two of them would ride. Together.

She should refuse. Instead, she took his hand and let him help her into the saddle. Sat tense, almost breathless, as he climbed up behind her.

And now she sat snug against him with her bottom cradled between his thighs and her back pressed against his chest. She felt his hands in her hair, pulling out the pins now, tossing them aside until her hair fell onto her shoulders, thick and blunt.

"There," he murmured.

And she wanted him to keep touching her hair, working his fingers through it, pressing his—dear God, pressing his face into it so that she could feel his hot breath against her ear.

But in the next moment he reached around her to grasp the reins and tapped the horse with his heels, and they were moving forward, then trotting, past the grand entrance to the house, breaking into a run and then a gallop down the shadowy tree-lined drive. Winston's body moved powerfully, at one with the beast beneath them. At one, it seemed, with *her*.

The night air whipped her hair like an ocean breeze coming off the water. The horse's hooves thundered like the roar of waves. It was exhilarating. They thundered over the stone bridge, down the straightaway that cut through the vast meadow, up a rise and along a crumbling wall that disappeared into a wood. And she felt him shift, and the horse slowed quickly, almost suddenly, at the top of the knoll overlooking the inky countryside, with stars peeking through silver-lined puffs of moonlit clouds speeding by high above them.

She felt his chest rise and fall behind her.

Felt him sweep her hair aside and press his lips to the side of her neck.

Felt his hands splay across her chest and drag down, down, over her bound breasts, her belly, her thighs. He gripped her, pressing his fingers into the soft insides of her splayed legs. Dragged one hand back up to her chest, the other to the vee of her thighs, and held her against him that way, cupping her intimately, holding her as if she were the only thing keeping him alive.

Her most intimate flesh seemed to melt beneath his touch, as if her breeches didn't exist.

But he didn't move.

Just held her, breathing into her hair.

Slowly, she uncurled her fingers from the saddle's edge. As if in a trance, she rested her hands on his knees.

Felt him inhale sharply.

His skin burned warm through his breeches. His muscles flexed hard. She already knew each one intimately, but now it was as if she'd never examined him at all.

"Miles," he breathed. "I want you to tell me to stop."

He said it even as his fingers began a slow caress between her thighs, sending liquid pulses of desire deep into her body.

Stop.

She moistened her lips, felt the kiss of cool night air. But the word didn't come out. His touch lulled her. Lured her. Awakened sensations she'd heard of but dismissed as the province of men.

But they were hers now.

In his arms—the duke's arms.

And now he was working the fastening of her breeches, and she *needed* to stop him. Now, before—

He found her.

A sound escaped her throat. A gasp, a small cry as he used her own moisture to circle her in small, tight motions constrained by her clothing. And it was as if she'd never been touched there at all, because she hadn't— not like this.

Behind her, the swelling inside his own breeches pressed hard against her bottom.

"You've got to tell me to stop, Miles, because— Ah, Christ." And now he was reaching beneath her shirt, tugging at the binding, then pushing it, shoving it up over one breast and then the other, and cupping her.

Rolling her already tight nipples in his fingers, sending spears of intense pleasure straight to the spot he was touching between her thighs.

She dug her hands into his legs and tried to form the word he asked, but couldn't.

"Winston…" Her whisper sounded more like a plea.

"Forgive me," he said against her neck. "Forgive me…"

And she might have forgiven him anything at all, because nothing existed except the pleasure coursing through her body and the solid heat coming off his, snaring her, making her cling to him and spread her legs wider instead of trying to slam them shut.

"Easy," he murmured. "There's scarcely room in here for me as it is."

Scarcely room—her breeches. He meant her breeches. They were tight across his hand—

She slackened her legs, but the tension had to go somewhere, and she arched against him, felt like screaming as his fingers slicked more powerfully, more rhythmically against her, and he plucked her nipples more firmly—

And now—

And now—

The nighttime swallowed her ragged cry as something inside her broke open, unleashing a pounding tempest of clenching, searing, pulsing deep, deep in her body, and the horse stepped restlessly beneath them and Winston issued a low command that sounded as if it could be meant for her.

But the pulsing went on and on and only finally began to fade, and his hands smoothed over her now, gentling her, as if catching her from a great fall.

And then there were only the sounds of the night and his breathing above her ear. She sat stunned.

He'd touched her *there*.

But it had been nothing at all like before. This time, she'd wanted the touch. And still his erection pressed against her, unsated. And any moment he would shift and guide her hand there.

He fastened her breeches.

Kept a hand on her belly and reached for the reins.

Urged the horse forward—away from the direction

they'd come, not back to the house. Coaxing the horse faster, faster beneath them.

And when they finally returned, they didn't speak of what happened.

He helped her dismount in the shadows by a far wing of the house, murmured good-night, and was gone toward the stables. As if nothing at all had taken place between them.

As if her entire body wasn't thrumming with the aftermath of his touch.

She stood in the shadows of the door, watching his form fade into the nighttime, then grabbed her wig off the hedge and let herself inside.

CHAPTER SEVENTEEN

HE WAS FAILING.

"Your Grace," a stable hand said, his voice tired. "Allow me—"

He thrust the reins at the young man and stalked out of the stables, into the night, around the side of the building and leaned against the wall.

Hot. Wet. Unbelievably sensitive, responding to his touch like wildfire.

He'd wanted to be with her. Just…*be* with her.

And he could have anticipated that would be impossible. Had probably known it even as he was telling himself, after speaking with Edward, that Katja would be enough.

A promise attempted but not fulfilled.

He was sliding headlong down a slippery slope, and he knew where it would end, because he couldn't keep his hands off her. What had she been thinking, coming to his room, interrupting his tête-à-tête with Katja with that nonsense about his medications? What had *he* been thinking, talking to Katja about Miles instead of talking to her about all the ways he wanted to enjoy her body?

He rubbed his jaw, smelled Miles on him, felt himself grow hard all over again. Katja was beautiful. Keenly intelligent. An exhausting and creative lover.

And he'd turned his back on her for his sharp-tongued medic in men's clothes, whose virginity made her entirely forbidden. But when she'd come to her peak in his arms... Ah, Christ. He'd been nearly mad with wanting to make love to her.

But he'd vowed not to do that.

He leaned his head back against the wall. Inhaled deeply. *And you didn't. You left her intact.*

He'd pleasured her, that was all.

He pushed away from the wall, paced to the end of the building. Was there anything wrong with that? Pleasuring her, as long as he didn't use her to pleasure himself?

He hadn't compromised her. Hadn't even pushed a finger inside her.

He'd merely...awakened her.

And perhaps this was the answer. He'd vowed not to *ruin* her.

It was a vow he could still keep.

MILLIE CREPT BACK to her room with her disguise hastily put back in place—disheveled, askew, surely hiding nothing.

And barely shut the door before she caught a movement at the far end of the corridor.

She leaned against it, heart pounding, thoughts tumbling in chaos.

Winston's hands. Her body. Deep, exquisite pleasure unlike anything she'd ever imagined.

She was losing her mind.

And Winston—he was losing *his* mind. Wasn't he? Turning his back on the princess and taking Millie for a nighttime ride? Touching *her* intimately, when he could have been touching Katja?

It didn't make sense.

She pulled off her wig, felt her hair immediately tumble. Went to the dressing table and tossed the wig in a limp heap next to her comb and brush.

Perhaps she'd misread Princess Katja's intentions. Perhaps the princess was not as willing as she appeared, was toying with Winston somehow, tempting him but then withholding her favour? And so Winston had found another outlet for his passions.

And had made Millie acutely aware of hers.

There was a sensitivity between her thighs…and on the peaks of her breasts against her shirt—there'd been no fitting the binding back over them once he'd pushed it away. Deep inside, her body pulsed.

She looked at herself in the glass—messy hair tumbling on the shoulders of a man's coat.

Miles Germain.

On the outside, perhaps. But on the inside…

A tremor of pleasure touched the secret places Winston had found.

And this had to be how men did it—rakes who lured young innocents, seduced them, coaxed them to surrender their virtues. In those moments when she'd felt as if her entire body were flying apart, she would have given him anything.

And no, clearly Winston was not fully committed to his supposed vow to change. And as for conducting himself in a moral fashion…

And now the princess was down the hall, possibly wondering if Winston would visit her room tonight.

Millie knew full well that he hadn't…arrived at his pleasure tonight. He hadn't asked her to touch him. Hadn't even reached for his breeches.

How would she face him in the morning? And face Princess Katja?

She reached up, gathered her hair and pulled it back, holding it there. Tightened her lips. She would face them as Miles Germain. Because she *was* Miles Germain. *Wanted* to be Miles Germain. Tonight hadn't changed that.

Tonight hadn't changed anything. She wouldn't let it.

"IT WAS VERY kind of you to stop by to check on Cara," the vicar said the next morning, after Millie had successfully avoided not only Winston and the princess but Harris and Sacks, as well.

The vicar's brows dipped a little, and he looked at Cara in a way that said he was not at all convinced nothing was wrong.

"I'm happy to do it," Millie said, all too glad for the distraction. She'd walked to the village this time to avoid the fuss and possible encounter with Winston that might come with ordering a carriage. But it was good—had given her plenty of time to lecture herself about last night and the imperative of keeping a safe distance from Winston. "Perhaps just a quick examination to be sure I didn't miss anything the last time, and to be sure nothing has changed."

"If you think it's best," Cara agreed, while suspicions lingered in her husband's eyes—until something out the window snared his attention.

"It's Winston," he said.

Millie's heart leaped into her throat. She looked, too, and saw Winston tying his horse to the post at the front of the garden. He came down the walk, his greatcoat swirling about his legs, and a flutter took wing in her belly.

He was admitted, entered the drawing room, and Millie's mouth went dry.

"Edward. Cara." Those devil eyes lit on Millie, piercing her with memories of last night. "Mr. Germain."

"Your Grace," Millie murmured.

"Mr. Germain has only just stopped in to make sure all is well with Cara," the vicar told him.

"Has he? I wondered where you'd gone this morning so early," he said to her.

He had? "I imagined you would be busy entertaining your company," Millie said to him.

"My company has returned to London."

For a moment Millie felt light-headed. "Has she."

Winston turned to the vicar. "I'd hoped to have a word."

"Of course, of course. We can talk while Mr. Germain is with Cara."

And then Millie followed Cara upstairs, and moments later they were in Cara's dressing room, closing the door behind them.

The princess was gone. What did that mean?

Cara turned to her the moment the door was closed. "Are you all right? You've gone rather flushed."

"Quite all right. The stairs…" Millie fanned herself, focusing her attention on her blessed medical bag. "But how are *you?*" she asked Cara. "Has there been any change?"

"None at all," Cara said worriedly. "Everything proceeds."

Millie reached into her bag. "I've brought some herbs. To strengthen the female systems, nothing more." She set the bottles on the table and turned to Cara. "If things continue, you won't be able to hide the truth from your husband much longer."

Cara wrung her hands. "I can't think of that. Not yet."

"You'll have to, soon."

"Likely not." She put a hand on her belly. "I've been turning my back to him at night, pretending to fall asleep right away. The other night, he..." Her cheeks turned pink. "He ignored my sleeping and started to..." She trailed off. "I told him my supper wasn't digesting well."

"I wish there was more I could do," Millie said. "But...there doesn't seem to be anything *wrong*."

"No, I suppose not." Cara circled her hand over her belly and let it fall. She came to stand next to Millie. "Has Winston yet guessed *your* secret?"

And Millie felt her cheeks flush again, and she reached for her medical bag, but there was nothing to be done with it now. "I learned not long after we arrived at the estate that he has known almost from the beginning."

"Now why does that not surprise me? I don't suppose there could be a woman within a mile of Winston and he would not recognize it, disguise or no. And yet, he seems content to let you continue in your disguise."

"He hired me for my medical skills. I doubt it matters to him what I look like, as long as he recovers fully."

She felt Cara observing her and was relieved when Cara went to the window. "I've long felt sad for Winston, leading such a reckless life. It can't be what he truly wants. Only look at the two of them… Winston walks as if the weight of the world is on his shoulders, do you not agree?"

There was no choice but to join Cara at the window. Below, Winston and the vicar walked together through the cemetery, disappearing around the corner of the church.

"I worry about him," Cara said. "He hasn't been the same since he returned from Paris. Oh, I know that's supposed to be a good thing—Edward says it is, that Winston may finally be soul-searching, and that would be such a blessing—but the light has gone out of him."

Millie stared out the window, barely daring to move or breathe because Cara's tone was so soft, so concerned.

"Has it?" she managed in a tone that sounded anything but offhand to her own ears.

"Sometimes I've thought Winston's worst qualities were born of his best. Such an amusing nature, always game for a bit of fun. When we were all young, he used to laugh at me for hesitating at whatever scheme he and Edward had cooked up, and then I would agree to join them, knowing full well I would meet Mama's tongue when we returned."

At that age, Millie had spent her days in the apothecary shop with Father. "What fun you must have had," she said.

"Yes." Cara's voice echoed softly from years in the past.

"Were you in love with him?"

Cara was quiet so long that Millie wished she hadn't asked.

"No," she finally said. "Well, certainly I…I thought I was, for a time." Outside, the two men came around the corner of the church again, headed toward the far end of the cemetery. "I think it would have been impossible not to, for any girl, really."

Millie tensed a little, remembering last night in vivid detail.

"Winston and I…" Cara paused. "It was a very long time ago. I was young, with a foolish heart." She sighed, looking out. "And he'd been drinking. It was all such a mistake. But I conceived. Of course, I didn't expect Winston to offer marriage. He couldn't, not to someone of my station. The child didn't live. There was a problem with the birth. It was a miracle I survived myself. But after I married Edward…"

Millie didn't need her to finish. After that birth, she'd been unable to carry a child to term.

"Oh," Millie breathed, feeling as if a claw had hooked inside her chest. She looked at Cara. "You needn't have told me."

"I thought you should know, because…" Cara searched Millie's eyes. "I've been worried that you might develop a tenderness for him yourself."

"Me—" Millie's gaze shot away from Cara and out the window before she could stop it, and of course, landed on Winston, who was facing Edward now but staring at the ground with his hands clasped behind his back.

"And below, just now, the way he looked at you…it wasn't the way a man looks at his medic."

A shiver ran down Millie's spine. "You needn't worry. There's nothing like what you're suggesting—everything is perfectly respectable."

"Forgive me, I didn't mean to suggest it wasn't."

"And of course, I feel *compassion* for Winston because of his injuries, but I have no intention of ever—"

Being with him.

Like Cara had.

"I never had any intention of it, either," Cara said now, a little sadly. "We broke Edward's heart, the two of us. Not that Edward and I had any kind of understanding," she added quickly. "It was nothing like that. But I knew—we both knew—that Edward was in love with me. But I suppose, Winston being the kind of man he is... No, the kind of young man he was, home from university, drinking and having his fun. And me, foolish enough to agree to go riding with him, never dreaming that once we found ourselves out in the countryside alone..." She stared quietly out the window. "We'd been such good friends for so long. And I was used to his wildness. And please don't misunderstand. I love Edward more than life itself. Sometimes I think I always did, and Winston just blinded me the way the sun will get in your eyes and for a moment it's all you can see."

And looking at Winston now, Millie understood completely.

"Please don't tell Winston I told you."

"No—I wouldn't dream of it."

"I'm just afraid it's all come back to haunt him. I can't think why it would, now, so many years later, but to see him suddenly trying to tame his life into some semblance of decency... And just look at him now, with

Edward. It's as if suddenly he can't bring himself to look Edward in the eye anymore."

Millie noticed that Edward was talking, and Winston was, indeed, looking in the direction of a nearby headstone.

"There must be a way for him to see that he can have decency and have light and laughter, too," Cara sighed. "He must have at least some friends who embrace a measure of morality. What he really needs..." She looked at Millie. "What he really needs is a wife. Someone strong enough to match him, but passionate enough to satisfy his thirst for excitement. There must be any number of women he knows who might suit. Perhaps in London. Women of his own rank, who would understand him."

Women, Millie thought, like Princess Katja.

"DID SHE LEAVE on her own volition or did he send her away?" Millie asked Harris and Sacks that evening, after managing to avoid Winston the entire rest of the day—something she could not continue to do and expect to keep her employment.

Harris shook his head at Millie, and Sacks shrugged. "There's no telling."

No princess, no guests, no dancing harlots.

"I just can't believe it." Harris sighed, leaning back in a chair in Millie's dressing room with a glass of wine, while Sacks sat nearby, elbows on his knees, gaze fixed on the floor.

Millie busied herself at her cabinet of medical supplies, arranging and rearranging things that had been perfectly organized to begin with, trying not to

think of what might happen now that there were no…
distractions left in the house.

None except you.

A nerve pulsed deep in her belly. No. She was no
distraction to him. At best, she'd been an outlet of some
kind. Now that there was nothing left to tempt him, perhaps his passions would cool and he would be able to
commit more fully to his supposed vow.

She glanced over her shoulder just as Sacks looked
up, worry in his eyes.

"Do you suppose he's dying?"

"Dying?" Millie turned away from the cabinet. "No.
He isn't dying. He simply…desires solitude."

And midnight horseback rides.

And talks with his vicar.

And…decency? It couldn't be true.

"No insult intended, Mr. Germain, but I wonder
whether he oughtn't consult a London physician," Harris said now, and Sacks nodded.

"Almost seems like 'is mind is going," Sacks commented.

Oh, for heaven's sake. "His mind isn't going," Millie
said. "Has he never tried to live differently since you've
known him? Never gone without company, or tried to…
change his habits?"

*It's not as if a man can truly change, not after so
many years,* he'd said. Yet he was partially committed
to trying? Why? Because of Cara? Because the accident had left him fearing for his soul?

Harris looked at her as if she was the one whose
mind was going. "Why would he want to change his

habits? He's a man who knows what he wants. He knows how to find the joy in life and exploit it to the fullest."

And now the light had gone out of him. At least, Cara thought so.

"He was 'imself in Paris," Sacks said with barely a trickle of hope, glancing up, then returning his gaze to the floor. "For a few days, anyhow."

It seemed an eternity ago.

"You 'ave very small feet," Sacks remarked a little absently. "Slender ankles."

Millie looked at him. Her breath stilled, and a quick retort came to her lips, but before she could speak, Sacks gave her a lopsided half smile and said, "Be mighty nimble in a prize fight, eh?"

Relief came so fast it made her feel sick. "I'd be beaten to a bloody pulp in a prize fight," she scoffed, and turned back to her cabinet.

"I can't understand it," Harris said. From the corner of her eye, she saw him stand up and drain his glass. "Everything ought to have returned to normal by now."

Sacks stood also, and they both headed for the door. "It's more like he's growing worse."

And then they were gone, and the only thing growing worse was her anxiety about seeing Winston again.

CHAPTER EIGHTEEN

"She left on her own volition," came the duke's voice from the doorway a short while later, startling her.

She turned abruptly. Winston stood leaning against the doorjamb, his blue banyan falling carelessly over his waistcoat and breeches. Just looking at him made her feel things she knew better than to feel.

"You've been in your secret closet again," she accused.

He smiled a little. "No. Only eavesdropping outside the door. So you don't subscribe to the theory that I'm dying?"

"Not at all."

"Nor the theory that I'm losing my mind."

"No." But he was making her lose *her* mind just by standing there watching her. Probably he was thinking of last night—how could he not be?—and how easily she had melted beneath his touch.

He wandered into the room. "If it turns out that I *can* change my habits, I suppose the two of them will have to grow accustomed to a quieter mode of living."

What was he *doing* in here? "They won't like it."

The duke laughed. "Nor shall I, I daresay." He stopped in the middle of the room and turned to her. "I thought I'd find out whether you've changed your mind about resigning from my employ."

The reason he imagined he might have changed her mind snapped in the air between them.

"No," she said briskly. "I haven't. And it's been nearly two days since I've inspected your wounds," she went on quickly before he could respond. "It ought to be done." And better to do it on her terms than his.

"Yes, I suppose it ought."

"Then let's do it now." With the door wide open and all of the staff awake. She gestured toward a nearby chair. "You may lay your things there."

She watched him glance at the open doorway, at the chair, at her.

"I would prefer to do it later. In my chamber, when I'm preparing for bed." His eyes flicked over her as if he were contemplating possibilities she could only imagine.

The memory of last night burned holes through all her efforts to block it.

"Very well." She managed the words more matter-of-factly than she thought she'd be able to.

Later. In his chamber. She'd done that exact thing a dozen times already.

"You haven't told me whether you revealed yourself to Cara," he said now. "Did you?"

"Yes."

"Why?"

The edge to his voice made it clear he was asking why she'd found it necessary to reveal herself—what malady had Millie perceived in Cara that made it worth the risk.

"I've already told you I won't answer that question. It isn't mine to answer."

"Edward grows more worried by the day."

"Then he needs to speak with Cara."

"He has spoken with Cara."

"I'll not interfere with the relations between a man and wife," she said, thinking now of everything Cara had revealed, understanding now Winston's concern and how much more worried he would be if he knew the truth. "Will you?"

She saw the moment he realized that, no, he wouldn't. "At least urge Cara to be open with Edward," he said. "Will you do that much?"

"I'll do what I can."

"Very well." He turned to go, his dark eyes still troubled. "Until later, then."

The room felt empty without him. A strong yearning filled her chest—so strong that she pressed her fingers to her heart as if she could ease the pressure.

She was here for his health, and only his health. Nothing about that had changed.

Nothing.

She returned briskly to her medical cabinet. Perhaps he imagined that because she was only his medic, because she was nobody of consequence and even her gender was hidden, that touching her as a woman didn't count.

That he could do with her as he pleased beneath a cloak of secrecy—one small outlet for vice in the face of his self-denial.

Tell me to stop...

Forgive me...

He could touch her while denying himself what he really wanted, like exchanging silk for burlap.

And she had soaked up his attentions like a dry sponge in the rain.

She stared at the bottles, the instruments, the gauze, and a feeling welled up from deep inside. She loved these things, felt a deep connection to them. They made her happy.

It was as if her very soul recognized these things and leaped with joy at the sight of them.

It had leaped the same way in Father's apothecary shop, as if each bottle contained magical secrets just waiting to be unlocked.

And once she left the duke's employ, she would have none of these things. She would have to start over.

The idea of leaving squeezed her chest. It shouldn't have. But she *was* dry. Dry and plain and alone and more than a little afraid of what the future would hold.

Yet last night, in his arms…

Even now, hot licks of desire smoldered in places she'd never imagined deriving any pleasure from at all. Between her thighs, a warm, heady feeling taunted her in the very place he'd touched, and already her mind drifted to an imaginary situation where he might touch her again.

Such as in a little while, after you inspect his wounds…

Oh, for heaven's sake. She marched forward, shut the door. She ought to be angry with him. Furious. What he'd done last night—what he'd done the other day in his bedchamber, ravaging her—was ten times worse than any peeping.

And when he'd touched her, every scrap of intelligence had disappeared. She'd become just like all the others. Just another one of his many diversions.

She had only herself to blame for that.

THE NEXT MORNING, Millie was at the top of a ladder searching an upper shelf in the library when Winston came in.

"I've brought you a present," he said, stopping at the base of the ladder.

"A present." She climbed down and saw a paper-wrapped object in his hands.

"Or I should say, I had it sent," he said. "I am acquainted with an excellent physician in London. I wrote to him that I had a passing fancy to learn about anatomy." He held out the gift. "The rest of the volumes are upstairs in your rooms."

Volumes? She took the gift, removed the paper. Could feel already that it was a book.

"He also sent some papers—some of the latest theories, apparently."

A Treatise on Surgery and Medicine, including a Complete Survey of Anatomy, Volume 1.

Her breath caught. He'd brought her a treatise on anatomy? She looked up at him, barely daring to believe it. "How many volumes are there?"

"Ten."

Ten. She looked at the bookshelves. "Certainly they should be added to your library," she said, even as her hands tightened around the volume.

"What would I possibly want with them? They are

yours, Mr. Germain, and I'll not go to the trouble of sending them back."

She felt light-headed. An entire set of medical volumes...hers? Even with the generous wage he was paying her, she never would have been able to afford this. She ran her hand over the spine. The gold lettering. Traced her finger along the bottom edge.

She looked up at him. "I don't know how to thank you."

But the moment the words were out she realized she could think of a way, and just that quickly she wondered...could that be why he—

"No thanks are necessary," he said a bit shortly, as if he'd read the moment of suspicion in her eyes. "Of any kind. I had them sent because I thought you would appreciate them, and not for any other reason."

She looked into those eyes that observed her too closely, and she felt a dangerous shift inside herself... a softening, opening, trusting.

"You are too kind," she said, and meant it.

His lip curved up on one side, as if she'd said something vaguely amusing, and he bowed. "I shall leave you to your studies, then."

Upstairs, Millie spent long minutes just looking at the volumes—all ten, stacked on her writing desk, with smooth new binding and crisp corners.

And they were hers. A giddy feeling skittered through her—a mad desire to read every word this very moment if it were possible. Each book felt like a treasure chest waiting for her to open the lid.

Winston didn't think she was silly for wanting to

be a surgeon. He couldn't, or else he would never have given her these. Would he?

And the sight of them there on her table made her feel oddly close to him. As if somehow, by touching them, she touched him simply because he had given them to her.

"I WANT YOU to show me what you've been doing in the conservatory," Winston called to her the next day, catching up to her on the walkway.

"I've only been cataloging the medicinal plants," she said. "Not particularly interesting."

"You must find it so."

They walked side by side now, and even in broad daylight in the middle of the open area between the east wing and the conservatory he felt...magnetizing.

There had been no hint that he planned to touch her again. And that fit perfectly with her theory about a vent for his frustration in the face of temptations he was trying to resist.

She hated that it cut a little bit, that she really had been...just a convenience.

Convenience for what? He took nothing.

He must have derived some pleasure from it, or else he wouldn't have done it.

"Well, yes," she said. "But I enjoy that kind of thing."

Inside the conservatory, she showed him the small number of African plants that were listed in the treatise she'd found. She led him down the path to the far end of the conservatory—her favorite place, where the caretaker had allowed the lush tropical plants to overgrow the path, creating green hideaways where plants grew everywhere.

"When the princess was here," she said, ducking beneath some low-hanging vines, "we found this one hiding among all this foliage."

"The princess came *here?*"

"Yes, the morning you were away in town."

"Yes, but…you brought her back here? In all these leaves?"

"I feared it might ruin her dress, but she insisted. And we found this," Millie said, putting one knee on a bench that was tucked among the foliage, pointing to the tangle behind it. "There—growing beneath that large leaf. Do you see it?"

She paused in the middle of an explanation when his attention strayed. "You find this boring."

He looked at her as if only just realizing she'd stopped talking about the plant. "Forgive me. I was listening."

"I didn't imagine you would enjoy this," she said in an I-told-you-so tone.

And he sat down on the bench, resting his elbows on his knees, letting his fingers lace together between them. "Even Princess Katja finds this fascinating," he said in frustration.

He looked so defeated.

"There must be some upstanding pastime you enjoy. Perhaps…writing? You could pen a novel, or a book of poems."

His eyes shifted from a spot on the ground to her face.

"All right, then, not writing. Is there no kind of sport

that could occupy your time? Perhaps fencing, or...or hunting?"

"It isn't that," he said on an exhale. "I've done those things. For God's sake, who hasn't? But a man can't fence and hunt every bloody minute of the day, any more than he can immerse his entire life in politics or scientific inquiry."

"Some men do."

"And where is their pleasure?" he demanded, looking up at her. "Where is their joy in life? Oh, indeed— I know men who immerse their entire lives in politics. One can hardly stand to have a drink with them, let alone spend any considerable amount of time in their presence. I'll not become one of them."

He leaned forward. Buried his face in his hands, and she heard him sigh. And she couldn't help it—she closed the distance between them and touched his shoulder.

He looked up. There was a long moment when she looked down into his eyes, let herself look at his face, tense now with frustration and defeat.

Slowly she lifted her hand from his shoulder and lightly traced the worry lines on his forehead. Smoothed her thumb above his brows, just to comfort him.

Along his cheekbone.

Time and breath seemed to still, as if she were watching someone else touch the hollow of his cheek. His jaw. His chin.

And then, lighter than a whisper, his lips.

They were warm. Firm. She traced them with the tip of her finger, barely making contact.

His eyes closed.

She brought her other hand up and caressed his cheek. Ran her finger along the hairline at his temple.

And then his arms came around her thighs beneath her coat, his hands covered her bottom, and he pulled her into the vee of his legs. Rested his forehead against her belly, smoothing his hands over the curves of her buttocks, the sensitive backs of her thighs.

She stroked his hair, watching her fingers tunnel through the black waves on the top of his head, feeling the flesh between her legs come alive even though he hadn't touched her there. Her belly felt soft, liquid, alive with yearnings as his hands circled, stroked, caressed.

Her hips.

Her thighs.

The front of her breeches.

Her breath stilled when his fingers found the placket. Worked the buttons.

She should stop him. This was a mistake.

But as he opened her breeches and pulled them low on her hips, pulled her shirttails free, it didn't feel like a mistake.

It felt like exquisite anticipation. He pushed her breeches even lower. Exposed her completely to his view yet in the shelter of her coat falling around her hips.

She didn't dare move. Her fingers rested on his shoulders. She closed her eyes, waiting for his touch…

And felt his hot breath against the lowest part of her belly. Felt his lips brush her skin, lightly…lightly… while his thumbs slipped into her woman's folds. Parted her. And his head dipped lower, and now she realized what he intended but it was too late. His tongue found her, and—

Oh, heaven.

Her eyes fell shut and she gripped his shoulders. Felt him exploring. Stroking.

Oh.

Sharp pleasure ripped through her belly, and she arched her hips toward him. He held her wide with his thumbs. Tasted her more deeply. Her flesh came alive, pulsing with need. Pleasure spiraled tighter, hotter.

He circled, stroked. Found places she hadn't known existed.

The pleasure keened through her, taking away sense. Reason.

He murmured something against her—told her to let go?

And there was something…something…

Oh, dear *God*.

Her body tightened, shattered in a thousand pulsing, brilliant pieces, and she strained against him, cried out raggedly as he caught each pulse with his mouth, drawing the exquisite sensations out of her until finally… finally…

There was only her breath in the silent conservatory.

I could make love with him, came a reckless thought. She could let him make a woman of her, right here, and nobody would ever have to know.

The pulses thrummed inside her, more quietly now, while Winston brushed his lips across her sensitive, pulsing folds, easing his tongue gently over her, caressing his hands over her tender thighs now with a softness she wouldn't have thought him capable of.

Would he be that gentle if she gave herself to him?

She felt him move to her inner thigh. Kiss her there, lingering. And then drawing her breeches up over her hips. She was weak-kneed as he silently helped her put her clothing to rights and fasten her breeches, and all the while she didn't dare look at him, couldn't think of a single thing to say, could scarcely think at all.

He put his hands on her hips. Urged her back a step, and another, and then he stood and put his fingers beneath her chin. He lifted her face so that there was no more avoiding his eyes.

"*That,* Miss Germain," he said, "is the pleasure of life."

CHAPTER NINETEEN

"WILL YOU NEVER again dress as a woman?" Cara asked the next day when Millie stopped by to make sure the new herbs were agreeing with her. The vicar was out for the afternoon visiting, so Millie and Cara talked freely in the downstairs drawing room.

Millie shook her head. "I could never do the things I wish to do otherwise."

"I can't believe you enjoy it as much as you claim," Cara said, tucking her chin. "No ribbons, no lace… Surely there must be *some* female trappings you long for."

Millie thought of her scarves, tucked away at the bottom of her trunk. Of Winston. *That, Miss Germain, is the pleasure of life.* She shook her head, unwilling to admit to Cara her longing for womanhood.

"Come with me," Cara said now, and led Millie upstairs to her dressing room. "I have a gift for you."

Cara opened a chest at the foot of her bed and lifted out a folded bundle. She shook it out and held it up.

A nightgown.

"I worked the lace myself," she said.

Millie reached out to touch the delicate lace cuffs. The linen was soft, decorated with pale green ribbons and more of the intricate lace.

"It's beautiful. But I couldn't possibly—"

"I want you to have it," Cara said, pressing the night-gown more firmly into Millie's hands. "You can at least indulge yourself as a female in the privacy of your bed-chamber." She reached out and touched Millie's arm. "You deserve that much for yourself."

Nobody had ever given her anything this special.

"Being a woman is a good thing, Millicent," Cara said, and smiled. "You should embrace it. For one thing, it means you're not stubborn or pigheaded."

"Edward isn't pigheaded."

"Bullheaded, then."

Millie held the nightgown in her hands and imagined putting it on tonight. Twirling in front of the glass and seeing it swirl around her. But she didn't dare.

It would go in her trunk with her scarves and the silver earrings.

"How is Winston?"

"Very well."

"Who was this visitor you spoke of yesterday? The one who left?"

"An acquaintance of his. Princess Katja, of Prussia."

"Mmm. She sounds like the kind of person Winston would be acquainted with. Did she look like a princess?"

Millie tried to smile. "Very much so."

"Oh, dear...I've pained you." Cara reached for her arm. Squeezed it. But pain was the last thing Millie felt when she was with him. When Winston touched her, she felt alive. Desired.

"Not at all," Millie said, because nobody could ever know what she'd let him do with her.

"Has he given any indication of how much longer he'll keep you?" Cara asked.

"I can't imagine it will be too much longer." If Winston's recovery was the measure, she should have left a week ago. "I fear he's only imagining his complaints now."

Cara looked worried. "I wish he would keep you on until…" She put a hand to her belly. "And not just because you've been helping me with this." She reached for Millie's hands, grasped them around the nightgown. "I like to think we've become friends"

Friends. Millie held the word in her mind like a delicate glass figurine while emotion welled up, making it difficult to speak. She thought of the camaraderie aboard the *Possession*. The vigil at her bedside after her brother had nearly beaten her to death. India's easy chatter. William's laughter. Katherine's trust.

She'd had friends once.

"Yes," she managed. "I like to think so, too."

But they couldn't be friends, not really, because Cara knew nothing about her. Cara didn't know that Millie had betrayed every friend she'd ever had—stolen from them, lied to them, even assaulted them.

Cara didn't know that Millie didn't deserve any friends.

For a man who had no interest in England, William Jaxbury bloody well seemed to find himself here often enough.

Twice in as many years was two times too many.

He practically leaped from the hired hack, dodged his way through the teeming wharf—handcarts, wagons, people wheeling crates and barrels and sacks in every direction. There were ships moored side by side as far as the eye could see, their masts a chaos of criss-crossing lines and yards.

He found the *Possession* and took its gangplank in long strides. In moments he was in his cabin, raking his hands through his hair, glancing out the window at the river and the sharp angle of the setting sun.

Winston. Philomena had found her an employment with *Winston*.

What the bloody devil was Phil thinking?

And now it was too late to start out. Or perhaps not. Arrive in the middle of the night, pounding on the door—that'd get Winston's attention.

If it wasn't too late to save a young girl he should have protected.

"If I didn't know better," Zayn Carlyle said in a quietly bemused voice from the doorway, "I would think you were anxious to leave England—and here we've only just arrived."

William turned. Leveled his gaze at his friend and passenger, a half-Egyptian dealer in armaments. Zayn knew bloody well he'd never wanted to come back here. Hadn't even needed to. He could have written to Katherine that he had successfully retrieved the *Possession* from Millicent and India, that it had been moored safe and sound in Malta as he'd suspected.

But he'd come in person instead. And he hadn't done it for Katherine.

He'd done it for Millicent.

Zayn sobered. "What's happened?"

"Miss Millicent Germain has spent these past weeks

with the most rut-hungry devil in all of England, that's what's happened."

And it was his fault, because he'd been too angry to think beyond the immediate future.

Zayn raised a brow, waiting for a name.

"Winston," William said. "She's been working as a medic for Winston."

Zayn's mouth turned grim.

William pinched the bridge of his nose against a familiar, strangling guilt. Horrific images in his mind of his own brutality toward Millie, albeit with reason. Of another man's brutality—the black-and-blue evidence of her brother Gavin's fists.

William had seen it with his own eyes. Had stood by Millicent's bed as she lay there, nearly dead.

Yet still, months later, he'd set the lash to her, five times.

For piracy, for her own good, to save her life.

Sod that. There'd been other choices he could have made. Surely there had, even then, even at the risk of his men's respect. "I only hope it's not too late," he said, grabbing a satchel, looking inside it uselessly and tossing it aside because he wasn't going anywhere until morning.

Zayn crossed his arms, frowning. "Are you certain you don't want me to accompany you?"

"No sense in connecting your name with this mess."

"Nonetheless, I shall gladly help in any way I can."

A pit opened up in William's gut. When he arrived at Winston's estate, he may well be too late to save her from the worst of it.

But no matter what she'd endured in Winston's employ, William would make bloody sure she never had to endure it again. He would offer his friend everything he could and hope it was enough to absolve him of his sins.

THE PLEASURE OF LIFE.

The headiness of it lingered on Winston's tongue the next day, after making visits to some of the farthest reaches of the estate, and then the village—where he'd learned that Miles had been to see Cara again while Edward was away visiting parishioners.

Edward said Cara insisted she was well but that he didn't believe her.

If she was well, why the need for secrecy?

Winston dismounted after returning from the village, handed the reins to a waiting footman and strode into the house, where no doubt Miles would have her nose in one of those new medical volumes.

And it made him feel...good. Seeing her eyes the moment she'd realized the volumes were for her made him want to give her...more. More things that would make her look at him as though he were the greatest man in the world.

Instead, he'd given her something very different.

And he wasn't going to think of that now. This time, he would demand that she tell him what was the matter with Cara. There would be no refusals.

He found her in the library, at her favorite desk by the window, exactly as he expected to find her: leaning over a book, finger on the page, peering at something very closely. The sight of her reminded him instantly of the conservatory, the gentleness of her hands on his face, the taste of her... But that wasn't why he was here.

"You will tell me what is the matter with Cara," he said as evenly as he could, "and you will tell me now."

She looked up at him as if she couldn't believe what she was hearing. "We've already discussed this. More than once."

And meeting her eyes was not the same now as it had been before their tryst in the conservatory. He could still feel the way she'd touched his face, the whisper of her fingers.

No one had ever touched him that way before.

"This is no longer a discussion." He said it because he had to, for Cara's sake, and Edward's. "I must ask you, as your employer, to tell me what you know."

"It's not mine to divulge," she said sharply.

"I know there's something the matter. You've visited her too many times."

"Did it ever occur to you that Cara and I might be friends?"

"Cara was *my* friend long before she was yours. She's my responsibility—"

"She's responsible for herself."

"—and I intend to see to it that she receives every means of treatment possible."

She bolted from the chair and faced him. "You think I would not insist on further treatment myself if I believed it necessary? I thought you trusted my judgment."

"I do trust your judgment." But this was different. This was Cara.

"No, you don't, or you wouldn't be demanding that I betray her confidence."

"All this sneaking around, secret examinations behind Edward's back—"

"How was I to know he would be away for the afternoon?"

"I *must* know what's the matter with her."

"Why?" she cried, exasperated. "Because you feel guilty?" And immediately her mouth clamped shut, and Winston felt as if he'd been punched in the chest.

And now Miles was shaking her head. "I didn't mean that."

"What did Cara tell you?" But Winston already had a good idea what it was, and it made him feel sick.

"It's nothing. I didn't mean that, and it's best if we don't discuss this further." She closed her book and picked it up.

"*What* did Cara tell you?"

"Good afternoon, Your Grace," she said, and headed for the door.

"She told you everything, didn't she?" Bloody hell. Miles knew it all—his sin, the baby, Cara's barrenness.

Miles paused. Turned, with her arms around the book. "You weren't supposed to know."

"*I* wasn't supposed to know? Perhaps I didn't want *you* to know."

"I won't tell anyone."

"I betrayed my best friend in the entire world—my two best friends—and that betrayal cost them both a lifetime of happiness, and there isn't one bloody thing I can do about it. Do you have *any* idea what that feels like?" he demanded. "*Do* you?"

"What if I told you I do? You aren't the only person in the world who has regrets.

"I wish I could tell you what you want to know— for your sake and Edward's—but Cara is my *friend*."

She said it forcefully, as if Cara were her only friend in the world. And then she turned back toward the door.

"Do not leave," he ordered. "I haven't finished."

She disappeared without bothering to respond.

And he stood there without bothering to go after her. Because she knew. She knew his blackest sin, and he had no idea what to do about it.

SHE EXPECTED HIM to follow her. Was surprised when he didn't.

She left her book on a side table in the entrance hall, went out the front door and into the gardens—straight down the very path she'd watched Winston take with the princess that day—all the way to the end of the third pond.

And then she turned around.

Faced the house.

From here it looked like a palace, sprawling in both directions, dotted with too many windows to count. It made her feel small.

And compared to Winston and his grandeur, she *was* small.

But she would not betray a friend ever again—not even knowing how tormented he must be. He was afraid for Cara, and she knew why, and she'd promised Cara she wouldn't let him know, but now she had.

Watching him just now, the look in his eyes made her heart ache. Regret. Shame. Resignation. They were Millie's closest companions. She knew better than he could imagine what it felt like to make a mistake that could not be fixed.

His pain sliced through her, reaching a place she did not want him to touch.

And she wished she could help him, but he'd been right that day in Paris. There was nothing she could give him that would undo the past.

CHAPTER TWENTY

AFTER A LONG WALK in the gardens and a bit of time in the conservatory, Millie retrieved her book from the entrance hall and returned to her rooms. Absently she closed the door, feeling the weight of the book in her hands, the smoothness of the cover, the crisp corner of the pages. Sitting down at her writing desk, she tried to read for a while but couldn't seem to concentrate.

The sky grew darker, and she lit a candle. Its warm glow flickered over the set of volumes Winston had given her.

She would take them when she left. She probably shouldn't, but she would.

And when will you leave?

Soon. She pulled the book closer, tried to brush the question aside with renewed attention to a section about the spleen.

How soon?

She focused on each word, each sentence. Studied the detailed plates, cross-referenced the diagrams to the text. But it was no use. Finally, she set the book aside and decided to prepare for bed even though it was much too early.

She removed her wig, jacket, waistcoat. Brushed her hair until it was smooth and shiny, went to the dresser…

and pulled out the nightgown Cara had given her. It felt soft and feminine in her hands. A great longing filled her—a longing for something she wasn't quite sure of—and she set the nightgown on the dresser.

Before she could leave, she would need to make plans.

She disrobed, washed and opened her jar of salve. Standing in front of the glass, she held up her hair, dipped her fingers in the salve, and began tending to the scars on her back.

Suddenly there was a knock, and Winston's angry voice came through the door. "Miles, I wish to speak with you about this afternoon."

"I can't!" Dear God—she snatched up the nightgown. "Not right now—" But the door was already opening. "Wait—"

There was no time to stop him as she fumbled with the nightgown, searching for the sleeves—

Winston came in. Saw her. His expression changed from upset to stunned in a heartbeat.

"What do you want?" she cried, hugging the nightgown to her chest.

"My apologies. I had no idea—" But now his gaze shifted past her, and his expression changed. "God's blood," he breathed.

She turned— No. Oh, no. The looking glass. "Please leave," she said, and turned so her back faced the wall, too aware that the nightgown she held concealed very little.

"Who did this to you?" he demanded.

"It's nothing for you to concern yourself with. In any case, it's of no consequence anymore." She did not want him to know the truth of her past any more than he wanted her to know his.

"It's of consequence to me," he said in a voice that was too low, too controlled. "Very great consequence. Is this Lady Pennington's doing?" His eyes had turned murderous.

Philomena? "No! Of course not."

"Your former employer? The one whose name you also refused to divulge?"

"*Please,* Your Grace, please leave, and let us not speak of it anymore."

"Have you committed a crime?" She could see him trying to figure out what act might carry an unusual punishment such as this.

"It was my brother," she finally lied, because he clearly was not going to stop until he had an answer, and Gavin may not have done this, but he had very nearly killed her with his fists a month before she'd been lashed.

"Your brother."

"*Please* don't make me discuss it." And that much was true. She didn't want to talk about the horror of that day, that she'd clung to the mainmast aboard William's ship as he'd punished her for her piracy. He would have been well within his rights to do much worse.

Even now, shame burned hot on her cheeks.

Winston's gaze on her gentled, almost looked pained, and he nodded. Looked at her dressing table. "You've been rubbing salve into the wounds."

"They're not wounds. They're scars." Ugly, horrible scars. And he'd already seen her nude once, but now he'd seen the worst of it. She would never look like Princess Katja, and she needed him to leave.

He went to the dressing table and, to her horror, picked up the tin of salve. "Let me help you," he said softly.

"I've already finished."

"I doubt that."

So she tried the truth. "I don't want you to see them again."

He dismissed that with a shake of his head. "Do they hurt?"

"No. Not anymore. But they're hideous."

He dipped two fingers into the salve. "Can't you trust me?" he asked quietly.

She was already out on a limb with trusting him—on horseback, in the conservatory—and so she dared a few steps past him, away from the wall, and presented her back to him, fully aware that she was entirely nude from behind because the nightgown she held only covered her front. But with those scars, it hardly mattered.

"The two in the center," she said now. "They're the hardest to reach."

He didn't say a word, but she felt his fingers touch her skin—warm, light, smoothing the salve along the ridge of one of her scars. And she knew exactly which one just by his touch—knew their pattern by heart. The first two lashes had landed across her shoulder blades in nearly parallel lines. The next two crisscrossed, making a lopsided X across the middle of her back. The final lash had struck her just above her buttocks.

Hang her! Hang her! She could hear the crew's terrifying shouts. The cheers that came with each blow.

She shuddered and felt his hand fall away.

"Did I hurt you?"

"No. Just a chill."

And so he began rubbing again—long, smooth strokes, gentle circular ones. Warm. Comforting.

And soon, more than that.

She felt him move to the lowest scar, felt his fingers skirt along the top of her buttocks.

"I want to know your name." His voice was low and rough, closer to her ear than it should have been.

Half-a-dozen excuses leaped to her tongue, but she didn't want them. Not right now. "It's Millicent."

"Millicent." He said it softly. "Of course."

His hands worked magic over her skin, igniting a slow burn on the inside, too, way down low. She knew the moment he finished with the salve, heard him set it aside, but his hands lingered.

She felt them on her shoulders.

He lifted a lock of her hair and let it slide through his fingers, and then pulled it back, away from her face, brushing his lips against her temple.

Her breath grew unsteady.

"So beautiful," he murmured.

The entire universe froze, suspended, except for his hand letting the hair slip from his fingers and reaching for her face.

Touching, barely touching. Her jaw. Her chin. Her cheek.

Beautiful. He thought she was beautiful?

"Hidden beneath your men's clothes," he murmured against her hair. "A secret goddess."

He caressed his hands down her sides, slipping them

around her in an intimate embrace. He kissed her ear, her temple. And then he simply held her, his jacket and waistcoat and breeches pressing into her unclothed back and bottom.

She imagined touching him in that way she'd hoped never to touch a man again, except now the idea of it made her feel soft and liquid on the inside, warm and yearning in all the places he had touched her.

She turned her face toward him. Her nose pressed against his cheek, and her mouth hovered by his chin. "Winston." His name was a breath on her lips.

"Mmm?"

"I want to touch you."

He stilled.

She felt her pulse at the base of her throat, waiting for his response. She breathed in the scent of his skin, felt its roughness.

After a long moment, he lifted her nightgown in his hands, so that they both held it now. "You'd best put this back on," he whispered roughly. Already he was searching for its opening.

And surely he wanted her touch—she could feel his hardness inside his breeches—but now he had found the bottom of her nightgown, and he moved back a little, and there was nothing to do but let him slip it over her head. She put her arms through the holes, and the nightgown whispered to her knees.

Finally, she turned to face him.

His dark eyes searched hers as if she was a wonder he'd never beheld. And she realized, now, that she wanted more than just to touch him.

She wanted him to open her womanhood.

His arms hung at his sides. A muscle in his jaw worked. "I need to leave."

"I wish you wouldn't."

He closed his eyes.

She hesitated, gripped by a moment of doubt. And then she reached for his placket. Found it beneath the vee at the front of his waistcoat and worked it open, loosing him into her hands.

He didn't move. She heard him let out a long, unsteady breath, eyes still closed, jaw tight now.

His member was large, heavy with desire. She smoothed her hands along it, circling it with her fingers, brushing her thumb over the soft, blunt tip. Her heart felt full as she stroked him—once, again, and again, and then sliding one hand down to gently cup his sac.

She heard his quick intake of breath, glanced up to find his eyes open and on fire, watching her touch him.

He took hold of her wrists, pulled her hands away.

He fastened his breeches with the unsteady motions of a man barely in control.

And then he reached for her, softly, just a hand on her face, and he dipped his head. Touched his lips to hers— barely clinging at first, then moving lightly, lightly...

And she was caught. He coaxed her lips open and gently, gently explored her. Nothing like the other kiss, none of the ferocity. More like the way he'd tasted her in the conservatory.

She pressed her palms against his chest, against the satiny texture of his embroidered waistcoat.

His hands cupped her shoulders. Skimmed down her back and rested on her buttocks, burning through her nightgown. He cupped her there, too, ever so briefly, all the while kissing, tasting, his lips soft as a prayer against her mouth.

He smoothed his hands up her sides, dragging the hem of her nightgown with them, and found her breasts. His fingertips caught her nipples, barely tightening around them, and a small cry escaped her. She clung to him. Felt his fingers tighten more, tasted the languorous brush of his tongue against hers, felt herself respond below with a warm, slick need.

As if he could read her body, his hand was there. Slipping into her folds, caressing her like he'd done before.

"Sit," he whispered, urging her backward, and she realized now that he meant to do the same thing he'd done the other times—pleasure her and then walk away, taking nothing for himself. But she didn't want to let that happen.

She put her hands on his chest, refused to do what he asked. "I don't want you to hide from me."

The corner of his mouth curved up, and his hot gaze touched her nose, her cheeks, her lips. "You have an interesting concept of hiding." Below, his fingers stroked the length of her slit.

"Then let me touch you." She ached to hold him in her hands again and feel that fullness in her heart again.

The curve on his lips faded. "There's no need for that," he said roughly.

"I know. But I want to."

His hands fell away from her body, and he stepped back. "Do you have *any* idea what you're saying?"

She knew exactly what she was saying, what she was asking for. She wanted this with him—knew he wanted it, too, and was only denying himself because he thought he had to, but there was only the two of them now and nobody would ever have to know.

"Good night, Winston," she said, and went into the bedroom, trembling now with the desire to know what womanhood felt like—warm and pulsing and ready for it. She gripped a bedpost. Leaned her forehead against it.

Heard him cross to the door in the other room.

Held her breath, imagining him opening it, waiting to hear it close again.

Instead, she heard the lock.

Heard a sound behind her and turned to find Winston tossing his jacket onto a chair, stepping out of his shoes, yanking at his neck cloth. Coming toward her with his hands at the front of his waistcoat working the buttons, abandoning them to reach for her instead and pull her to him, crushing his mouth against hers, digging his fingers into her hair and kissing her deeply. Fiercely.

And she reached for his placket again, and he let go of her but didn't break the kiss, worked his buttons, shrugged free of his waistcoat at the same moment that she caught him in her hands. But this time he pushed his breeches down. Broke away just long enough to yank them off, get rid of his stockings, pull his shirt over his head, whisk her nightgown away.

And then he was lifting her, naked, onto the bed, and he planted a knee between her legs, bracing one arm by her shoulder, dipping down to kiss her breasts. He took one in his mouth and she arched toward him, reaching between their bodies to find and hold him again.

He groaned against her skin. Pulsed in her hands.

Kneaded a breast and pulled its nipple taut, and then licked it, loosing new pleasure between her thighs. His knee came up higher, pressed against her flesh, and she moved against it.

Stroked him—up, down, teasing his sac with her fingers, gasping at the wicked things he was doing to her breasts.

Knowing what would come next, yet not knowing at all.

And oh, heaven, he felt glorious, and she let go of him with one hand to caress his thigh, his tight buttocks, his flat stomach and hard chest. He abandoned her breasts and buried his face at her neck, kissing her there with his breath coming hot against her skin. She feathered her fingers through the coarse hair on his chest, splaying her hand against him.

He eased his knee back and reached between their bodies. Took her hand from his shaft, moved to his side, and raised up on one elbow, bracing himself over her while he parted her with his fingers.

She looked into his eyes—those devil eyes that were heaven to her now, looking at her with need and desire, as if she were the greatest temptation he'd ever known.

"So beautiful," he whispered, as he delved deeper between her legs. She opened them wider, already knowing his touch. Craving it again.

He leaned down to kiss her, taking her mouth completely as he stroked her. His touch was a refiner's fire, burning away the ugliness of the past, and she pressed into it. Sighed—gasped—with new pleasure when he circled her opening and dipped inside.

He circled again, pushed his finger farther inside

her this time, spearing fresh need with it, and she lifted her hips.

"Easy," he murmured into their kiss.

He went on like that, pushing his finger in her and then tracing her opening, each time stoking a need that came from deep in her belly, as if her womanhood was crying out to be found, until she couldn't stand it anymore and *she* cried out against his lips with desire—frustration—she didn't know.

And then his finger left her. He brought his other knee inside her legs and nudged them even wider. She felt his hand on her hip, shifting her. And something else—his shaft—rubbing against her thigh now. Touching her where his fingers had been, sliding up and down against her slick folds slowly, deliberately, sending excruciating pleasure searing through her flesh. She dug her fingers into his hair, made a noise when he broke their kiss to suckle her breasts, heard him breathing now—hard, barely-in-control breaths.

She felt him splay her with his fingers. Felt him shift between her thighs, felt his shaft push at her opening.

And time seemed suspended as she clung to him, feeling him breach her and rock himself in, in, in, a little farther each time, until suddenly—

Dear *God,* he braced himself on both elbows above her and thrust himself once, swiftly, all the way inside her.

She cried out in pain, surprise, and her eyes shot to his face, and there was just enough time to see the apology in his eyes before he brought his mouth down on hers again, tangled his tongue with hers and began moving between her thighs—slow, sure thrusts that seemed to touch her very core, each one opening her a little more, coaxing pleasure from the pain.

Building a rhythm inside her.

His hand found her breast again, caught her nipple, and fire speared down below. Need. She began to move with him, wanting to feel…to feel…

Oh.

Her breath turned ragged and the fire turned wild inside her, building…building…and she couldn't keep her legs still so she lifted them, hooked them around him, reaching for him with everything she had.

And the fire took her. It ripped through her in great throes of release that clenched and gripped him as he thrust again, again, again, kissing her madly now, holding tight to her breast on one final thrust that held and held and held.

His shaft throbbed and pulsed inside her. He broke the kiss and pressed his forehead against hers, breathing…breathing…while shudders racked her body and she pushed herself as close to him as she possibly could.

And he finally released his breath, and his arms came around her tightly, possessively. He buried his face in her hair and just held her.

WINSTON THOUGHT HE'D known everything there was to know about being inside a woman's body.

Now it seemed as if he'd never known at all.

He rolled onto his side, taking Millicent with him, keeping himself buried in her tight sweetness. Thoughts crowded at the edges of his mind, but he didn't want them. He only wanted her.

Her passage still pulsed, so exquisitely tight around him he almost couldn't take it. But he couldn't stand to pull out of her. Not yet.

He tried pushing farther inside her—as if that were possible—but stopped with a hiss when her body fisted around him and he was too bloody sensitive after that insanity of a release to do anything but lie perfectly still and breathe.

Feeling her skin, soft and warm against his.

Smelling her hair.

Letting his lips linger against her ear, her jaw, her lips.

Her arms felt small yet fierce around him. Her legs, too, tangled around him, splayed wide to cradle his hips and accept his body into hers.

You've done it again.

The thought crept in, seeking a place to take root in his foggy mind.

He turned his head, just a bit, just enough to see her face because she was so beautiful he couldn't stand not to look at her. Her hair was a silken curtain of mink pooling on his shoulder and the pillow. Her eyes were liquid brown and looking at him with something he'd never seen in a woman's eyes in bed before: Trust.

You don't deserve it.

He cupped the side of her face—innocence cradled in the palm of sin. "Did I hurt you?" He barely recognized his own rough voice.

She shook her head. "Only a little."

"Good." But a terrible feeling had begun to pool in his gut.

He tried to ignore it. He trailed his fingers down

her throat, along her collarbone, across the tops of her breasts. Those tender nipples stood firm and berry-pink from his lips and teeth and hands. He smoothed his hand down her side and over her hip and thigh to her knee where it hooked around him.

Remembered that moment—the one where there had been no going back because he was already inside her, had already breached her maidenhead, and there was nothing left to do but take everything.

Fifteen years.

"My leg hurts," Millicent whispered.

And of course—he was lying on it. So he shifted, and the movement made him slip from her body, and he glimpsed a sheen of moisture on her inner thighs before she closed them.

Moisture from her deflowering.

By him, when he'd sworn off virgins after that mistake with Cara and hadn't even been tempted by one in all these years.

He pulled her close and tucked her face beneath his chin. His clothes lay strewn about her room. Her night-gown lay atop his breeches, a limp scrap of linen that had been no protection at all.

"What do we do now?" she asked against his throat.

He had no bloody idea. Somehow he had to make things right, but he couldn't stand to think of that now.

She would need to wash.

"Now," he said, pushing himself to his elbow and then fully upright—pausing to brush his thumb across her lips because, holy God, they looked so plump and perfect. "You wait here."

He got out of bed and walked into her dressing room

to her pitcher and bowl, seeing his naked body in the glass as he wrung out a cloth and wished the water weren't so cold. When he returned to the bedchamber, she was out of bed and picking up her shift off the floor. He caught a glimpse of those scars, and fury rose up inside him.

He needed to know who Millicent really was. Her family, her history. He needed to speak with Lady Pennington.

Why? Why the devil do you need to know any of that?

"I thought you'd want this," he said, and offered her the cloth when he'd intended to bathe her himself, but then he'd assumed she would still be in bed. He picked up his shirt, pulled it over his head, watching her.

He wanted to commit murder on her behalf. The way she'd looked earlier, clutching that damned shift while she stared at him in horror and shame…

He'd wanted something he couldn't even identify. Wanted to protect her, though clearly it was too late for that.

He pushed his arms through the sleeves and flexed his hands, itching to find the whoreson who had whipped her and tear the man limb from limb.

And despite all that, he'd taken her virtue. Which made *him* the whoreson. But God help him, when she'd said she wanted to touch him… And he wasn't going to do it. He was going to walk out that door—because he'd promised, and he was trying, and—

God.

She had her shift on now and was tugging to straighten it, and she looked beautiful. Vulnerable.

Self-hatred edged in on all sides, but there was little

point to that now, so he closed the distance between them and took what he wanted instead.

A kiss.

Those soft lips, moving against his. That slender body, melting against him even now, when she had to be raw and sore from their lovemaking, because he hadn't gone slow.

He couldn't.

Not with her, not after holding back for so long.

He held her face in his hands and drank of her for long, long minutes. Loved the feel of her arms around him, her tongue mating with his, sweet and trusting.

And knew that he'd failed completely at everything he'd set out to do.

CHAPTER TWENTY-ONE

MILLIE HARDLY SLEPT after Winston returned to his rooms. He didn't stay—couldn't, not with Harris and Sacks and the rest of the help, not unless she was willing to risk being entirely exposed as very definitely not "Mr." Germain.

She didn't feel like Miles Germain.

She felt…womanly.

In the morning, hours after the fact, she lay there in the very spot where it had happened, and the tenderness between her legs testified to the truth that she had become a woman, fully and completely.

With him. Winston.

He'd called her beautiful. Had touched her *scars*. And she'd let him. And it had felt so, so good to be cared for, even if he was only being kind.

But last night, as he'd filled her and they'd moved together…

She felt she knew him.

The clock chimed. It was later than usual. She needed to dress before any servants arrived. She made herself get out of bed, hurried through her morning routine to be dressed before any servants arrived.

Finally she fussed with her wig, unable to get it quite

right, feeling unaccountably grumpy about having to wear it all the time in the first place.

She tugged at the wig, leaning toward the glass. Bloody thing...*now* it decided it didn't want to fit properly. She pulled it off and three pins came loose, and half of her hair came tumbling down.

She looked at herself in the glass and paused. Lifted her hair, brought it to her nose.

Inhaled his scent. Remembering.

A duke could always use a personal medic, couldn't he?

She let her hair go, took out the rest of the pins, brushed out her hair and gathered it back up. Five extra pins beyond the usual number, and all was secure.

She really needed to cut her hair.

Later. She would do it later, after she left Winston's employ, when she was on her own as Miles Germain and would not be able to afford the risk of an ill-fitting wig.

She pulled the bagwig back on. And still it didn't look right.

She looked like a woman in a man's wig. Had her gender been this obvious the entire time?

Surely not. Harris and Sacks would never have been able to keep quiet if they'd suspected.

She patted the bagwig down more firmly and opened her jaw to draw out her expression. But her cheeks were still flushed pink, and her neck...

She leaned closer. There was a slight abrasion on her skin where Winston's jaw had scraped her when he'd moved over her.

But nobody would know that's what had happened.

She tugged at the front of her waistcoat and turned to the side to make sure the binding was having its proper effect.

There was a knock, and her attention shot to the door. A mass of butterflies came alive in her stomach, and for a moment she didn't answer because what did one say to the man one had given one's virtue to the night before?

But it was only Harris.

"There's a visitor here to see you," Harris said, while Millie closely watched his face for any sign that he saw the same things she'd seen this morning in the glass. There was no hint that anything had changed. "He said his name is Sir William Jaxbury."

William. Here?

"Mr. Germain, are you quite all right?"

"Yes," she managed, and swallowed past a rising panic.

"If you'd rather I sent him away—"

"No. No, I shall see him. Thank you." She started down the corridor and then paused, looking back. "Harris, has His Grace risen yet this morning?"

"He has, and he's gone out for a ride on horseback. I would expect him to return shortly."

Then there might be enough time to find out what William wanted and send him away before Winston ever knew he was here.

Downstairs, she entered the grand salon and saw William's familiar figure in front of the window.

She stopped just inside the threshold. "William."

He turned. And seeing him now, a terror ripped through her. Blood rushed in her ears like the deafening shouts of the crew.

Hang her! Hang her!

Her stomach knotted tightly. Sickly.

"Please don't do this to me now," she begged before he could say anything. Horrible memories rose up, putting a panicked waver into her voice. "I've told you I was sorry, and I would go back and change it if I could, but I can't."

"Millie—"

"It was an accident." She approached him now, because she couldn't afford to be overheard. "I didn't set out to do it. Truly, I didn't." But she'd done it—hit him over the head, locked him away, taken over his ship. And now he had come to England to bring her to justice.

"I'm not here for retribution," he said in a low voice, coming toward her now, and she began to shake. His blue eyes weren't laughing like they usually did, and his mouth was tight, and the scar down his cheek made him look ferocious. He still wore his gold earrings, but dressed, today, in a crisp jacket, waistcoat and breeches embroidered with oriental patterns. "God knows I've punished you enough already," he said raggedly.

And she'd deserved it. She'd deserved worse than what William gave her. He'd given her the lightest punishment the crew would have tolerated and remained loyal to him as captain. But that didn't change the fact of the ugly scars that would crisscross her back for the rest of her life.

Because of him.

Because what she'd done to him first was worse.

"I don't understand."

"I sail for Italy in a week, and then to Turkey." He

put his hands on her arms. "I want you to join my crew. Be my ship's surgeon."

There was a heartbeat when Millie's mind went numb.

"You can't." She shook her head. "You wouldn't. Not after—"

"Sod all that," he said fiercely. "None of it matters anymore. At least, not your part in it." He looked at her, eyes regretful, mouth grim. "I won't ask your forgiveness. But I won't hurt you again. You have my word."

He thought he needed *her* forgiveness? "You had every right—"

"I was the *captain*. Could have done as I bloody well pleased."

"No, not as angry as those men were. You had no choice."

"I won't discuss this anymore. Bad enough what I've done…but I could murder Phil for sending you here." William's blue eyes glanced over her, taking in her disguise. It wasn't the first time William had seen her dressed like a man. "What the bloody blazes was she thinking? Tell me he hasn't compromised you."

He. Winston. "Don't be ridiculous. I'm his medic, nothing more."

But her mind and her body were still steeped in last night, and she felt her cheeks warm, felt the truth written all over her face for her old friend to read.

"Bloody *hell*." His eyes turned ice-cold, and he closed the distance between them. "You can't stay here. You'll come with me, right now."

What? "But my employment here isn't finished—"

"Your *employment*—for Christ's sake—never should have begun."

"The duke was going to Greece—"

"And he went to your bed instead."

"Sir William," came Winston's sharp voice from the doorway.

Millie's head whipped around, and William released her, striding toward Winston. "Sodding bastard," he said, and landed a fist across Winston's jaw.

"William!" Millie screamed. Already a handful of servants were rushing to the doorway, and Winston was still on his feet, putting a hand to his lip, which she saw now was bleeding. But he did not raise his hand to strike William in return.

"To what do I owe the honor, Jaxbury?" Winston said.

William flexed his fists as if he was considering throwing another punch. "I think you know bloody well."

"William, don't. Please." And now Winston was looking at her, and she could see the questions in his eyes, and they were questions she didn't want him to know the answer to.

"I'll not see you harmed further, Millie," William said, without turning. "Putting a stop to it *today*. Go upstairs, pack your things and come with me."

Today.

"I'm not ready to leave today." But she should be. William was offering her...everything she wanted. But to leave Winston, now, after last night...

"I can assure you that I have no more desire to see

Miss Germain harmed than you do," Winston said coldly.

"Bollocks. Your reputation is well-known."

"I don't need to tolerate this in my own house."

William turned to her, and now they were both looking at her. Waiting.

And she needed to go with William. She *should* go with him. There was nothing for her here. Except Winston.

"I can't," Millie said.

"Devil take it, Millie." William started toward her, but Winston stepped in front of him, blocking his way.

"She's given you her answer. I have no doubt she'll let you know if she changes her mind," he said.

Millie thought for a moment William wasn't going to leave. But he backed down and turned to leave.

William offered an opportunity she would never have again. Otherwise, when she left Winston's employ, she would be alone. She followed William out over Winston's objection.

"He doesn't know," she told William when they couldn't be heard. "He thinks I'm merely one of Philomena's acquaintances. He doesn't know the rest, and I don't want him to." Winston respected her now. He wouldn't if he found out all the awful things she'd done. "Please—you must go."

"Tell me you don't fancy yourself in love," William said.

"I'm not a fool."

"Then let me help you." He took her by the shoulders. "Let me give you back the life you had aboard the *Possession*."

SHE PROBABLY SHOULD have gone with him. Today, just like he'd said.

Instead, she'd told him she needed more time and she'd promised she would consider his offer.

But she couldn't simply leave Winston. Not after last night, without so much as a...

As a what?

She didn't know. But now she was in the house, and Harris said Winston wanted to see her in the library, and now she would have to face him.

He sat at the large desk, sorting through some papers. She watched him for a moment, saw that his lip was cracked and red where William had hit him—defending her honor, when she was the one who had asked Winston to stay with her last night.

Then he looked up, and she met his eyes, and suddenly she wasn't sure how she would be able to make herself leave at all unless he dismissed her.

He stood, came around from behind the desk. "How are you?" he asked, concern in his eyes.

"Very well." Except it turned out that last night had not been an end to anything, because here she was wanting to reach for him all over again.

He looked at her for a long moment, as if trying to decide whether she was telling the truth, and then he nodded. "Good," he said, in such a low voice she could barely hear it. And then, more evenly, "How do you know William Jaxbury?"

She'd already rehearsed her answer. "He's a friend of a friend." It was true. "Lady Pennington, in fact." That, too, was the truth.

"A very close friend, apparently."

"Please accept my apologies. I had no idea he would…"

"Discern the truth?" Amusement barely whispered across Winston's face as he looked at her, let his gaze roam over her face, her body, clothed now as Miles. "He's not your lover, I know that much."

"William?" The idea almost made her laugh. "He's like a brother to me," she said, and immediately realized how much that simple statement revealed.

Winston regarded her for a moment and then reached for something on the desk, a letter, the two halves of its broken seal stuck like thick blood to the paper. "My presence is required in London. I shall be leaving immediately, and I expect to be there at least a week, perhaps more."

London. The word and all it implied burst into her mind in vivid detail. They would never be alone in London. A pain caught her in the chest, and now she realized she should have accepted William's offer on the spot.

"It was time I was on my way anyhow—"

"I want you to come with me—" They'd spoken at the same time, and now he cut off. "On your *way,*" he said.

"You won't need a medic in London."

"That's neither here nor there. For God's sake, do you really imagine that I would—" He stopped, as if he wasn't quite certain what he'd been about to say.

And with every passing moment his life in London was piecing itself together in her mind, one entertainment, one acquaintance after the next. Every form of carnality was to be found in London. Every kind of temptation.

It wasn't hard to predict what would happen once he got there.

"I can't remain in your employ forever," she said. "I don't want to. You already know that."

"I'm only talking about a few more weeks—the time I'm required to spend in London, until I'm able to return to my estate. Perhaps a bit longer, just to be certain."

"Certain of what?"

"Of my health." He made a frustrated gesture. "Of my complete recovery. In case anything should happen—anything that might aggravate the freshly healed injuries."

It was ridiculous. Nothing was going to slash open his wounds. He was perfectly sound now, and they both knew it.

Yet he wanted her to stay.

The fact of it surged hotly inside her, almost like the thrust of his body, except fuller and more completely. And there was no doubt, if she stayed, what would happen between them.

Just a little bit longer.

It wouldn't hurt to stay with Winston just a few days more.

"Very well," she said. "I shall go with you to London."

CHAPTER TWENTY-TWO

FROM THE MOMENT Winston arrived in town, it began—
demands, invitations, callers…his life, the way it had
always been. As if there had never been an accident,
never any useless vow or crisis of conscience.

London didn't care about one young woman's virtue
or the fact that he had taken it when he had no right to,
or the even more damning fact that he couldn't quite
regret it.

He presented himself at the palace, listened for two
hours about the excessive power of Parliament, and then
met for two more hours with a handful of malcontents at
Westminster and heard about the king's overreaching.

But he wasn't quite concentrating on business.

He couldn't touch her again. He knew that much.

Even though he wanted to. Because making love to
her was a madness beyond compare to anything. He'd
never experienced anything like it, and he couldn't quite
reconcile the idea of never experiencing it again.

Which was why, when his business was finished,
he went to White's instead of going home. Had supper
there, and plenty of company, and just enough distraction to keep him from changing his mind.

He should never have brought her to London in the

first place. But he needed more time. For what, he had no idea.

The one thing he could *not* do was compromise her and simply leave her.

He'd just finished a game of billiards when the much-celebrated Captain James Warre, Earl of Croston, approached him.

"Thought you were convalescing in the country," Croston said, picking up a stick.

"The country became a bit claustrophobic."

"For you, I don't doubt it." They started a new game, and Croston took the first shot. "You appear to be completely recovered," he said.

"Mmm." Winston lined up his shot, sank a ball in the corner pocket. "Excellent medical attendant."

"So I've heard. Miles Germain, is it?"

Bloody hell. "You know him?"

"*Miles* Germain? Can't say that I do."

Winston had been about to line up his next shot, but now he straightened. Looked at Croston, who stood on the same side of the table. "Perhaps you know my medic by a different name."

"I shall face hell at home if I do not do my duty and warn you off her. My wife won't tolerate anyone treating her ill. Nor shall I, for that matter. In a very real way, I owe her my life as much as I owe it to Katherine."

Winston knew of only one connection between Croston, his wife, Katherine, and William Jaxbury.

"You're telling me Miss Germain was aboard your wife's ship."

"I know firsthand what an excellent medic she is," Croston said. "She did a very thorough job restoring my health. I'd have her as ship's surgeon aboard any vessel of mine without question."

Winston finally bent down, lined up his shot. After the disastrous shipwreck when Croston had been found and pulled to safety by Katherine Kinloch, he'd been tended to by Millicent. Ship's surgeon. It explained everything.

He missed the shot. "Was it *Miles* Germain that tended you, or Millicent?"

Croston gave a laugh. "I've never had the privilege of meeting Miles."

And now Winston wondered if *he* had ever met Millicent. But a picture was coming together—one that was scarcely credible. He imagined her aboard a sailing ship. It wasn't as difficult an image as he might have thought. Her sensible demeanor, her no-nonsense expectations. He could imagine her doing just about anything aboard a ship, from doctoring the sailors to hoisting the sails.

If she'd sailed with Croston's wife, she must have done even more than that. She'd likely helped take ships. Perhaps fought Barbary pirates, although that was difficult to imagine, as small as she was.

Millicent was as much a renegade half-pirate as Katherine was. But where Katherine had her title to protect her, Millicent would never be accepted in society and had, apparently, even been rejected by her own family. All because…

She wanted to live a life that was closed to her unless she became someone else.

Miles Germain.

And through it all, she'd managed to guard her virginity. Until him.

Croston sank two balls before missing a third.

Winston thought of something else. "Did your wife take the lash to her?"

"Good God, no. Katherine wasn't that kind of captain. I've never seen a more devoted crew." Croston frowned. "Why do you ask?"

Croston didn't know about the lashes. And for Millicent's sake, Winston wasn't going to tell him. "You wouldn't happen to know anything about any…injuries she's received?" He rounded the corner of the table, took his next shot. Glanced up to see Croston's mouth settle into a grim line of comprehension.

"You're talking about the beating she took. I don't know what permanent damage it might have left—little on the surface, I would imagine. But her brother beat her nearly to death. We were all quite concerned that she might leave us."

"When was this?"

"Months ago. But she was able to pull through, fortunately. Convalesced in Katherine's town house."

"The man ought to be hanged, taking the lash to her like that."

"Lash?" Croston looked at him. "I don't recall any lashings. All blows from the bastard's fists."

Winston could hardly comprehend what he was hearing. Millicent had been beaten and lashed?

"Then she's been back to see him?"

"As far as I'm aware, she's been out of the country until she arrived with you. What's all this about lashings?"

Which meant that she'd lied. And why in God's name would she do that?

"A misunderstanding, apparently."

At home in the wee hours, he stood for long minutes outside her closed door, one hand braced on the jamb, reciting all the reasons he should not go in.

Finally he pushed away and went to his room.

MILLIE HAD JUST finished Miles Germain's morning toilette when Winston knocked on the door. She knew it was him—could recognize the way he knocked. Raprap. Two solid thumps.

She drew in a breath to calm a sudden flutter in her belly as she opened the door.

"Good morning, Your Grace," she said in her most formal tone, in case any of the staff were listening. In this house, so much smaller than the house at the estate, she'd noticed after only a day that they seemed to be everywhere all the time.

He gestured for permission to come in and closed the door behind him.

"Good morning," he said. His voice was low. Familiar. With a hint of uncertainty? "I shall be out most of the day," he said now. "I wanted you to know."

"Thank you." He could have had Harris or Sacks tell her.

He hadn't come to her last night. She'd lain awake a very long time, listening, wondering, but had fallen asleep before she heard him return.

It was impossible not to wonder, now, whether he'd found more suitable company instead. The possibility hurt a little, deep inside her chest.

Winston cast dissatisfied eyes over her clothing. "I'm coming to despise that bagwig and suit," he said.

"I can hardly change it now." Here, in London, where rumors would spread from the staff throughout town like wildfire.

She wondered briefly what she was doing here. She would scarcely get to see him, was positive that when she did see him, it would lead to…more.

He reached for her hand and drew circles on her palm with his thumb. "True enough," he said. He was regarding her very intensely, as if she were a puzzle he was trying to solve.

And she couldn't stand another night like the last one, so she asked, "Will you be late tonight?"

"I don't know." He searched her eyes, possibly trying to determine whether she wanted him to be late, or…

Something else.

She moistened her lips. His eyes darkened.

"I should tell you," he said, "that you're free to return to the estate if you wish."

Did he want her to return?

"I would rather be here." With him holding her hand, lacing his fingers through hers now, holding more tightly, sending delicious sensations through her with just that simple contact.

He moved closer. "What will you do today?"

"I don't know." It was impossible to think and stand this way at the same time. "Read, most likely." And think about what to do next, and whether to accept William's offer, and what was going to happen tonight when Winston came home.

"I've put a carriage at your disposal should you wish to visit anyone." He paused. "Do you have any acquaintances in London? There is Lady Pennington, of course. I understand she's in town."

"Yes. Perhaps I shall see her." There was also Katherine, whom she still hadn't been able to come up with words for, and her little daughter, Anne, whom Millie had hurt most of all when she'd left Katherine and returned home to her brother. And India, whom Millie suddenly longed to see. But most likely, none of them would want to see her. "I doubt I shall need the carriage. I don't have any friends to see." It was true. And it made her heart ache fiercely, but she tried to hide it with a smile. "I'm not terribly fond of London."

"Why not?"

"Memories," she said after a moment. "Of a different time."

Now he brought her hand to his lips and pressed a kiss to her palm. "Perhaps, later, you'll tell me about them."

She put her hand against his face, touched him and imagined what it might be like for a woman to call him her own. How it might feel to be with him and know that one never had to leave.

It was a feeling no woman would likely experience.

Her least of all.

"I CAN'T STAND LONDON," Sacks muttered a while later when Millie found him stitching a quick mend to one of Winston's jackets—a friendly face among a sea of strangers, even if he didn't know the truth about her.

"I should think there would be plenty of entertainments here to keep you distracted," Millie said.

Just then, Harris appeared in the doorway. "Mr. Germain, you have visitors. Lady Pennington and Lady Taggart."

Philomena. And India!

He raised a brow at her. "You keep very high caliber company, Mr. Germain."

"Old acquaintances," she said. "From my former employment. I can't imagine what they could want," she added for good measure.

This was a disaster. If there was one person who could divine the truth of what she'd done with Winston just by looking, it was Philomena.

Millie would have to lie as she had never lied before.

Downstairs, Millie found them in the salon.

"Millie!" India squeaked before clamping her mouth shut.

"I knew you should not have accompanied me," Philomena said under her breath.

They exchanged formal greetings, as any man of Miles Germain's station might do with his betters, and then seated themselves at the grouping of chairs closest to the window and farthest from listening ears.

"I came as soon as I heard Winston was in town," Philomena said in the lowest conceivable voice, perfectly pitched to prevent servants from hearing something they shouldn't. "I've been beside myself since the moment I heard Winston had returned to England. I was much relieved when William was going to take care of the matter, but then he returned from Winston without you. Whyever did you not come with him?"

And Millie realized that William, bless him, had not told everything he'd learned during his brief visit.

"I wasn't finished with my employment," she explained reasonably, and shifted her attention to India.

"And it still isn't finished?"

"Just a few more days, to make sure nothing is aggravated by his activity in London." She sounded perfectly calm, perfectly detached. Just as a medic should be. But now as she looked at India and her heart squeezed, she was almost afraid to ask. "Did you receive my letter?" It had been weeks since she'd written it—before her employment with Winston.

"Oh, *yes,* and all is forgiven—never doubt that." She reached for Millie's hand and immediately let it go. "I should have written back, but I wasn't sure, with you in Paris…and with so many things happening. Millie—I mean, Miles…" A happy glow flushed India's cheeks. "I am with child!"

"India—I'm so happy for you."

"I love Nicholas so much," India whispered earnestly, still glowing. "You have no idea. It isn't like I feared it would be at all. He's…*magical.*"

"A man always seems magical until one tires of his repertoire," Philomena said. "Now tell me…Miles… whyever did Winston not go to Greece?"

"His Grace changed his mind."

"Well, yes, I'm aware of that. But *why* did he change his mind? Because of the accident, I assume. Were his injuries even greater than we were all led to believe?"

"They were quite severe," Millie said. "He's been longer in recovering than expected." She managed to hold Philomena's eyes, managed to keep her head up and speak in a matter-of-fact tone.

Philomena pinned her gaze on Millie. "And you've been at his estate all this time."

"He's been convalescing."

Philomena narrowed her eyes at that. "I know very well that several men whose presence I can barely tolerate in the best of circumstances traveled to Winston last week—and not for any convalescing. And Lord Hensley was included in the party."

"You didn't tell me that," India whispered, horrified. "Millie..." She started to reach for Millie's hand but stopped herself.

"I should have gone to Winston as soon as I heard he'd returned," Philomena said. "For your sake."

"His excesses did not seem to concern you in Paris," Millie whispered shortly.

"Endless hours of grueling travel is hardly the same thing as the intimacy of a man's own house. The things I've heard about the goings-on at Winston would burn even *my* lips to repeat them."

"Oh, Millie," India breathed. "Has it been very awful?"

"They only stayed two days, and Winston hardly spent any time with them at all. I scarcely saw Lord Hensley."

"Winston's injuries must have been very grave indeed," Philomena said, searching Millie's eyes. "And Winston has not suspected you at all? You're certain?" Her eyes glanced over Millie's clothes.

"Not even the smallest suspicion."

India leaned forward. "Will you not sail with William, then?"

"Yes...I very likely will." But it was too hard to think

of leaving and all it implied—never seeing Winston again.

"Katherine thinks you should," India said now, and reached for Millie's hand regardless. She smiled gently. "You should go see her. I've asked her forgiveness for taking the ship, and all is right again. You mustn't leave London without making amends."

CHAPTER TWENTY-THREE

MILLIE USED THE CARRIAGE, after all.

Still dressed as Miles Germain, she adjusted her waistcoat and tugged at her wig in the last minutes before arriving. Katherine had seen her dressed in male clothes before, but for some reason, Millie suddenly wished she could face Katherine as herself.

This *was* herself now, she supposed, and climbed out nervously when the carriage stopped and the door was opened.

She was admitted into the entrance hall with a severe scowl from Katherine's butler, but a few moments later she heard a voice that made her forget all her nerves and uncertainties.

"Millie!" Anne's delighted cry carried through the entrance hall, and Millie's heart sang even as it squeezed with awful regret. "Millie, are you really here?"

Millie hurried to the base of the stairs as the little girl descended, holding her governess's hand but straining against it with excitement, grasping for the spindles to help her go faster.

"Not so quickly, Anne," Miss Bunsby said, casting a disapproving glance at Millie.

"I'm here, Anne," Millie said, knowing full well she deserved every bit of the young woman's disapproval.

"I've missed you so!"

But she didn't deserve Anne to miss her. Not after the way she'd left Katherine's house all those months ago, too full of pride and anger to stay, and Anne had been the most hurt.

All of that and more was there in Miss Bunsby's eyes. The last time they'd seen each other, they'd argued bitterly about Millie's leaving Katherine's house without telling anyone.

Pride, Millie realized now. She'd had too much pride to accept the love of friends, thinking it was charity.

But in the next moment none of it mattered because Anne threw her arms around Millie, and Millie crouched down and hugged Anne tightly. "I've missed you, too, little Anne," Millie said. "Very much." How could she have grown so much in only a few short months?

Tears filled Millie's eyes and she blinked fast.

"You're wearing men's clothes," Anne said, patting Millie's jacket with small hands. "You're not wearing a gown like Mama does."

"No," Millie said. "But your gown is beautiful."

"I'm almost a lady now," Anne said proudly. "My new papa says so."

"And he's exactly right." Captain Warre had always known just how to make Anne feel special.

And now, coming down the stairs, was Katherine. She wore a simple yet elegant gown of light blue covered with embroidered ivory flowers, and she looked regal. Katherine always did. Millie straightened, suddenly nervous, wondering whether Katherine's mercy had been reserved for India alone.

"Mama, it's Millie!" Anne cried.

"Yes, dearest. Isn't it wonderful? Hello, Millicent."

But dear, blind Anne could not see that *wonderful* was not the expression on her mother's face.

After a few more words with Anne, Miss Bunsby took her back upstairs, and Katherine led Millie into an adjoining salon. Before they could even be seated, the words that Millie couldn't seem to put on paper began to roll off her tongue.

"My offenses against you are unforgivable," Millie said, through a throat thick with emotion. "I don't expect you to accept my apologies. But I want to look you in the eye and make them nonetheless. I betrayed you in the worst possible way after you showed me nothing but kindness, and I don't expect your friendship—I don't deserve it—but..." Now she lost her voice completely.

Katherine regarded her through those same intelligent, light brown eyes that Millie knew so well—shrewd, exacting...compassionate. "Thank you," she said, and reached for Millie's hand. "I'm glad you came...I've been worried about you."

"I don't deserve it."

"You've never believed you deserved anything unless you earned it," Katherine scoffed gently. "You have so many excellent qualities—courage, strength—yet pride was always your worst fault."

"I know," Millie said. "If I could go back, I would do everything differently."

"But we cannot go back, can we? We can only move forward. As far as I'm concerned, what happened is forgotten." Her eyes sparkled. "And William tells me a position awaits you aboard the *Possession* once more."

"Yes."

"You were the strongest member of my crew in so many ways, Millie. William will be fortunate to have you."

Hearing Katherine say that, fresh tears burned Millie's eyes. "And I will be fortunate to sail with him," she said, and it was true. The terrible fear that had lived inside her dissolved away in the light of her former captain's approving smile.

And now Katherine pulled her into an embrace, and everything was just as it used to be—better, even, because the old tension between them was gone. She had her friends back. All of them—Katherine, Philomena, India and even William.

What more could she possibly ask for?

WITH EACH PASSING HOUR, London threatened to pull him back into his old life.

The luncheons he used to take at the finest brothels in town, where the food was just as succulent as the women.

The friends who expected entertainments to resume immediately at Winston's town house and who were obviously perplexed by the excuses he made.

The invitations to various routs, the illicit solicitations for his company by women whose living came from other men's accounts, the promises of delights at any number of scandalous festivities about town.

Everything that had taken up his time for years.

Even the discussions he'd come to London to help broker did not stop the tide of others' expectations.

And as the day wore on and his frustration grew, he thought of Millicent.

Last night, he'd made up his mind not to touch her. But this morning, he hadn't been able to resist seeing her. Touching her, after all, if only to hold her hand.

He burned to hold much more than that.

He took supper at the temporary residence of a member of the French court who was anxious for entertainment, and in the interest of international relations ended up in one of the very brothels he'd avoided at luncheon, only to drink quietly in a chair while the proprietress— a woman whose charms he knew intimately—tried valiantly to tempt him before finally giving up, insisting that he must be ill.

"I've never seen you like this," she said with genuine concern. "I fear something is dreadfully wrong. Have you seen a physician?"

No. He'd seen a medic—a ship's surgeon—and sitting there while other men enjoyed themselves, he made up his mind that he would see her again.

All of her.

Tonight. And he wouldn't think about the consequences or the reasons he shouldn't or how he might make things right.

He would sink into her, experience the unique madness of it and, for a few hours, forget all about London's demands and expectations, forget that he may never really succeed at turning his back on any of it… Forget everything but Millicent.

BACK AT WINSTON'S town house after her reunion with Katherine, Millie marveled at her good fortune.

All was forgiven. It didn't seem possible.

She felt lighter. Happier, as though she'd been given a precious gift. Suddenly the future seemed... manageable. She would have the money she'd earned as Winston's medic, and she would have her salary as ship's surgeon. And, if she was lucky and nobody had found it, she would have the sum she'd hidden away aboard the *Possession* months ago.

But you won't have Winston.

It was a dangerous and nonsensical line of thinking that she tried to ignore.

It was late when Winston returned. Millie's heart leaped when she heard the low rumble of his voice as he said something to Sacks in the corridor. She got up from where she'd been writing, went to her dressing room door, listened.

She heard the faint click of his door and deflated a little.

Still in her waistcoat and breeches—just in case he might ask for her—she returned to her writing desk, where the letter she'd been writing to Cara lay nearly finished. Candlelight flickered over her careful script. It hurt to think of leaving her new friend behind. But when the truth finally came out, there was no doubt Cara would have the best care. And if anyone could possibly understand why Millie couldn't stay, it was Cara.

She looked at the door. Wondered about Winston's day. His evening. Who he'd seen, what he'd done.

Perhaps he'd taken a lover tonight.

She sat down, staring at the page.

Perhaps there'd been more than one.

Her stomach contracted into a tight, painful lump.

It wasn't as if she hadn't known what he was like when she'd made love with him. But at the estate that night, beneath his gentle touch, it had been so easy to imagine he was changing into the man he'd said he was trying to be, and that giving herself to him would turn out to be more than a disastrous experiment.

Disastrous?

No, it hadn't been that. It was an exquisite, sensuous experiment that only made her yearn for him in a way she'd never dreamed possible. And that was worse.

A knock startled her. "Yes?"

Sacks poked his head into the room. "He's asking for you."

"Of course." Anticipation took wing. "I'll be there momentarily."

With a nod, Sacks withdrew.

Now Millie checked herself in the glass—another thing that there'd been no reason to do before she'd entered the duke's employ.

A plain young man with too-rounded features stared back at her.

And suddenly she didn't want to see him like this. But what other way was there? This was what she'd chosen. What she wanted. Once she left his employ, she *needed* to be Miles Germain—there would be no hope of respectability otherwise.

But she also wanted…more.

More of him.

More of that delicious feeling of being a woman that he'd awakened so thoroughly.

But she knew the kind of women who would flock to him in London. Women like the princess, who would not be wearing bagwigs and breeches. For all she knew, he was asking for her in her capacity as a medic.

She took her candle and went to his room, where he stood staring into the fire. Just the sight of him—broad shoulders encased in shimmering, embroidered silk, narrowing to firm hips—made her breath turn shallow.

"You wanted to see me?" she said.

He turned. And now everything inside her felt shallow, tense, warm. He was so utterly handsome, firelight playing across his devil's face.

"Yes."

She saw his eyes roam over her, knew exactly what he was seeing because she'd seen it herself moments ago. And for the first time ever, she wished she'd been wearing one of those gowns like Philomena wore—sparkling, tight, accentuating every curve.

The kind that ladies of quality wore.

The kind she'd never owned. Never even *wanted* to own.

"Are you feeling unwell?" she asked when he didn't say anything.

Now he came toward her. Stopped next to the settee. "I don't know what I'm feeling."

"Perhaps a calming tea—"

"No. No tea." And then, "Come here." His voice was low. Soft. Unmistakable in its intent.

She set her candle aside and went to him.

He reached for her. Silently removed her wig and tossed it aside, undid her hair and let the pins fall where they may.

Dug his fingers into its mass and kissed her deeply.

He smelled of perfume and snuff. Tasted of port and frustration.

"I'm so glad you're here," he breathed against her lips.

The clock on the mantel chimed half past midnight. A coal snapped in the fire, sending a spray of sparks into the flue.

He kissed her once, twice, a third time, then buried his face in her hair and inhaled deeply. "I told myself I wouldn't touch you again."

But he was touching her again now, drawing his fingers along the side of her neck, pushing her coat from her shoulders, smoothing his hands down her back, curling them possessively around her buttocks in a way that made her feel so utterly feminine.

He kissed her again, deeply, and she wound her arms around his neck and let him pull her intimately against him.

After long minutes he worked at her waistcoat, let it fall to the floor, as well. Dispensed quickly with the rest until she stood before him in only her shirt, and now it didn't matter that she had no sparkling gown, because the look in his eyes made her feel...desirable.

He drew her toward the settee, pulled her down with him, on top of him, so that she lay cradled between his powerful thighs. And still he cupped her bottom, but now she felt him pulling her shirt higher, higher, exposing her, while her belly pressed against his hard sex and he was kissing her so very sweetly, drinking at her lips as if she were the very elixir that kept him alive.

The room's air touched her bottom, followed by warm fingers against her flesh, exploring now. Caressing their way between her thighs, coaxing her open for him.

She did.

She felt him at her opening, his finger circling in the moisture there, and a noise escaped from deep in her throat. She pushed herself against it and felt him breach her. Felt him inhale even as they kissed.

And then he was pulling, tugging her shirt over her head until she was naked on top of him and he cradled her breasts in his hands, stretching up to kiss them. Suckle their tips. Pleasure pooled between her legs and she melted in his hands, desperate to feel him moving inside her again.

She felt him working his placket, freeing himself. Urging her to straddle him, guiding her, seating his sex at her opening.

Thrusting upward. Filling her on a hiss of breath.

She gasped at the tightness of it, the depth, as if he'd speared all the way to her heart. His eyes were dark, burning with desire as he withdrew and then pushed inside again just as deeply. Guiding her into a rhythm and then pulling her forward, feasting exquisitely on her breasts.

"Ah, God," she heard him breathe against her skin. "Forgive me."

But there was nothing to forgive. He was heaven beneath her, and she moved her hips with him. He was beautiful madness, building her pleasure with hard, sure strokes.

Her hair tumbled around her shoulders, and she felt like a goddess in his hands. Felt herself tightening, spiraling, straining against him—and breaking, crashing around him in a flood of pleasure while he pushed up, up, up into her, and stilled, arching beneath her, letting out a strangled curse as he lost himself inside her.

She could scarcely catch her own breath in the aftermath of such intensity. But before she realized what he was doing, he caught her around the waist and stood up, still buried in her, and carried her into the next room.

She clung to him, pressing her face against his damp neck, breathing his scent.

He laid her down on the bed, carefully, staying joined with her, moving over her to kiss her. She reveled in his weight between her thighs. Ran her hands down his back, over the embroidered silk of the waistcoat he still wore, pulling it up to grasp his bare buttocks and pull him closer.

Yes.

This was what she wanted.

Him. She wanted *him*.

CHAPTER TWENTY-FOUR

MILLIE AWOKE IN the nude.

It took a moment to realize that the curtains she stared up at were those that draped Winston's bed, and that she lay sprawled across that bed.

And that he lay next to her, asleep.

But just that quickly, memories pooled and eddied in her mind.

They'd made love on the settee, and again on the bed after he'd carried her in here, and yet again, much later.

Her eyes shifted to the doorway...to the arm of the settee, barely visible in the next room. His dressing room—

Her gaze shot to the clock on the mantel, scarcely readable in the darkened room, but slices of daylight edged the window curtains, which meant...

Morning. And—

Sacks! He could be here any moment.

Next to her, Winston lay on his stomach, breathing in the slow, even rhythm of a man deeply at rest. Carefully she sat up, looking around for something to cover herself with, finding only his crumpled shirt at the foot of the bed. She reached for the shirt and clutched it to her breasts as she climbed from the bed.

And still Winston slept.

For a moment she watched him, and everything they'd shared filled her so completely she felt as if her chest might burst. Perhaps...

Perhaps she *could* stay. Everything could remain just as it is now, with her continuing to act as his personal medic...

His personal mistress, more like.

Oh, dear God.

And it was worse than that, because tomorrow she would receive the week's pay, which meant—

No. No, that wasn't what was happening. He was paying her for her medical services, not... She clutched his shirt more tightly to herself and glanced down at her bare legs and feet.

He wasn't paying her for this.

Tears filled her eyes. He wasn't. And she certainly hadn't done this for any sum of money. She'd done it because she'd wanted to. She'd wanted *him.*

And that was the entire problem.

She hurried into the dressing room to find her clothes, brushing away tears that slid down her cheeks. She needed to leave. *Wanted* to leave.

But she also wanted to stay.

More tears leaked from her eyes as she quickly gathered her breeches, shirt and waistcoat from the floor, hastily pulling the shirt over her head, stuffing one leg into her breeches, nearly losing her balance—

The door opened.

Frantically she stuffed her other leg in just as Sacks entered the room. She looked up at him and froze, her face wet with tears.

He looked at her. His eyes widened in shock. "Good God."

She tried to straighten, but her breeches were only half-on, so she ended up on the settee. "Sacks, please..."

His eyes shot from her to the doorway leading into Winston's bedchamber and then back to her. Voices came from outside the room—chambermaids.

Sacks turned abruptly, shut the door, bolted it.

Turned back, nodded toward the bedchamber. "Is he awake?"

She shook her head.

His brows furrowed. "All this time...?"

She nodded.

"And you and 'is Grace have been—"

"No," she said quickly, and now the tears started coming again and she pressed a fist to her mouth to try to stop it. "No, it isn't like that."

"Here, now." He came over, crouched down and helped her with her breeches, quickly hiking them up over her knees, letting her do the rest. "We'll get you dressed and to your room."

"Please don't tell anyone," she begged in a whisper as she blindly tried to button her waistcoat.

"Never mind about that, just put this on," he said, helping her with the coat and then handing her the wig. "And this."

She tried to pull her hair back.

"Just put it on," he said. "Like this." He pulled it down with the ends of her hair hanging out and ushered her to the door, pushing her behind him as he opened it and looked out. "Wait here."

He was gone for a few seconds, and when he returned, "*Now.* Quickly."

He kept her at his side, shielding her as they walked briskly down to her rooms.

"No wonder you've got such small feet," he muttered, and then they were inside her dressing room and he shut the door behind them.

She looked at Sacks and pulled the wig off her head. "Promise you won't tell. Please."

"I'm not going to tell anyone." He exhaled, looking at her. "Did he take advantage or are you plying your trade?"

Plying her trade? "No! No, I'm not a…" The tears stopped her again, because now she was thinking of her pay coming tomorrow.

Sacks cursed. "He *never* touches the 'elp. And I've never known 'im to take advantage. I can't *believe* 'im, doing something like this."

"I only dressed this way so that I could work as a medic," she sniffled, hating how helpless she sounded.

"You don't have to explain it to me," he said "I know what it is to have to scrap for a living. I've seen women do stranger than this to get by. A damned sight stranger." He looked her over and shook his head. "Here, now, let's find you a fresh shirt, and then I'd best hie myself back to 'is room before he wakes. Oh, and I almost forgot." He reached into his pocket. "Harris said this came for you."

It was Philomena's writing. She tore it open while Sacks pulled a shirt from the drawer and set it out for her.

I must see you immediately. I will send a coach
for you at 12:00.

It was already nearly eleven. Philomena wanted
to see her? Millie tried to imagine why. Worse, she
tried to imagine hiding the truth from Philomena's all-
perceiving gaze.

For her own sake, she would have to.

"THIS IS ALL my fault," Philomena declared the moment
Millie walked into the lovely upstairs drawing room
with its robin's-egg-blue walls, clotted-cream trim and
floral drapery. "I blame myself entirely. But Winston
will *not* use you ill and toss you aside. I won't stand
for it."

Philomena could not have divined the truth this
quickly. "Don't be ridiculous," Millie said. "He hasn't
used me ill."

Philomena framed Millie's face firmly in her hands.
"He most certainly has. It was written all over your
face yesterday. It's written all over your face now. You
shared his bed last night, didn't you?" Millie's stomach
tightened. Dear God. "No, you don't need to confirm
it," Philomena went on. "It couldn't be plainer what's
happened. And I shall never forgive Winston for it—but
we can use the situation to your advantage."

Millie felt light-headed. "What are you talking
about?"

"Your compensation."

"I already have my compensation. He has recovered
from his injuries, and I've received my wages for tending to his health—"

"You shall receive a good deal more than that."

Millie shook her head and took a step back, breaking Philomena's hold on her. "I don't need more than that."

"Millicent. Your feelings for him haven't caused you to change your mind about your future, have they? About that school?"

"Of course not." But just this morning, her feelings were murkier than they'd ever been before.

"How much did he give you in wages?"

Millie told her the sum, and Philomena raised a brow. "Handsome, indeed. But you shall have more than that."

"I'll be leaving at the end of the week with William."

"Millicent…" Philomena's blue eyes turned shrewd. "You've always been exceedingly practical. What's done is done, and I take full responsibility, but now we must face this situation squarely for what it is—" she came forward again and took Millie's hands "—and what it can become."

Millie stared at her.

"Men like Winston pay their favorites extravagantly. Let us not mince words. Surely you agree that the virtue he took from you is worth the price of your schooling and then some."

Millie felt sick. "No." She shook her head. "No, I…" *Gave it to him.* But Philomena would wave that away with a flick of her wrist.

Philomena let go of Millie's hands. "Tell me you haven't fooled yourself into imagining he might marry you."

"Of course not."

"I am not suggesting you become anything you

have not already become. For the sum he's paid you already—"

"That wasn't what it was for!"

"I've never known you to be a fool, Millicent. Or impractical. At this very moment, Winston's seed could be taking root."

Dear God. Dear *God*. "I know." She'd let herself be swept away by Winston and her own desire, but now, hearing the facts spoken aloud brought a lick of panic. "I *know*."

A child. Winston's child.

"What will you do aboard a ship then?" Philomena asked, kindly but firmly. "How do you imagine you'll do what William expects of you when you're waddling across the quarterdeck heavy with child? I doubt that's what he had in mind when he made the offer."

A hole opened up in the pit of Millie's stomach. "There could well be no baby."

"And if there is?"

"Katherine sailed with a child."

"*Katherine* had no choice. You must command from Winston everything you will need should the worst become reality. You already enjoy his company... I assure you, you will do far better now than you ever could as his medic."

Stricken, Millie's hands started to tremble.

Philomena's eyes softened. "I would never recommend that you lose your heart to Winston, but seeing that you've lost it already, isn't there part of you that would be glad to stay close to him?"

There was. Heaven help her, there was. She just never imagined...

"I will call my dressmaker immediately and we must have you outfitted for tonight. We must waste no time. He will be at the Rogersfield gala tonight, and he must see you there, and he must see a woman who could command the attention of any man she wished. He must see that you are not a waif. He desires you, that much I could tell."

Millie thought of those times at his estate, the way they'd laughed together. The care he'd taken with her, the torment in his eyes when he'd spoken of the accident in Paris. His mistake with Cara.

He cared for her. He respected her.

They were…friends. Weren't they? And yet…

The practicalities and realities of their relationship reared up, and she wanted to stay with him so badly, had given so much of herself to him, and suddenly— unbelievably—she was thinking of how much Phil knew about the ways of the world, and how possibly…

Perhaps…

Millie took a deep breath, feeling like a different person as she nodded.

Perhaps Phil was right.

WHEN WINSTON CAME home to dress for the evening, he was told that Mr. Germain had gone off in Lady Pennington's carriage and that he had not yet returned.

"What time did he leave?" Winston asked Sacks as his neck cloth was being tied.

"Noon, Your Grace."

He wondered if Lady Pennington might be helping Millicent arrange a new employment.

He didn't like that idea at all. Not that he had any right to an opinion.

Maybe they should return to the estate. The pressing need for his presence was becoming a clear exaggeration. He could beg an emergency and take Millicent back there, where...

What?

Where every night could be like last night. He could tolerate her disguise indefinitely if, at nights, he could have her—just her, stripped of everything except her passion, her determination. When he was inside her, he felt washed clean of all that came before.

It didn't make any sense. He'd wronged her gravely, and what he did with her was a blacker mark against him than any of the rest. And yet it felt...more pure.

"Did Mr. Germain say anything before he left?"

"Such as what, sir?"

"Anything about his plans. Whether he might be seeking other employment, for example."

"Is Your Grace thinking of dismissing 'im, then?" Sacks asked.

"His employment was only supposed to last until I recovered."

"He did seem a bit out of sorts."

"Out of sorts? How?"

"Can't say, really."

"Unhappy?"

Sacks raised a brow. "Most definitely, sir."

He'd hurt her. She was an innocent—if not sheltered—and now that carefully guarded innocence was gone, and instead of mitigating the situation by refusing to touch her further, he'd indulged his own needs and ignored how it might affect her.

He'd taken her on the settee—that settee right there—setting her atop him and driving up into her as if she were experienced, when, in fact, it had only been the second time she'd ever taken a man inside her. And then, later, the third time and the fourth.

As if she were a whore.

Not that she hadn't responded to him. The fire between them burned hotter than anything he'd ever experienced. But her awakening pleasure was no excuse for tumbling her for hours in his bed. Had he ever even *been* in bed with a woman that long?

And then he'd fallen asleep—must have, because he didn't remember her leaving. Had she been unhappy even then? Creeping back to her rooms, virtue in a shambles, wondering what she would do next?

And now she'd been with Lady Pennington all day.

It made too much sense. The only question was, how much would Millicent tell?

None at all, most likely. Millicent valued respect above all else. It was the reason "Miles Germain" existed in the first place. And however much he might be weary of seeing her in that awful disguise, he couldn't help admiring her for it. Her tenacity, her sense of purpose, her refusal to let anything stop her from pursuing her gifts to the fullest.

Not even him.

MILLIE STARED INTO the glass in Philomena's dressing room and scarcely recognized herself.

Jewels winked from her hair. Embroidered silk in

a richly hued pink floral pattern shimmered in candlelight, fitting Millie's body perfectly, accentuating slender shoulders and a trim waist. Soft lace fell from her elbows, graced her low-cut décolletage where stays pushed her breasts high and round. Panniers made her skirts flare at her hips. Yards of fabric and lace draped all around her.

She looked…beautiful.

Like someone else entirely.

Like a duke's mistress.

"Here," Philomena said, moving to an ornate jewelry box and lifting out a heavy necklace of pearl, opal and ruby. "You'll wear this."

"Philomena—"

"Don't you dare change your mind now, Millicent," Philomena said, placing the magnificent necklace around Millie's neck and fastening it.

Miles Germain was gone. The face that stared back at her now was feminine, uncertain. Philomena rested her hands on Millie's shoulders. In the glass, her eyes softened. "I have a good deal more understanding of these matters than you do, and I've known Winston for a very long time."

Millie's chest tightened. She swallowed. "Perhaps the accident changed him," she said, hating how small she sounded and how fearful her eyes looked, and hating even more how much she wanted Winston to approve.

"Do not lose your heart to him, Millie." Phil adjusted a lock of Millie's hair that curled artfully at the curve of her neck. "It will only leave you bitter and aged when you must finally accept that he will not return it."

"I haven't lost my heart." She hadn't. Of course she hadn't. She knew better than that.

Philomena was studying her critically in the glass. "You look too innocent. Smile a bit— No, not that much. Just a tiny curve at the corners. Yes. Like that."

Phil moved out from behind her, reached for a small jar and held Millie's chin in her hand, fixing her eyes on Millie's mouth.

"Philomena, I don't want—"

"Hold still…" She dabbed a bit of color on Millie's lips— "Just a tiny…tiny…smidgeon. And this…" Philomena added a small black beauty patch high on Millie's cheek. Finally she smiled. "Much more appropriate. Nothing too garish, but it takes the edge off that innocence."

Millie looked past Phil. Just these two small changes completely changed her face. Her lips looked lush. The beauty mark lured attention to her eyes.

"Now try that smile again," Philomena instructed.

Millie curved her mouth.

In the glass, she saw the very kind of woman that Winston preferred.

CHAPTER TWENTY-FIVE

THE BALL WAS an endless crush of glittering quality.

Millie stayed by Philomena's side, the practiced phrases she'd been taught soon rolling easily off her tongue, even as it seemed that every pair of eyes regarded her suspiciously.

She did not belong here. Surely everyone could see that.

And yet her connection to Philomena—however circumspectly explained—had gentlemen bowing and kissing her hand and women curtsying politely, if not warmly.

"Remember what we discussed," Philomena reminded her in a low voice behind her fan. "When we see him—and Winston always attends these things, even if only for a short while—you must be the picture of calm indifference. We want him to see exactly, precisely, what he has under his nose."

Indifference. Yes, that was what they had discussed.

She still wasn't sure she could accomplish it. But she would try.

Hope she barely dared entertain pressed at the edges of her mind. She imagined the expression on his face when he first saw her, how much more intensely his eyes would darken with desire tonight than when she dressed in her men's clothes.

Millicent, she imagined him murmuring on a breath of wonder. *You look magnificent.*

For the hundredth time she surveyed the sea of faces, expecting any moment she might see him yet almost wishing she wouldn't.

Perhaps he wouldn't be here, after all.

"Where is your fan?" Philomena asked.

"Here." Millie had forgotten all about it, and it hung from a cord on her wrist.

"Open, open— Yes, just like that. Now close…"

Millie did as Philomena had taught her, and Philomena nodded. "Good. Now just remember that when we— Ah, here is someone you will be happy to see!"

"Millie?" India stared at her. "Oh, my *heavens.* I can't believe it! You look *beautiful.*" And then, scolding, "Auntie Phil, you didn't tell me you were going to do this."

"I wanted it to be a surprise," Philomena said smoothly.

India held up her fan and spoke behind it. "Is it because of Winston?"

Millie's pulse shot up. "Well, I—"

"Certainly not." Philomena laughed lightly. "I only wanted Millicent to be with friends in London, and what better place to be with friends than here?"

"You'll have men positively *swarming* around you," India said. "Which I know you'll hate, but you *must* keep an open mind. And only look," she said, lowering her voice, "here are two that I know are eligible. Nicholas," she called to her husband, waving him over with her fan even though he was already headed this direction. "Look who I've found."

India's husband joined them with two young gentlemen at his side. Millie already knew Nicholas Warre, Lord Taggart, better than she wished. The last time she'd seen him, he'd paid her a tidy sum in exchange for her role in helping him trick India into marriage.

"Miss Germain," he said, bowing politely. "A pleasure to see you again." He introduced his companions, both ridiculously out of her reach even if she had entertained hopes of marriage. She felt their eyes on her, and her skin prickled.

"Do excuse me," Philomena said now. "There's someone I must speak with. I'll only be a minute or two. India, look after Miss Germain, won't you?"

She smiled encouragingly at the two young gentlemen and disappeared into the crowd. Now Millie was forced to make small talk about the music, the food, the general affability of the company, and all the while her nerves grew tighter and tighter, expecting Winston at any moment. She wanted to search the faces, but she didn't want to embarrass India and Lord Taggart by being impolite, so she continued with the conversation even though she was starting to feel ill.

He'd never been the kind of man to maintain prolonged relationships before. What if Philomena was wrong, and he refused to do so now?

But they couldn't go on with her in disguise. Philomena was right about that.

She would not be abandoning Malta, the surgical school, her hopes for a life as a surgeon. She was simply…securing that future for herself. Just like Philomena said.

"WINSTON," A VOICE CALLED, and devil take it, Lady Pennington was bearing down on him, gliding across the ballroom floor as if on ice.

Lady Pennington was beautiful. Stunning, really, with perfect breasts slimming down to an impossible waist. A young widow—the ideal companion. There was a time he would have paid a decent sum for the opportunity to explore that luscious body.

Yet standing here with her now, he hardly felt a stir. There was only one body he could seem to think of lately.

"Paris must be entirely shuttered without you," he began, deciding he would take this opportunity to see if she would divulge any information about her day spent with Millicent.

Lady Pennington fluttered her fan. "I have no doubt that it is. Why did you not tell me you'd changed your mind about Greece?" The fan snapped shut, and she swatted him lightly on the arm.

"Forgive me for not realizing I answered to you."

"Don't be ridiculous. But a change of plans might have made a difference to Mr. Germain, who can only have me to blame for disappointed hopes of a Mediterranean adventure."

"Indeed."

She took his arm, and he found himself being guided toward a secluded corner. "I shall come straight to the point, Winston," she said now. "About Millicent."

He tensed.

"I shan't ask whether you've trifled with her, because I already know you have. It was written all over her face as soon as I saw her."

Anger flashed. "If you breathe a word to anyone, so help me—"

"If *I* breathe a word." Those jewel-like blue eyes narrowed up at him. "Have you taken any precautions at all to protect her reputation? To protect her from conceiving?"

"Her reputation is as safe as ever." And if she conceived…he would arrange to care for the child.

"And what do you plan? Use her until you tire of her, and then toss her aside?"

Rage burned so hot it nearly blinded him. "Excuse me, Lady Pennington. It's been a pleasure."

"Do not walk away from me, Winston." She skillfully blocked his way. "I referred a medic to you. Not a plaything."

He knew that. *Forgive me,* he'd said to Millicent last night, as if that meant anything at all. The old adage about actions versus words screeched through his brain.

He was not going to discuss this with Lady Pennington. "And I will be forever grateful for your recommendation," he said.

She cocked her head to the side. "Will you."

"As you can see, I am quite recovered."

"Indeed. I only wonder whether Miss Germain will recover."

"She is nothing if not resourceful. And I understand she spent the afternoon in your company."

"Indeed she did, and I'll have you know that I will not stand for you to cast my young friend aside. Where you play, Winston, you must pay—and I expect you to do right by her in that regard."

Now she had his attention. He stilled on the inside. "Please—do explain how you expect me to do right by her."

"Do not play dumb with me. An apartment of her own in London. Lavishly furnished, of course. And a very tidy allowance. No less than a hundred a week— and I do not mean that she must use that sum to dress herself. You will see to that, as well."

"Will I?"

"This is no game, Winston. My young friend may have made any number of mistakes, but ruining herself was not one of them—at least, not until I delivered her into your hands. And now I expect you to ensure that she profits handsomely from your seduction. And in the meantime, I will be moving her out of your household to await your arrangements."

"Absolutely not," he said.

"She cannot stay with you."

"*She* is not staying with me. *He* is staying with me— or perhaps you forget that it is *Mr. Miles* Germain that you referred to me."

"That makes not one whit of difference to me, because it was not *Mr. Miles* Germain's field that you plowed." She smiled at him. "And it shan't be *Miles* who becomes your mistress. I assure you, any man in London would fall over himself to have Millicent at his disposal."

He laughed, because he wanted so fiercely to strangle the very life out of her for what she was suggesting. "Millicent would never do that. Not for me or anyone else. Apparently you don't know your *young friend* as well as you think you do."

She smiled and reached for his arm. "Escort me into the other room, will you? There's someone there I would like you to meet."

A COLD FEELING snaked through him.

He walked with her into the next room, through the crush, until Lady Pennington paused. He followed the line of her gaze.

And saw Millicent.

She was scarcely recognizable, but it was her, all feminine curves in patterned pink silk. Jewels sparkled around her neck and at her ears. The breasts that for weeks had been secured beneath their binding swelled enticingly above her décolletage. There was no hideous bagwig now—her hair was piled atop her head, save for a few locks left curling at her shoulders, and it shimmered twenty shades of mink in the candlelight.

She stood with Cantwell's daughter, India, her husband, Nicholas, and two young men Winston didn't recognize but whose purpose was easy to guess. She was laughing.

And clearly he was the one who didn't know her.

"Do come and say hello, won't you?" Lady Pennington singsonged.

Dumbstruck, he followed her over.

Felt, in the moment that Millicent's gaze shifted and their eyes collided, as if he'd taken a fist to the gut.

There were the usual greetings. One of the young men was a knight from the north of England, the other a gentleman from a family whose name he didn't recognize.

"Winston," Lady Pennington cut in smoothly as he

was kissing Lady India's hand, "I have saved the best for last. Do meet my young friend Millicent Germain."

And now there was no more avoiding her. He met those soft brown eyes—the very eyes he'd looked into last night as they'd found release in perfect unison on his bed, when he'd felt almost as if he was part of her, and she of him.

Now those eyes were finely edged with pencil. The face that had been flushed pink and warm with pleasure was now dusted with powder, and the sweet lips he'd devoured as he moved inside her were lightly stained. And she was breathtaking—every bit as beautiful as any woman who had ever tried to capture his interest.

More so.

And he could hardly stand to look at her.

"Miss Germain," he murmured. "A great pleasure."

She curtsied low, and he bowed, but he couldn't bring himself to reach for her hand and bring it to his lips.

"Likewise, Your Grace."

He saw the uncertainty in her eyes and wondered if she feared he would not like what he saw or that he might reject the scheme Lady Pennington had so obviously devised.

And that Millicent, apparently, had embraced.

A feeling cut through him—betrayal? Disappointment?—even though he was the one who had wronged her, and he had no right to feel anything but remorse.

"You must be very careful of him, Millicent," India said now in a tone of mock seriousness. "He has the blackest of reputations."

Winston smiled a little. "You wound me greatly. And cause Miss Germain unnecessary alarm. I'm quite sure she has no reason to fear my reputation." Now he bowed to Millicent. "Enjoy your evening worry-free, Miss Germain." And, "Lady Pennington. Always a pleasure."

CHAPTER TWENTY-SIX

HE GAVE AWAY NOTHING.

Millie's pulse raced as he walked away, and her heart sank. Not even a flicker—nothing to indicate whether he approved, whether he found her more attractive now.

Enjoy your evening worry-free. What did *that* mean?

"You did very well," Philomena said to Millie behind her fan. "I am exceedingly proud of you. Only let him think for a little while about what he's seen."

"He didn't seem pleased," Millie whispered back.

"Of course not. It would have been tasteless for him to show it. But never fear...I've already spoken with him, and all shall be settled before the evening is through."

Settled. With Millie no longer Winston's medic but his mistress.

It seemed, suddenly, as if her stays were strangling her.

And now India was talking to her, telling her something about Lord Taggart's sister, and Lord Taggart was conversing with one of the young gentlemen while the other seemed enthralled by Philomena, and the air was filled with music and voices and perfume, and somewhere in this great sea of people Winston was considering... What? How much he should pay her?

One of the young gentlemen asked Millie to dance, and she started to decline, but Philomena interrupted. "By all means, Millicent. What an excellent idea."

He led her through the crowd, closer to the orchestra, where a lively line of people whirled and twirled and laughed.

Pay her. Winston was going to *pay* her.

It wouldn't be like it was now. She would dress herself up, make herself available, and he would visit her—or perhaps, too often, he wouldn't—and she would give herself to him, but even if she still gave from the heart, he would never believe it.

He would make love to her knowing he was paying handsomely for the privilege.

And she would store up money for her future knowing it all came because of what she let him do with her in bed.

She felt sick.

"Excuse me," she said to the young gentleman, pulling away from him just as they reached the line of dancers. "Please forgive me. There's—"

"Is something the matter?"

"There's someone I must see. Please," she said even as she was already walking away, "forgive me."

And she pushed through the crowd, looking for Winston.

You're already receiving wages in exchange for your favors.

The truth of it burned her cheeks, soured her stomach.

She scoured the rooms, searching, searching, praying he hadn't left already, knowing it was really too late, that she was already here tonight as a whore. She'd become the thing she feared most without even realizing it.

He wasn't in the main ballroom, wasn't in the antechamber. She noticed people coming and going through a door, so she went in and found herself in a sort of corridor, a labyrinth of rooms that were just as full of people as the main rooms.

She had to talk to him and put an end to this. It couldn't wait until tonight—she wouldn't be seeing him, anyway, because Philomena would refuse to let her return.

One room, the next, the next... He was nowhere to be found.

And it began to hit her that this could be the last time she saw him at all, because she couldn't be his medic, *wouldn't* be his whore, would have to accept, now, that—

Oh.

Millie stopped short in a doorway and stared at the laughing group inside.

At Winston.

He didn't notice her. His attention was on a woman who was dipping her finger in his drink and drawing a wet trail across the tops of her—

"Ho, there! Come in, come in—always room for beauty," a man said, coming up to her.

"No, I—" Couldn't tear her eyes away from Winston, who only now looked her way, laughing and licking his finger after catching a bead of liquor from the woman's bosom.

Millie's heart constricted, her lungs, everything, so

sharply that it seemed as if she would not survive this moment, but by a miracle her voice returned.

"Forgive me. I have the wrong room." She turned and fled. Blindly, not toward the party but away, to another room and out a pair of doors that led to a stone balcony populated with knots of people talking, drinking, laughing.

Frantically she looked from one side to the other for an escape.

"Well, aren't you a pretty thing?" came a horribly familiar voice from nearby, and Millie turned abruptly.

Lord Hensley. He stood talking with another man, and both of them were looking pointedly at her décolletage.

"Looking for someone?"

"No. No, I was just…" What she'd just seen had her dazed. Confused.

"Now, now." Lord Hensley reached out, caught her hand. "What's the hurry?"

The other man laughed and shook his head. "I think I'll rejoin the party," he said meaningfully, leaving them.

Lord Hensley was close enough to smell the liquor on his breath. "Perhaps there's some fun to be had at this tedious event, after all," he said. Eyes greedy for flesh wandered over her body.

"Let go of me." He didn't recognize her. But she recognized him too well, and she tried to pull her arm free, but he tightened his grip. He was drunk, as he'd been so many times before, all those years ago when she'd been a governess to his children. But she wasn't in his employ any longer.

"Let *go* of me," she said sharply.

"Now, now, my dear, you don't mean that."

She had no way to defend herself—no weapon of any kind. She tried digging in her feet, wrenching at her arm. Trapped inside whalebone and panniers and skirts, there was little she could do.

He pushed her toward the shadows, dipped his nose to her cleavage. "Mmm, love a bit of perfume between a woman's breasts."

She shoved at him, afraid of the attention screaming would bring, terrified of what would happen if she didn't scream. "My aunt will be looking for me," she tried, even though Philomena was not her aunt, and now that Lord Hensley had pushed her into the shadows behind a large column, she couldn't see anyone.

"Your aunt, hmm? Saucy little thing." He bent his face toward her cleavage again.

"No— Stop!" She struggled against him, but he was holding her more tightly now.

And then suddenly he was being yanked away from her.

"Hensley." Winston's voice was ice-cold.

"Winston!" Hensley exclaimed. "Good God, didn't know what was happening there for a minute— damnation, no need for this." He pulled away from Winston and brushed his jacket where Winston had grabbed him. "Just having a bit of fun. You understand."

"Miss Germain is not available for that kind of fun," Winston said sharply.

"My mistake, my mistake. Couldn't have known." He offered her a slight bow. "My apologies for any inconvenience, Miss Germain, and..." His brows dove, and he looked at her more closely. Tucked his chin. "Germain...you're not the same chit who left us in Venice without a governess...?"

This time Winston stepped in front of Millicent. "No. She is not. I suggest you return to the festivities."

The threat was palpable. It was not a suggestion.

Hensley withdrew and left them alone.

Winston turned to her. "Was *he* the employer?"

"Yes."

"And you said *nothing* the entire time he was under my roof enjoying my hospitality?"

"*Say* something? Surely you're joking."

Winston looked down at her, his face unreadable in the shadows, and there were more important things now than Lord Hensley and a party that seemed as if it had taken place months ago.

"Is this the end you've had in mind?" he asked now. "To become my mistress?"

"No." It wasn't. And how could she ever have imagined, even for a moment, that it was? She'd come this close to giving up everything for him—the life she'd wanted for years. The opportunity William offered her that could make that life a reality.

"You already had a position as my medic for as long as you wanted," he said almost angrily.

She wanted to reach for him, but she couldn't. It felt as if a great stone wall had sprung up between them. She wanted to be with him so much she didn't know how she would bear the pain after she walked away. There was so much more to him than anyone knew, hurts that lived far beneath the surface.

But there was no future for them. At least, not one she wanted.

"I can't be your medic." Her heart hurt so terribly she could hardly speak the words past the clog in her throat. "I can't be anything to you. This was a mistake—Philomena was wrong, and I never should have listened."

She heard him exhale. "Or perhaps she was right," he said a bit tiredly. "Perhaps I owe you this—more, even, after what I've taken from you."

"Taken." Was that what he thought? "You didn't *take* anything from me, Winston. I *gave*. And I did it because I *wanted* to give." She shook her head. "But I can't give you anything more." Her next words were the most difficult. "I'm leaving your employ. Leaving England."

"Leaving *England*."

"With William Jaxbury. He's offered me a position as his ship's surgeon." And even now, part of her wanted Winston to ask her not to go.

He was quiet for a moment. "I see."

Her throat tightened. "It's the perfect opportunity."

"Yes, I suppose it is."

And it hurt, more and more with each passing second, but it was just as well that he didn't beg her to stay because she would have had to tell him no.

He stood looking at her, the gold embroidery on his jacket catching the faint light from the torches farther down, his skin giving off the hint of a perfume that wasn't hers. "Is there anything I can do to make things right?" he asked.

"I already have everything I need," she said quietly. "You don't owe me anything. Go and have your fun."

"Millicent, what you saw in there—"

"You don't need to explain. I know what kind of man you are, and I've never pretended you were anything different." She looked up at him, blinking back tears. "You're the only one who's done that."

HE WATCHED HER walk away and disappear through the doors into the ballroom.

It wasn't as if he didn't know it would end. It wasn't as if he could really have kept her as his medic forever.

Forever?

His chest hurt. He rubbed the base of his throat, trying to ease the tightness.

"Winston."

He turned, saw a familiar figure coming onto the balcony. "Taggart."

"Problem?"

"No." Winston realized he was still pressing his throat and let his hand drop. "Taking the air."

Lady India's husband smiled a little. "That doesn't sound like you at all." And then, "India thought her friend Miss Germain might have come out here, but I don't see her."

"She just went inside."

"Ah. Well, then, no doubt India's found her by now. Suppose I ought to leave you to your air-taking and go inside myself before India finds some trouble to get into." He laughed. "I don't have to tell you about that. Enjoy the evening." He started to walk away.

"Taggart."

Nicholas turned back.

Leave it alone. "Was Miss Germain with India in Paris?"

Nick went from smiling to serious in a heartbeat. "Yes. Before the wedding."

"She was aboard that ship with your wife, wasn't she?"

That ship. The one that Lady India—and if he didn't miss his guess, Millicent—had stolen right out from under Katherine Kinloch's nose.

"What is it you want to know, Winston?" It was clear Taggart didn't want to discuss any of this. Winston couldn't blame him—nor did he care.

"I want to know how she might have come by a lashing that left her back looking like the devil's tally stick."

Nick's voice dipped, quiet and low. "Some things are better left in the past."

"It isn't in the past for her."

"If you're concerned about having her in your service," Taggart said, "I'll tell you this—Miss Germain is a desperate young woman who will do nearly anything to accomplish her ends. I won't pretend there's any love lost between us. But she is India's dearest friend, and I can't deny that she has suffered greatly. But if I were you, I should keep my valuables safely locked away."

He took a step to leave, but Winston blocked his path. "Tell me who did it."

"It wasn't me, if that's what you're thinking. But if you want to know Miss Germain's secrets, you'll have to ask her yourself."

CHAPTER TWENTY-SEVEN

SHE DIDN'T TAKE the books he gave her.

They sat on the table in her room in two neat stacks, he saw in the early hours of the morning. Winston had stayed later at his club than was advisable because he didn't want to face…

This.

So he didn't face it. He stopped torturing himself and went to his rooms, tried to sleep in linens that still smelled like her, arose the next day and went about his business—and the next day, and the day after that, until he was no longer needed in London and he decided to return to his estate and find out how Cara was faring.

If he had to, he would bring the best physician in London to Winston until Cara was determined to be perfectly well. And this time, the physician would answer the questions he was asked.

"A CHILD?" WINSTON stared at Cara and Edward, standing in their drawing room at the vicarage, scarcely believing what he was hearing. "You're certain?"

"Yes," Cara said, flush with happiness, looking up at Edward, who put his arm around her now. "Nothing is ever *certain,* of course not, but…" She looked at Winston. "I know we're going to be blessed."

"I'm..." Speechless. "I'm exceedingly happy for you. For both of you." And seeing their joy, knowing the deep affection they had for each other, he felt a moment of envy.

"I thought surely Mr. Germain would have told you by now," Cara said.

"I could have held a pistol to her head and she wouldn't have told me. I won't say I didn't consider it, for Edward's sake."

"I shouldn't have kept it from him," Cara said.

Edward squeezed her shoulders. "No, you shouldn't have."

"I was just...so frightened."

Of course she was. And they all knew the reason— it sat in the room like a fourth person nobody wanted to acknowledge. And in a way it *was* a fourth person. It was the child he and Cara had created that hadn't survived.

But now Cara was smiling at him in a very suspicious way. "You said *she* just now, when you spoke of Mr. Germain." She glanced at Edward, then back at Winston. "It's no secret among us anymore that she wasn't a *Mr.* Germain at all. Please tell me she's come back from London with you."

"I'm afraid not." It shouldn't have been so difficult to say. "She has...left my employ, actually. Left England, in fact, on a ship bound for the Mediterranean. I understand she's spent some time there working as a ship's surgeon—"

"A ship's surgeon," Edward said. "Can it be possible?"

"Of course it's possible." Cara laughed. "She passed for a man, after all."

With Millicent, Winston was beginning to think anything was possible.

"She had an opportunity she couldn't pass by," he told them. There was that tightness in his chest again. "It was perfect timing, actually."

And now Cara was looking at him more closely than before, and he shifted his weight under her too-knowing gaze, and for the first time it occurred to him to wonder whether Millicent might have said anything to Cara about him. Them.

Edward and Cara exchanged a meaningful look, and now Edward broke away from her. "Walk with me to the church," he said to Winston. "I left some business unfinished for Sunday, and I was just on my way there when you arrived."

They turned just as Cara came forward and reached for Winston's hand. The contact startled him, but she squeezed tightly and he could not let go. "You're a good man, Winston," she said, searching his eyes. "Deep down, you are."

THE TWO MEN walked in silence along the stone path that led to the church. Through the wooden door worn smooth with age, into the cool, shadowy interior lit by slender windows all around the upper part of the walls. Their footsteps echoed as they walked down the center aisle.

Edward went to the pulpit. Winston sat in the front pew, leaned forward with his forearms on his knees, staring at the smooth stones in the floor, listening to Edward's rustle of papers.

"I compromised her." Winston heard his own voice swallowed up in the empty church. He hadn't meant to say anything, hadn't wanted Edward to know, but there it was.

"Who?"

"Miss Germain."

"Ah." Edward was quiet for a moment, and still Winston stared at the floor. "Your medic."

Winston's head snapped up. "She *was* my medic. That was all. She was no whore. She was an innocent. Untouched. She was like the bloody Virgin Mary, for Christ's sake." The words resounded through the church just as Winston realized what he'd said and where. "Apologies."

Amusement edged into Edward's eyes. "With a few adjustments, you could deliver from the pulpit."

"I'm glad you find this amusing."

"So what are you saying? Are you in love with her?"

"*Love?* No— No. It's nothing like that. It's…" What the devil was it? "Just another of my carnal vagaries." Even he didn't believe that.

"Was she unwilling?"

"No." Winston stood up, paced to the front of the church. "But she should have been. I had no right to do it. No *intention* of doing it." He leaned forward and gripped the wooden railing that separated the congregation from the altar area. "There hasn't been a single defilement in all these years. I haven't let it happen again. Until now. I've ruined another life just at the moment that you and Cara finally—"

"Winston…"

He turned his head and looked at Edward, who stood with his hands resting on the edges of the pulpit. "If it weren't for me," Winston said hoarsely, "you and Cara would have any number of children by now."

"Winston, don't do this."

Winston let go of the railing and went to the pulpit. Looked Edward in the eye. "I want you to tell me to go to hell."

"I don't need to. You've done a good job of sending yourself there, and without reason."

"Without *reason?*"

"All these years— Winston, all has been forgiven since the very first. Nothing can be gained from re-hashing it now."

"But you shouldn't have forgiven me. You should have called me out. Bloodied my face. Said at least *one word* in anger. But you didn't. Even after what I did, even when year after year went by and my two best friends had no babies because of me. I didn't *deserve* your forgiveness."

Edward was quiet for a moment, then sighed. "I didn't do it for you, Winston. After that mess happened, I had a choice. I could either lose my best friend in the entire world and the woman I love more than life itself, lose both of you to hatred and anger, or I could forgive. *That* was my choice." Edward brought his finger down hard on the pulpit. "I forgave for myself, so that *I* wouldn't carry that burden."

And in doing that, Edward had lifted the burden for all of them. Winston had kept his two closest friends, and Cara had married the man she loved.

The significance of it took his breath away.

"My God," he said after a moment. "The debt I owe you…" Even if he knew how to keep that vow he'd made, even if he kept it for the rest of his life, it would never add up to this.

Edward just shook his head. "Forgiveness cancels debts, my friend. You don't owe me anything. That vow you think you made… You didn't make it to anyone but yourself. And the only one who hasn't forgiven you is you."

He hadn't. He couldn't.

Edward came out from behind the pulpit. "Forgive yourself, Winston," he said firmly. "Here. Now. Do it today, and free yourself from this burden. You don't need to carry it anymore."

Winston tried to comprehend what Edward was saying.

Forgive *himself.* That was all Edward wanted.

THEY WERE NEARLY off the coast of Spain. Squalls could come up quickly, but for now the sky was clear, and the only clouds were in a long, barely visible bank on the western horizon, somewhere out over the open ocean.

From inside William's great cabin, looking out through the bank of windows at the stern of the ship, Millie watched the waves erase the ship's wake behind them. "I don't *want* to stay with them," she said, turning away from the windows now. "There's no reason for it. I shall be perfectly fine here."

Pacing at the end of the table, William exhaled and rubbed the back of his neck. "Going to be too dangerous here, in your condition."

Millie glanced at Zayn Carlyle, who sat leaning back in one of the chairs with his hands clasped across his stomach, gazing thoughtfully at the center of the table. "I've got a sister in Cairo and one in Alexandria," he said evenly, looking up at her. And then, with a hint of teasing in his dark eyes, "And a friend in Tripoli who could possibly be convinced to accept another wife."

William flashed a grin at Zayn. "Could leave her with a band of Bedouins in Algiers."

Zayn allowed that with a lift of his brows. "Or a nunnery in Rome."

"Now you're just being ridiculous," Millie said, and headed for the door, but William caught her by the hand, and she stopped.

"Watched Katherine go through this," he said. "If I'd had anywhere else for her to go, believe me I bloody well would have sent her there."

"William, you're the closest thing to family I have." She put a hand on her belly. "The closest thing *we* will have."

She saw him glance behind her at Zayn, and she knew exactly what they were thinking.

The baby had a father.

"We don't need him," she said flatly. "I won't take anything from him. You already know I won't."

"The child will need an education," Zayn commented. "Legitimate or not, Winston will be able to pay for the finest schools in Europe and use his influence on the child's behalf." It was said in Zayn's quiet, matter-of-fact way.

Millie was learning that sometimes Zayn could be infuriatingly practical. And it was difficult to tell, but sometimes she imagined he was flirting with her. It made her feel...good. Desirable, and not just by a man whose taste ran to any female who happened to be available.

"I don't want to hear about Winston," Millie told Zayn now. And then, to William, "And I don't want to hear about being abandoned with strangers. I belong aboard this ship, I've proven myself, and I shall prove that my condition won't change anything. I'm going back to the infirmary."

She left them there and made her way back to her own realm in the center of the ship, a small room where her herbs and tinctures and instruments were locked in cabinets safe from the lurch and roll of the ship. A table fixed to the floor gave her a place to perform whatever procedure might be necessary.

In here, she was in charge. And not William, not Zayn, not anyone would take this away from her.

She thought of Anne, Katherine's beautiful little daughter, and hoped suddenly, fiercely, that her child would be a girl. A girl who would grow up aboard the *Possession* and learn to be strong. Independent. Millie would teach her medicine, and William would be like a father to her just as he had to Anne before Katherine had married Captain Warre.

But Millie wouldn't be marrying anyone. She didn't need to. The small fortune she'd been forced to abandon aboard the *Possession* months ago had still been there, hidden inside a wall in the lower cargo hold. Added to her wages from Winston and what she would earn sailing with William, it would ensure a living for herself and her child well into the future.

There wouldn't be enough for the school, but the school was out of the question now, anyway.

She *didn't* want to hear about Winston. It hurt too much. And it made her long for that feeling of being wanted that she'd felt when he held her. Those two nights they'd lain together, for a few hours it had seemed as if nothing in the world could come between them.

It was just an illusion. She'd known that even if, during that short time, she'd let herself forget.

Now, finally, she was at peace. She wasn't the girl she'd been on the *Possession* when she'd sailed with Katherine. Nor was she the desperate young woman who had stolen her friend's ship in a mad attempt to carve out some kind of place for herself. She felt calm, comfortable, accepting of life—even now, with a child taking root in her belly.

She was a medic, a sailor, a friend.

A woman.

And by this time next year, she would be a mother.

CHAPTER TWENTY-EIGHT

WINSTON STOOD IN the drawing room at the palazzo of his friend the Marquis de Trecenza, in the arch of a window, looking out over the city of Valletta and Malta's Grand Harbor. Ships dotted the water—every kind of craft from two-man rowboats to frigates in full sail. He followed the harbor to where it joined with the sea, and beyond, where a few ships could be seen on the approach.

Perhaps, today, one of them would be the *Possession*.

One of the benefits of his rank was being acquainted with others of similar rank, and his friend the marquis had attained a high enough level within the Knights of Malta that it was no trouble to have a man at the port's sanitation office put on notice to send word when anyone from a ship called *Possession* presented papers for entry into the city.

He was not going to live his life without Millicent.

That night at the ball, he should have told her she was the most beautiful creature he'd ever beheld and promised her anything she wanted—not walked away and turned his back on her as if he didn't want her at all.

If he had, she would be richly settled in a town house of her own, where he would spend every night in her bed making love to her until he was too exhausted to move, and then he would fall asleep with her in his arms. And when he awoke, he would make love to her again.

Is this the end you've had in mind? To become my mistress?

His own accusing words damned him now. As if she was the one who wanted something from him, and not the other way around.

These past weeks he'd come to understand exactly how wrong that was.

But he would not make that mistake again.

This time, he knew exactly what he would say. And he knew exactly what to offer. He could see it now, barely, across the city: the famed hospital of the Knights of Malta, where the School of Anatomy and Surgery was located.

He would be her patron. Buy a house here, where they could live while she completed her studies. And when she was finished, he would provide her with whatever—

"Mi scusi," said a voice behind him, and he turned abruptly to find his host's butler. "A messenger arrived a few minutes ago," he said. "A ship called the *Possession* arrived in the harbor this afternoon, and members of her crew were given papers to enter the city just a short while ago. One of them is a person with the surname Germain, apparently with a small party staying at the home of Jacques Martel."

Just then the marquis came into the room. "I understand there is news."

"Jacques Martel," Winston said. "Do you know him?"

He shrugged. "A wealthy merchant, well respected by the knights of the Order...not married...very active in shipping and trade."

A friend of Jaxbury, no doubt.

After the marquis apprised him of a few more details—the man lived very close by—Winston walked out onto the street, on his way to pay a visit.

TEN MINUTES LATER, Winston presented himself at Martel's house. He didn't wait long before Martel came out to greet him.

"Forgive my unconventional introduction," Winston said after explaining who he was, "but I understand that you are hosting some friends of mine that I would very much like to see."

"Si, infatti." Martel bowed. "I am most honored, and of course, any friend of the marquis is a friend of mine. Come and join us in the courtyard."

Winston's pulse spiked. He followed Martel through two rooms and out an arched doorway to an interior courtyard filled with potted trees and flowering vines, where a small group sat at a table, laughing...

It took him a moment to recognize her, and when he did, her smile cut him to the bone. He'd never seen it before—not like this, brilliant and unguarded.

"A friend and countryman of yours has come to pay a call," Martel said cheerfully, and now she saw him, and the smile died on her lips.

Winston forced himself to acknowledge the two men—Jaxbury and...Zayn Carlyle. And now Winston knew everything he needed to about Martel and his connections with trade.

"Winston," Carlyle said, standing and offering a bow. "What an unexpected surprise."

"Indeed." He should have guessed Carlyle and Jaxbury would be acquainted. But right now he only cared about one thing. He bowed a greeting to Jaxbury.

And faced Millicent.

He'd been expecting Miles Germain. But what he saw was someone very different.

There was no wig. Only her own mink-brown hair falling in a braid that came forward and ended just below her collarbone. She wore a man's jacket—plain, dark blue—and a man's shirt and breeches. But beneath it he glimpsed a colorful scarf tied around her waist, angling down over one hip. And the hilt of a short sword.

Silver dangled at her ears.

Another colorful scarf circled her head, part turban, part West Indies pirate, with its fringed ends dangling in the back to her shoulders.

She acknowledged him with a simple "Your Grace" that grated on his nerves.

He seated himself between Martel and Jaxbury, accepted a glass of wine, tolerated a half hour of talk about Mediterranean commerce during which Millicent offered a number of opinions about the viability of establishing business in several port cities in the Levant. She sounded as conversant in shipping as she did in medicine, and he realized she'd taken more from her years sailing with Katherine Kinloch than just experience as a ship's surgeon and a sharp hand at cards.

It was clear that Martel didn't quite know what to make of her and found her unconventional appearance amusing. It was just as clear that Jaxbury and Carlyle would tolerate no disrespect of her.

Daylight faded, and torches were lit in the court-yard, and Millicent's skin took on the warm glow of sunset and firelight. She scarcely looked at him except when he spoke.

He shouldn't have imagined it would be easy.

All he needed was to talk to her. *Touch* her, because it was killing him to watch the expressions play across her face, the hints of smiles touch her lips as she con-versed, the fingers that had once curled around his cock wrap delicately around her glass.

And it infuriated him to feel as if he needed Jaxbury and Carlyle's permission to talk to her when he never needed anyone's permission for anything, but finally he couldn't stand a minute more.

"If neither of you have an objection," he said dur-ing a pause in conversation, "I'd like to request a word with Miss Germain in private."

Millicent's gaze shot to his face.

"By all means," Martel said, clearly intrigued by this development. "Make use of the green salon—we walked through it when you arrived."

"I'm sure anything His Grace has to say to me can be said here," Millicent objected, but Carlyle slid his quiet gaze her direction.

"Grant the man an audience, hmm?" Carlyle spoke up.

And now it was thanks to Carlyle that she stood up and walked past Winston into the house.

The green salon had a view out the front side of the house and could not be seen from the courtyard. Millicent stopped in the center of the room and looked at him squarely with that same no-nonsense stare he'd grown so used to during those first days after Paris.

All he'd meant to do was talk, but now he reached for her instead and slid his hand to the back of her head and kissed her before she could have time to object.

The fire was instantaneous, tearing straight to his groin, reminding him ruthlessly that he hadn't been with a woman since Millicent—that he didn't want any woman *but* Millicent, and that he wanted her *now,* any way he could have her.

Her lips were soft. Sweet. She responded, opening for him, and she tasted just the way he remembered. And he was almost insane enough to pull her down on one of the settees and take his chances before anyone got a mind to check in on them, but he didn't have a death wish.

And she broke the kiss anyhow, pulling away from him, looking up at him with bruised lips and disturbed eyes. "What are you doing here?"

He breathed in, deeply, trying to quiet the need inside himself. "I have a proposal for you." He felt restless, impatient, and his words came out more rushed than he'd meant them to. Her eyes widened a little, and victory surged through his blood. "I would like to be your patron," he said. "For the surgical school. I'll pay everything—your living expenses, whatever you need for your study." Surprise. Comprehension. They passed across her face in quick succession, urging him on. "I've missed you," he said. Drew in a breath, told her what he wanted. "I thought I would stay here in Valletta with you while you complete your studies."

She stared up at him as if dumbfounded. And then, even as he watched, her lips firmed and her eyes cooled. "I left my whoring days behind when I left London," she said flatly.

"Don't you ever say that again." The response shot off his tongue on a lick of outrage. "You were no harlot."

"Then what would you call it, Your Grace?"

"Don't call me that."

"We were lovers. And you paid me."

"I paid you to be my medic—"

"And now you wish to pay me again, and for what? You need no medic now, and we both know you're perfectly capable of finding company—and at a far more reasonable price. In any case, I've changed my mind about the school."

Changed her *mind?* "I don't believe that." Not for a minute. He knew her too well. "The school was the one thing you wanted more than life itself."

"It was a passing fancy, nothing more. I'm ship's surgeon aboard the *Possession* now, and I have everything I need. I'm perfectly content."

"Devil that." *He* wasn't content. "I didn't travel all this way to have you pretend indifference and ply me with lies."

"Why *did* you travel all this way? I can't believe it was simply to find me." She looked him up and down. "Perhaps you're on your way to Greece, after all?"

"You know bloody well that isn't it, that everything has changed since you—" He broke off. Since she'd what? Left his employ? His bed? Left *him?*

"What I know," she said firmly, almost gently, "is that you and I have nothing to discuss. My life is at sea, and we both know there's no more place for you there than there is for me in London." She walked past him. "Goodbye, Winston. I'll let them know you had to leave."

SHE DIDN'T RETURN to the courtyard. She made it into the next room, and then the next, fully expecting Winston to follow her, but he didn't. She was in a small unlit library that faced the street, and there was just enough light outside to see him walk past as he left.

She could barely breathe past the grief ripping her inside.

I've missed you, too.

His kiss still burned on her lips, and she wanted more—she wanted to touch him and to feel him touching her and to lose herself in his embrace until it felt as if they were one person and not two. And she wanted so desperately to believe that he'd come all this way because...

Because what?

She wouldn't be a fool. What she'd seen in that room at the ball in London—that was the true Winston. The real man that could not ever really be snuffed out, not by injuries or good intentions or anything else.

He was a rakehell. A blackguard.

And he wanted to pay for her schooling.

The idea of it keened straight to that place inside her that couldn't accept that the school would not be possible now. A house, where the two of them would live while she pursued her studies...

Or until he tired of her and withdrew his support. Or

worse, until he learned she carried his child and realized it would *not* be just the two of them, but so much more.

He wants a mistress. He hadn't wanted that in London, but he wanted it now. And she may have been desperate when she'd listened to Philomena's advice, but she wasn't desperate now, and she didn't need to listen to anyone but herself.

HE WAS NOT staying on this island without her.

Winston waited the next day, watched Martel's house until he saw Jaxbury leave. He followed Jaxbury through the narrow streets toward the waterfront and cornered him just before he started down the stairs to the wharf.

"I want to buy passage aboard your ship."

Jaxbury didn't seem surprised to see him at all, and he smiled. "Got a yen to see Turkey?"

"Perhaps I do."

"Not going to make it that easy for you, Winston." Jaxbury turned toward the stairs, but Winston blocked his path.

"Damn you," Winston said. "This is no game."

"Exactly. This is Millicent's life. So far all I've seen is you enjoying a Mediterranean stay with an old friend. Your presence here proves nothing to me."

Winston wanted to blacken Jaxbury's laughing eyes. "One word, and I could have your ship delayed here for weeks."

"You do, and I'll guarantee you won't see Millicent for even one hour."

It was too much. "Do you have *any* idea what Millicent means to me?"

Jaxbury raised a brow. "No. Perhaps you'd better explain it—and have a care to do a better job than you did with her last night. Whatever you said put her in a very foul mood."

The fact of it made Winston feel helpless. If she didn't want him to help her attend that school, he didn't know what else to offer. "I'm doing everything I know how," he said tightly.

"To give her what?"

"Bloody well more than a ship's cabin and a sailor's pay."

"Setting sail for Marmaris tomorrow," Jaxbury said, unmoved. "You're welcome to follow us there. Perhaps by then you'll have figured out a way to get back in her good graces."

Jaxbury tossed Winston a smile and headed jauntily down the steps.

CHAPTER TWENTY-NINE

WINSTON WASN'T GOING to follow Jaxbury anywhere. He was going to board the *Possession,* but he was going to need help.

Back at the marquis's house, his friend just shook his head. "*This* is why they say love is madness," he said. "But if you are going to do this, you should do it tonight under cover of darkness. I can arrange the papers you'll need and a boat to row you out, but climbing aboard the ship undetected...*that* will be up to you."

It wasn't difficult, in Valletta, to find the clothes he would need. Winston gathered a few belongings, some rolls, a jar of water, and by the time night fell, he was ready.

Gliding across the inky water in the Grand Harbor, the oarsman's every pull seemed to splash deafeningly as they headed out. Ships' lanterns glistened faintly on the waves, and the sounds of the city at night drifted across the water—voices, laughter, music.

"There," the oarsman said, nodding toward a ship up ahead.

Winston studied it now, looking for signs of anyone on board. Someone was keeping watch—there was no doubt of that. The only questions were how many and how closely were they paying attention.

He hoped they were paying most of their attention to cards and a bottle of rum.

The rowboat slipped into the shadow of the *Possession*'s giant hull. The water wasn't calm—nothing broke the waves coming in from the sea. The ship lolled as the oarsman rowed into position below the net of ropes hanging over the side. They lingered in the ship's shadow, looking up, waiting to see if anyone had seen the rowboat approach.

Nobody appeared at the railing.

Winston slung his sack over his shoulder, stood up and grabbed the net. The thick rope was wet and difficult to grasp, but he pulled himself up. Found his footing and began to climb—one square and then the next, easily now as the rope grew drier and drier, until he reached the top and pulled himself over the railing and onto the deck.

He turned, crouching down, watching for any sign of movement.

There was a bark of laughter—voices drifting up from a hatch in the deck a few feet away.

The men left on guard were down there, likely drinking and gaming exactly as he'd expected. He made his way aft, toward the door that would lead to the captain's cabins. He may not be a sailor, but he'd been a passenger, and he knew it was possible to access the holds from here.

It was dark, almost pitch-black. He felt his way, found the stairs, went down, and now it *was* pitch-black. He struck a match. It flared. Gun deck. The flame lasted just long enough for him to get his bearings and then snuffed out.

Ten minutes later, he was tucked among the cargo in the hold, and he leaned against a wall to wait. And he waited, and waited, all night and all morning and most of the next day, until he was sure the ship was in open water.

Then he went to find Jaxbury.

TWO DAYS OUT of Malta, Millie finally stopped crying over Winston.

All these emotions had to be the pregnancy. They couldn't be her. She didn't cry over irrational, senseless things.

He'd asked her to become his mistress, she'd said no, and that was the end of it.

She came up from the infirmary to the quarterdeck in the evening and ducked out of the way as sailors heaved on lines and the boom of the mainmast began to shift.

And then something caught her eye.

She looked.

Looked a little closer. And her heart leaped into her throat.

Winston.

Here, aboard the *Possession,* dressed like a common sailor, acting like a common sailor—except nothing about him could ever be common. He was too strong, too beautiful, too—

She spun on her heel and went to find William. Found him in his cabin, leafing through his logbook and smoking his hookah.

"What is Winston doing aboard this ship?" she demanded.

"Snuck aboard."

"Without your knowledge? I find that difficult to believe."

"Under way by the time I realized."

"I want you to put in on Sicily and force him ashore," she said.

"Take too much extra time. Besides—" William inhaled off the hookah, exhaled a puff of smoke "—I'm rather enjoying watching him suffer."

"*I'm* the one who's going to suffer." Millie jabbed at her own chest. "Me."

William looked at her. "Went to a bloody lot of trouble to join my crew, don't you think?"

"He went to a bloody lot of trouble to get what he wants, regardless of anyone else's feelings."

"What he wants, being you," William clarified.

"He doesn't want me. What he wants is—" Suddenly she wasn't sure *what* he wanted. "He wants a mistress."

"Seems like a damned lot of effort just for that."

"I haven't heard any proposal of marriage, have you?"

And there it was, out in the open, with William watching her through the smoke of his hookah, and her standing there with her arms falling at her sides, scarcely believing the words she'd just spoken aloud.

"Not that I want a proposal of marriage," she said now. "Or would ever expect one. He's a duke. And I'm not a fool." Not a complete fool, anyhow. Besides, "Pity the woman who ends up his wife. He'll be in every bed in the hemisphere but his own." She looked down, fussed with the cuff of her sleeve.

"Might be worse things than being a duchess."

"And perhaps I could have tea on the moon, as well," she snapped.

"These things can be arranged." William's blue eyes glittered. "Been thinking perhaps I ought to arrange it on your behalf." His mouth curled with satisfaction at whatever coercion he was imagining.

"I already have an arrangement."

William exhaled three perfect rings. "Your babe could well be Winston's heir."

"*She* is nothing to him. Only imagine what he would say if he knew— Dear God. William, you didn't tell him—"

"Of course not," William said sharply.

"You must promise me you won't breathe a word."

"Took some balls to climb aboard the ship and hide among the crew, don't you think?"

"No," Millie said, even though William was right, and now her insides were beginning to tremble because Winston was here, aboard the ship, and there was no denying it was because of her. "It took impertinence." William just looked at her. "And dishonesty. *Promise* me, William."

William turned back to his logbook. "If Winston finds out about your child, it won't be from me."

BEING ABOARD THE SHIP, with nowhere for Millicent to run, should have eased the tension inside him.

It hadn't.

And Winston didn't know one bloody thing about sailing—had never needed to lift his hand to a single task he didn't want to, let alone been shouted at for being slow to learn—but he welcomed the task now.

The boatswain ridiculed him, goaded him, shouted orders at him, and all the while Winston's brain stored each piece of information carefully away. Each day he made fewer mistakes.

He put his full attention toward pulling lines. Raising and lowering canvas.

And developed horrible, stinging blisters on his hands.

He watched Millicent when he could and tormented himself with all the ways he wanted to make love to her.

The other sailors accepted him easily, which in itself was somewhat disconcerting. He might have liked to think there was something about him that could never pass for a common sailor.

But there was something about the sea that stirred his blood in a way he'd never noticed before. Before he'd gone to Malta—and not counting the channel crossing on the way home from Paris—his last voyage had been to Spain, and he'd been preoccupied with a Spanish contessa who'd been practically insatiable.

Now, in the afternoon as they were passing by an island on the southeastern end of Greece, the boatswain came over as Winston was coiling a line. "If I didn't already know ye weren't a seaman, I'd bloody well know now," he said, shaking his head. "Go see the surgeon an' take care of yer hands."

Millicent.

He could have gone to see her before now. But he hadn't missed the looks she gave him when she was on deck. And he didn't know what to say to her that he hadn't already said in Valletta. And so he stayed away.

"I don't need the surgeon," he told the boatswain.

He'd already torn up one of his older shirts and made bandages to wrap around his hands.

"Go." The boatswain jerked his head toward the hatch. "Ye'r no use to me if yer hands swell up an' fester."

Winston went. He already knew she was in the infirmary; he'd seen her go below not long before.

Her little infirmary was dark, lit by a lantern, and she was grinding some herbs and measuring them into a spoon. He stood for a moment in the doorway and watched her before she'd seen him. Her braid fell over her shoulder when she leaned down to check her measurement. He followed the line of her back, over the curve of her bottom to her legs, encased in breeches like before but looking not the least bit masculine now.

And then she straightened. Turned.

"Winston."

And for just a moment, before her eyes cooled, he saw a spark.

"The boatswain sent me." He held out his arms. "My hands."

"I suppose it's no surprise," she said, already opening a cabinet and taking out some lint and a roll of bandage, and then taking a bottle of something from another cabinet. She set them all in a boxed area where they couldn't fall to the floor when the ship rolled. "Come here, under the light."

He moved closer, breathing the scent of her, wanting to touch her but holding himself in check as she unwrapped the strips of linen he'd tied with his teeth. She hissed when she saw his palms, raw and bleeding from blisters that had long since torn open.

She looked up at him with his hands cradled in hers, and her eyes were anything but cool. "Why are you doing this?"

"You haven't given me a reason why I shouldn't."

"Winston—" She exhaled. "You're not a sailor. You're not even a laborer. You've never done this kind of work in your life, and you're not *meant* to. You have an estate waiting for you in England, a valet, servants—" her lips curved a little and she shook her head "—and you can't wear a banyan in the crews' quarters or they'll all laugh at you."

The tender way she was looking at him took his breath away. "They already laugh at me," he said. "And for some reason I left all my banyans behind." *And you still haven't given me a reason,* but he wasn't going to say that for fear her eyes would cool again. "Cara told Edward that she's with child," he said instead.

"Oh…" Millicent breathed, looking up from his hands. "How is she? I've been so worried."

"Well and happy, the last I saw her. She and Edward were very hopeful."

"I'm so pleased." She truly was, he could see it in her eyes, and it was one of the things he loved about her.

And he couldn't help it now—he touched her cheek. "Millicent…"

"Winston…" She reached up, pulled his hand away, her voice barely a whisper. "Don't."

"I'm doing this for you."

"You shouldn't."

Her rejection reached inside his chest like a fist. He wanted to grab hold of her, force her to look him in the eye and tell him she didn't want anything to do with him, even though he... *he* wanted...

What?

To find something, anything, that would make her his and make it so she could never walk away.

Something like marriage?

The idea assaulted him out of nowhere.

He could marry Millicent.

Marry her.

Marriage would make her his. Irrevocably, permanently his.

But...

Good God.

She dabbed something on his palms and the sting startled him.

"You should be used to this by now," she chided softly as she looked down at his hands, packing the raw places with a layer of lint.

He stared at the top of her head, stunned by his own thoughts.

Millicent, his duchess.

She wrapped bandages to keep the lint in place and tucked them in securely. "There," she said. "Much better than those strips of shirt."

"Yes." He held his hands palms up, flexed his fingers. "Much better."

But even if he offered her that, would she accept it?

CHAPTER THIRTY

THE MIDNIGHT SEA was calm when Millie took her turn on watch. A half-moon sat overhead, surrounded by stars, lighting a few cloud wisps that drifted by on faster winds up in the sky.

Millie stood on one side of the quarterdeck in the shadows between the railing and the stairs that led to the upper deck, leaning against the wall that enclosed the main cabins, looking at the glittery streak of moonlight on the water.

I'm doing this for you.

She didn't know what that meant. But it was an intoxicating feeling knowing he was here because of her. And it had felt so good to tend to him today—to touch him, if only his hands.

The memory of his fingers against her cheek made a nerve leap in her belly even now.

Voices and laughter drifted from the crews' quarters below, where the men were still drinking and gaming. She blew out a breath, laughing a little at the idea of His Grace down there swilling grog with them. He wore no wig now, no embroidered silk or neck cloth. Sacks would be speechless.

What would happen when they reached Turkey? He couldn't go on like this forever. He would have to accept that she would not agree to be kept by him no matter what he offered. And then he would leave, and it would finally be over.

Just then a movement caught her eye, and she sucked in her breath. It was Winston, emerging from below.

She eased farther into the shadows beneath the stairs, partly hoping he wouldn't see her, partly hoping—knowing—that he would.

Gentle waves lapped the hull, and the ship lolled softly from one side to the other as she watched him survey the lower deck and, not seeing what he was after, turn.

He was facing her now.

She could see his face in the moonlight. Knew that the sailor on watch up in the crow's nest could see him, too. But here, beneath the stairs, she was hidden from both—for now.

Her heartbeat was a steady thump behind her chest as he worked his way closer. She breathed in the salt air, a waft of aromatic foliage from the Grecian shore, felt the solid wood against her back.

Just the sight of him made her go soft on the inside. Which was exactly why she should scoot out from beneath the stairs, confront him and insist that he return below. He wasn't on watch until three.

Instead, she watched him pause in front of the stairs. Look through them, just as she was doing.

He veered to the side.

Her breathing turned shallow.

And then he was there, standing to her left between the stairs and the railing, looking at her. She opened her mouth to speak.

"You're not on—"

He silenced her with his hand on her face and his thumb against her lips. The bandage around his palm felt a little coarse against her cheek. And then he kissed her. She didn't stop him. He felt too good, and she wanted him too much.

She could taste the sailor's brew on his tongue. Could tell, from the lazy but thorough way he was kissing her, that he'd imbibed a great deal of it. "You're drunk," she whispered against his lips, not quite ready to push him away.

"Not at all," he murmured. "I'm pleasantly sotted."

And now he was backing her against the wall, sheltered by the stairs and the darkness. It was time—past time—to scoot away from him. Instead, she pushed her hands beneath his jacket, splayed them across linen. Instantly his kiss went from lazy to demanding.

And instead of leaving, she drank him in. Dragged her hands over hard muscle to his hips. His buttocks.

He pushed himself against her. Found her breasts, cupped them, teased their peaks through her shirt and shift, and her intimate flesh came alive with need. There was no doubt now what he intended, but still she urged him closer. Pressed herself against the hardness at the front of his breeches.

This time, she worked his placket herself. Freed him into her hands and stroked his hot sex while he pulled her shirt from her breeches, pushed it up, covered a nipple with his mouth. She swallowed back a scream when he pulled her—hard—with his lips.

And then he was working her own breeches loose. Pushing them over her hips and reaching between her thighs, delving inside her, straightening to kiss her again while he plunged a finger inside her—two—three—

Oh.

And then he pulled his fingers out and turned her in his arms, pushing her breeches to her knees. He pulled her back against him, holding her tight with one hand cupping her breast and the other splayed across the vee of her thighs, delving inside, holding her folds apart while he sought her from behind with his sex. Found her.

She felt the large tip of him push into her body. His hips thrust forward against her bottom, and his shaft speared into her opening, filling her. In front, he found her pleasure and stroked little circles over its bud. Pinched and rolled her nipple, kneading her breast, while behind, he pushed powerfully up into her again, again, again.

Winston.

Her lover.

She felt the pleasure building. Spiraling. His lips pressed hot against the crook of her neck while he thrust into her. Her channel melted around him, warm and accepting. She clung to the wall, gasping, swallowing back the sounds that tried to escape her throat.

He breathed her name against her skin. Murmured something…

So beautiful. God.

Bent her a little more, thrust into her harder. Faster. And release came just as hard and fast, pulsing its explosion inside her, and she cried out a little. Bit her lip. Exhaled raggedly through her mouth to keep from screaming.

And when it was finished he leaned against her, trapping her between his body and the wall with his arms still around her and his face buried against her neck. Breathing. Holding her in a way that she wished could go on forever.

"Why did you leave?" he asked against her skin.

"You were completely recovered. There was no reason for me to stay," she managed, still shuddering inside with the aftermath of release.

"I wanted you to stay."

"You want a great many things, Winston." She felt him slip from her body, felt moisture warm on the insides of her thighs.

"Yes," he breathed near her ear. "I want you to be my wife."

Everything inside her stilled, and all she could hear was the pounding of her own heart. "You don't mean that." He was more than pleasantly sotted. Even now she could smell the liquor on his breath.

"I want to make love to you every night, as many times as I wish, without anything to stop me. Ever."

Which had absolutely nothing to do with her being his wife. They were the words of a man entirely in his cups.

"You should go below," she said, easing away from him and reaching to pull up her breeches. "Try to sleep before your watch."

"The ball, in London…"

"I don't wish to speak of that."

"You were beautiful. But you're more beautiful now. Like this." No, not in his right mind at all. "I owe you my apologies," he said now.

"You owe me nothing. You can't be anything except what you are."

"Then let me show you what I am." He cupped her chin in his hand, brought his face an inch from hers. "What we just did…" He searched her face. "Could never be done with any woman but you."

If only that were true. Right now, he was holding her so tightly, so possessively, that she could almost imagine it was.

"I can't be what you want me to be," she said.

"Millicent…I need you."

A terrible sadness gripped her heart. "Forgive me," she told him softly, "but I do not need you."

HE'D ASKED HER to be his wife.

Winston worked near the bow of the ship the next morning, pulling a line while another man tied it off. The ship cut through the blue water, her white sails billowing above.

I want you to be my wife. He'd uttered those words, and Millicent was right. He hadn't meant to. But the idea had been there, planted in his thoughts, and after he'd spent himself inside her, she'd felt so damned right in his arms that the words had slipped out.

Perhaps… Good God. Perhaps he *had* meant it.

"Hard to credit she could take over a ship," the man he was working with said, jarring Winston out of his thoughts. He realized the man had followed his line of sight and that he'd been staring at Millicent.

"Pardon me?"

"Her." The man nodded his head toward Millicent. "Only a few months back. Her and another scrap of a thing—blonde girl. Locked Cap'n Jaxbury away and took over the ship. I'm the only man still aboard from that crew. Never will forget it."

The man had Winston's full attention now. "Are you saying she took the ship by force?"

"Aye, that's what I'm saying."

Millicent and Lady India, mutineers. It was a capital crime.

The man lowered his voice. "And if you ask me, I wouldn't be turning my back on her if I was Cap'n Jaxbury."

And now, a puzzle was coming together in Winston's mind. An unholy rage was building inside him. "And how did Jaxbury punish this insurrection?" he asked tightly.

The man made a noise. "Tied her to the mainmast and gave her the lash, that's what he did, and as long as I live, I'll never—"

The words weren't finished before Winston was walking away. Striding across the lower deck, the quarterdeck, with his eyes fixed on the upper deck where Jaxbury stood with Carlyle, Millicent and a few others.

He climbed the stairs. Walked up to Jaxbury, grabbed his shirt and laid his fist into Jaxbury's jaw.

Jaxbury reeled, and almost immediately someone grabbed Winston from behind, but Winston was too angry to care. "*You're* the whoreson that whipped her," he raged.

"Winston, no!" Millicent cried. "You don't understand— I deserved it."

"Devil that." Already there was a commotion down below, and Winston realized it was Carlyle that held him, but his eyes were fixed on Jaxbury, whose lip was bleeding now.

"I did what I had to," Jaxbury said.

"You marked her for life." He imagined Millicent screaming, crying while Jaxbury brought the lash down mercilessly in front of the crew.

"They wanted to hang me," she told him desperately. "William saved my life."

"Winston," came Carlyle's calm voice at his ear, "this isn't the place. Don't make her talk about this in front of the crew."

And then came a shout from the crow's nest. "Corsairs!"

Instantly Jaxbury raised a glass to his eye. Winston's attention snapped to the direction the man pointed. Jaxbury barked some orders, and the crew disbursed below. The boatswain shouted for Winston, and he bit his tongue not to tell the man to go to the devil.

He returned to the lower deck, helped with the sails. Half an hour later, they hadn't outrun the ship. A xebec, he'd been told—small and fast, built for overtaking larger, lumbering merchant ships.

"She's going to catch us," one of the sailors said grimly. "We're going to have to fight her off."

And now Winston no longer cared about protocol. He went to the upper deck and faced Jaxbury again. "What's going on?"

"Go back to your post, Winston."

"And you can go to the devil. What's happening? Where is Millicent?"

"Going to be overrun by sodding corsairs if you don't

return to your bloody post. Ready the cannons!" Jaxbury shouted, and a chill ran down Winston's spine.

"Where is Millicent?"

"I need you at your post, Winston, or so help me—"

Devil that. He'd find her himself. He went below, to
the infirmary, didn't find her there. Walked through
the gun decks, where a dozen men were scrambling to
pack powder and cannons.

"Winston!" someone shouted. "Man that cannon!"

He ignored the order and exited the far door. He
found her in her cabin loading a pistol. And now he realized what she was doing: readying for battle.

"No," he said absolutely. "You are not going to fight.
I won't allow it."

She looked up at him, her face already set for what
lay ahead. "This isn't for you to allow or disallow. We
need all hands—including yours."

"I won't have you killed."

"It's our duty to fight them. Yours and mine both."

"I want you to stay here. In your cabin."

"Absolutely not." She was angry now. "If you weren't
prepared for what happens at sea, then what are you
doing on board this ship?" she demanded.

"You know bloody well what I'm doing here."

"No. I don't. Do you have any idea what it takes to
command the respect of those men up there? What they
will think of me if I don't fight with them? This is my
life, Winston, and you will *not* take it from me."

He didn't want her to need the respect of those men.
He didn't want her to need anything at all.

But then there wasn't any more time to argue because the sound of a cannon exploded through the air, and men's shouting came from above.

She ran up to the deck, and he followed her, refusing to let her out of his sight. Cannons exploded from the starboard side. Jaxbury's orders bellowed above the shouting and chaos, and the xebec took a direct hit to the bow, but the *Possession* took a ball on her stern that wiped out a corner of the upper deck, and now the xebec was close enough to throw her grappling hooks.

On deck, all was chaos.

Already, Barbary pirates were shimmying up ropes and trying to climb aboard amid a volley of pistol fire.

Millie had darted away, separated from him by nigh on half Jaxbury's crew, and suddenly there was nothing to do but fight.

Men screamed to his right, his left. He parried, jabbed, thrust, sliced. Felled one pirate, then another, while his pulse screamed in his ears with the agony of dying men.

There was more cannon fire. Part of the xebec exploded near its stern—a direct hit to its store of gunpowder.

Flaming bits of wood shot into the water, arced over the *Possession*. One of her sails caught fire, and a handful of sailors raced to cut it down and snuff it out, chased by a pair of pirates.

Winston stabbed one in the back. Jaxbury grabbed the other and slit his throat.

Blood ran slick on the deck planks.

"Where is Millicent?" Winston shouted.

But another pirate rushed them, stopped just in time by one of Jaxbury's crew, and then Jaxbury was gone, shouting a string of orders, just as Winston spotted Millicent near the bow firing her pistol point-blank at a pirate trying to climb up the nets from below.

His stomach turned.

The xebec took another direct hit. And another, even though it was already engulfed in flames.

Winston dispatched another pirate, shoved the body aside, whirled around to confront the next...

But there wasn't another.

All the pirates were dead.

Immediately he plunged through the chaos looking for Millicent. And found her on the lower deck, crouched over one of the crew, who was covered in blood.

AFTERWARD, AN EERIE calm settled over the ship as they watched the xebec list, flaming in the water, sending billows of smoke into the air as she inched beneath the waves. Millie's shoulder burned, too, but there wasn't time to think of her own wounds because she was tending to others.

She felt the blood seeping into her shirt, felt it begin to run down her shoulder and under her armpit. Still she tied tourniquets, shouted orders for men to be carried to the infirmary, triaged the worst of the wounds.

"Millicent!"

She heard Winston shouting for her, but there wasn't time to think of him. "Take this man below—immediately! I'll tend to him first." She headed for the ladder leading down, but a hand curled around her arm and stopped her.

"Are you all right?"

Winston was ragged, covered in blood, eyes fierce.

"Have you been wounded?" she asked.

"No. But you—" His eyes landed on her shoulder. "God's blood."

"I need to go below. Either help me or move out of my way!"

Somehow she managed to stay upright through twelve ball extractions and an amputation. One of the men died—there was nothing to be done about it, his innards were torn up beyond repair.

She was vaguely aware of Winston there, handing her instruments, mopping up blood, working with William and two others to hold the men still while she worked.

Her shoulder burned with pain so sharp it made her arm numb.

And when at last she heard William utter the words, "That's the last of them," she collapsed to the floor and the world went black.

CHAPTER THIRTY-ONE

IT TOOK TWO bloody days to reach Rutledge's shipyard off Turkey's Mediterranean coast.

Winston sat by Millicent's bed while she tossed and turned with fever. Every moment, his mind tempted him with visions of the worst. And he might have begun this voyage as part of Jaxbury's crew, but with Millicent at death's door, he wasn't going to do one bloody thing except stay by her side.

Sir Noah Rutledge and his wife, Josephine, lived in a villa overlooking the harbor.

Getting Millicent off the ship was a devil of a thing, but they managed it, and now she lay in a room at Rutledge's villa, where his physician was doing everything he could for her. Winston stood at the side of the room with Jaxbury, watching the physician work. When he'd finished attending to Millie and gone, Jaxbury signaled that he wanted to talk to Winston outside.

"You've done enough," Jaxbury said. "She's with friends now."

"What the *sodding devil* is *that* supposed to mean?"

"You know bloody well what it means. This isn't an aristocrat's adventure, puttering about the Mediterranean trying your hand at being a sailor. This is our lives. *Millicent*'s life."

It was almost exactly what she said to him aboard the ship before the fighting broke out.

But it was his life, too. And he felt more alive now than he could ever remember feeling before. And it wasn't because of some new and creative pleasure he'd found. He'd never been in so much pain.

"You're not helping her by acting as if you're going to be there for her when you aren't," Jaxbury said.

"It would seem that I already am here, would it not?" Winston asked coldly.

"And what are you going to do when she awakes? Ask her to be your mistress again? Become a part of my crew for the rest of your life?"

Actually, he'd been planning to ask her to marry him. But... *This is my life, Winston, and you will* not *take it from me.*

Jaxbury shook his head. "You've got nothing to offer her, Winston. Don't make her any more attached to you than she already is."

"Understand me well, Jaxbury...I'm staying right here until I'm satisfied she's out of danger." And then he would lay his whole life at her feet. And if she wanted her life at sea more than she wanted him, then—and only then—he would leave.

MILLIE AWOKE IN a bedroom draped in colorful, shimmering silks. Sunshine streamed through windows built high on the walls.

"She's awake. Aunt Josephine, she's awake!" And then, "Miss Germain...Miss Germain, can you hear me?"

"See if she'll take some water, Pauline."

Millie turned her face and tried to lick her lips, but her mouth was cotton dry. She tried to move, but her shoulder burned like fire.

The anxious face of a young woman in traditional Turkish dress peered at her, clutching her hand. "Here," she said, "just a little bit." She dribbled some water from a spoon into Millie's mouth.

Another woman joined her, perhaps Philomena's age. Beautiful, with upswept auburn hair and kind, hazel eyes. "We've been so worried about you," she said, taking Millie's hand. "You needn't be afraid—I am Josephine Rutledge, and Katherine Kinloch is a dear friend of mine from many years ago. Your captain, Sir William, is well acquainted with my husband, Sir Noah."

Millie moved her hand over her belly. "My baby..." she rasped.

Was still there. She felt the gently rounding bump, and all the tension drained out of her.

"I shall call Winston," Josephine said. "He only just stepped out this minute."

Winston. "Wait." Millie reached toward Josephine. "Tell me he doesn't know—" she moistened her lips again to speak "—about the baby."

"If he does, he hasn't spoken of it. Ah—here he is now. Winston, she's just awakened."

And then he was at her side, lowering himself into a chair by the bed. "Millicent," he said, and took her hand, brought it to his lips and dropped his forehead against it and closed his eyes as if in prayer. When he looked at her again, he was so unbelievably handsome it took her breath away. "Thank God."

William came into the room. "Millie," he said, mov-

ing to the side of the bed across from Winston. He bent
down and kissed her forehead. "How are you feeling?"

"Awful," she said, and tried to smile, but her lip
cracked.

"Noah will bring the physician," Josephine told
them. "Sir William, come and help me choose something delectable that might tempt her."

William hesitated, Josephine's ploy only too obvious, but followed her out with a promise to Millie that
he would be back shortly.

And then Millie was alone with Winston.

"William is still upset with you," Millie said.

"You mustn't worry about that." He still had her hand
in his, was still looking at her as if he was afraid to look
away in case she lost consciousness again.

It all came back to her, the fighting and the terror,
the carnage afterward. The fight between Winston and
William just before.

"Someone told you what happened." Her mouth was
still so dry. "That I took William's ship."

"Shh...you don't need to talk." He spooned some
water between her lips the way Pauline had done.

"I didn't want you to know." She looked away from
him. "I was so desperate, so angry... I didn't know what
would happen to me if I were separated from India. I
was so afraid." She paused. "I've done so many shame-
ful things."

Winston's lips thinned, and his fingers stroked hers.
"If we compared our past shames, I guarantee I would
come out the winner. In any case, your friends have all
forgiven you, haven't they?"

She nodded against the pillow.

He reached out with one hand and softly brushed the hair from her forehead. Even like this, his touch was pure magic, warming her on the inside. And she realized now what she hadn't wanted to admit before: she loved him.

The truth had been sitting inside her, waiting, but she hadn't dared consider it—and now that she had, her eyes began to fill with tears.

She loved him.

Winston, the devil duke, who could not love her in return.

"Millicent," he said now in an alarmed tone, catching a tear that fell, "it doesn't matter to me. You could have sailed with Blackbeard himself and I wouldn't think less of you."

She tried to smile, but that wasn't it at all, and she couldn't tell him. And right now she loved him so much she would almost rather be his mistress than not be with him at all.

Almost.

MILLIE STAYED IN bed the next day, still too tired to do more than sit up. Everyone visited with her, read to her, talked with her. Josephine's uncle Elias even played draughts with her. She saw Winston, but he didn't stay at her side as he'd done when she first awoke. Most of the time, now, he wasn't there.

By the second day, Millie was well enough to sit outside in what Josephine called "the women's courtyard."

"The Ottomans have a marvelous concept called the *harem*," Josephine was saying as they sipped tea in the dappled shade beneath an arch covered with flowering vines. Millie wore one of Pauline's colorful Turkish gowns that was easy to slip on and wrapped around her comfortably without disturbing her shoulder too terribly. "An entire wing of the house just for the women. I told Noah I absolutely wanted one." She smiled mischievously. "He's very suspicious of what goes on here."

Millie smiled, cradling a small glass in her hand. She sipped the apple tea, breathing in the scent, trying to take comfort in the breeze that smelled of earthy Mediterranean foliage and salty Mediterranean air. "Every manner of feminine plots and plans, I'm sure."

"Exactly." Josephine looked at her across the table. "You are unhappy."

Millie's eyes filled with tears. It had been happening too much lately, and all because of one person. "Has Winston said anything to you about leaving?" she asked.

"Not at all. Do you expect him to?"

"I've hardly seen him since I awoke," Millie said, looking down into her glass.

"Men do strange things sometimes—exactly the opposite of what we might expect."

"With Winston, I've always known what to expect."

"You know, I did spend many years in London before we came here. Lord Winston and I are old acquaintances—and by that I do *not* mean intimate acquaintances—but I'm all too aware of his reputation. You might say he's always been very…predictable."

Millie inhaled. Sipped her tea. "You must think me such a fool."

"Millicent, the man who stayed here the past days was not the Winston I remember."

Winston *had* changed. It was true. Millie knew that

in her heart, and hope rose up, but she didn't dare entertain any hopes.

"The Winston I remember would without a doubt have tested the waters to see exactly how devoted a wife I am to Noah. He would not have spent his every moment with a feverish young woman who couldn't even talk to him, let alone... Well, let us just say the Winston I remember would have sought more lively entertainment."

The Winston Millie had first met in Paris would never have pursued anyone to the Mediterranean. Why go to such trouble, when there were so many willing women within arm's reach?

From the moment she'd first let him touch her, she hadn't been the same.

"I don't need him," she told Josephine now.

"No, I don't suppose you do." Josephine looked at her thoughtfully. "But the heart hardly cares what one needs, does it? The heart is mostly concerned with what one wants."

HE WAS A bloody coward.

Winston stood at the edge of the villa's main courtyard, with his hands on the stone railing, looking through the trees at the turquoise water below. There wasn't to be a moment's peace, because Rutledge joined him at the railing.

"Thought you might like a drink," he said, offering Winston a glass of arak.

"Thank you."

Rutledge looked out at the view. "Never loved anything so much as a warm Mediterranean afternoon and a fine glass of liquor."

Winston needed to figure out how and when he was going to ask Millicent to marry him.

"If you've got intentions toward Miss Germain," Rutledge said after a moment, "perhaps you ought to let Jaxbury know about it."

"My intentions are none of Jaxbury's goddamned business." Winston knocked back a swallow of the milky-white arak, felt the bite of licorice on his tongue.

"He sees Miss Germain as his responsibility."

But Millicent was Winston's responsibility. He wanted her to be, for the rest of his life. He wanted to care for her, hold her, give her everything he had.

"I love her." The words came out without him meaning them to, and he looked sharply at Rutledge, who merely regarded him in return. "I'm going to ask her to marry me."

"Congratulations," Rutledge said.

"Bit soon for that, isn't it?"

"What do you mean?"

Winston looked at him. "What if she doesn't accept me?"

Rutledge raised a brow. "Forgive me, but what woman would not accept a man of your rank?"

"Millicent," he said flatly.

And then something behind them caught Rutledge's eye. Winston turned…and saw Millicent standing there at the corner of the house, fully within earshot of their conversation, looking at him in disbelief.

Rutledge sipped his drink and turned away from the railing. "I think I had better go see what Josephine is doing."

I'M GOING TO ask her to marry me.

Millie stared at Winston, caught, unable to pretend she hadn't heard what he said.

Her heart raced wildly, and everything except him seemed to fade away. It was difficult to breathe. She felt suspended in time with his words pulsing inside her.

"Millicent…" His voice was rough. The breeze toyed with his dark hair while he watched her with eyes full of longing…and love.

He came forward, wearing his simple sailor's clothes, and took her hand. He touched her face, a gentle brush of his fingers against her cheek and his thumb along her lips.

"I love you," he said. "Since the moment I met you, there hasn't been anyone else. Not even in the weeks we were separated. And there never will be. I can't even stomach the thought of it. When I thought I might have lost you—" His expression darkened, and he let out a breath. "Nothing could compare to the fear I felt."

Perhaps she hadn't known what to expect from Winston at all.

But he didn't know the whole truth. He didn't know about the baby. "Winston—"

"Shh." He put his finger over her lips. "There's something I've been wanting to ask you. I meant to ask the second you awoke. I've been a coward these past two days, unable to find the right time, the right place."

"Winston, there's something you need to know."

He shook his head. "You've already said you don't need me. I know that," he said, searching her eyes. "But is it possible you could want me? Choose me?"

Dear God, yes. *Yes.* But—

"Millicent Germain…" He sank to one knee in front of her and took both of her hands, kissing them, and looking up at her. "Will you please do me the honor of becoming my wife?"

His question soared through her, filled her heart, made her blood sing. And new tears sprang to her eyes because he loved her that much, and because…

"I am with child," she confessed instead of answering, barely able to push the words out past the fear that the news might change everything.

It took all of her willpower to make herself meet his eyes. And what she saw there was…

Shock…and joy.

"A *child?*" He got to his feet. "Truly?" His gaze raked over her as if she'd suddenly turned to glass. "Good God, you shouldn't be standing." He glanced toward the table and chairs on the patio, and then— "Holy *hell*. The attack on the ship, the fighting—" Stunned, he looked at her belly, and she could see him reliving the terror of those hours knowing now that the baby, too, had been in danger.

"I won't hold you to what you've asked me," she said, and tried to step back, but he wouldn't let her. "If you need time to consider—"

"Time to *consider?*" He pulled her closer and held her gently, mindful of her shoulder. "Millicent, the only thing I want to consider is how quickly I can make you my wife. Please tell me you can trust me that much."

Emotion clogged her throat. He really, truly wanted her for his own. The truth of it took wing, and she reached for his face, standing on tiptoe to kiss his lips. "I do trust you. And I love you—so much more than I know how to say. And yes—" an unsteady smile tugged at her lips "—I will be your wife."

It was like a dream, and she barely had the chance to accept that it was real before he kissed her in return—deeply, thoroughly, lovingly—with the Mediterranean sunshine caressing them with its warmth and the sound of waves drifting up from the turquoise sea below, whispering through the ancient olive grove clinging to the terraced hillside.

"I vow myself to you, and our child, completely," he told her, pulling back just enough to look into her eyes. "You have my solemn promise. Forever."

EPILOGUE

"EDWARD, TALK WITH Winston and make him see reason," Millie said, seated on a picnic blanket near the old mill in the village at the Winston estate. "He'll listen to you."

Sunshine filtered through the trees onto the grassy spot by the river. Food enough for an entire regiment spilled out of a giant basket she and Winston had brought from the estate. Millie brushed a crumb from her greatly rounded belly and reached for another currant cake.

Winston plucked a dandelion flower and twirled it playfully beneath her chin. "If by *reason* you mean I should have allowed you to continue your studies until you were in danger of becoming a live birthing exhibition in front of the other students…"

"Winston! That would never happen." The flower tickled, and Millie rubbed her chin, checking her fingers to see if he'd left a smudge of yellow pollen. Amusement creased Winston's eyes, and even now her breath caught just looking at him.

The most magnificent man in all creation. And he was her husband.

"I daresay they would all be shocked as well as educated." Cara laughed, shifting baby Matthew on her lap. Her cheeks were pink, and her eyes glowed with happiness as she looked down at her child and adjusted his sleeves. "I still can't believe you managed to conceal yourself in scholars' robes for four months."

"Four *very short* months." By the time they'd traveled to Malta and Winston had used his influence to gain her admission to the surgical school, there hadn't been much time before her pregnancy made it difficult to continue. Not that there was the least doubt that everyone knew the new young "man" at the school was the Duchess of Winston, but waddling belly-first through the corridors would have stretched the limits of what people were willing to ignore.

In any case, Winston had insisted they return to England before she became so heavy with child that traveling would be dangerous. He'd been completely deaf to her argument that she could continue at the school and bear the child at their new home in Valletta.

But now, seeing Edward and Cara's beautiful baby boy, she couldn't regret that they'd returned. It was a wondrous thing to share in their joy, and not only that, Millie would have Cara by her side when her own time came.

"Afraid I can't help you," Edward told Millie now with a smile. "I'm in full agreement with your husband on this."

Millie reached out and put her finger beneath Matthew's tiny little hand. He curled a fist around her, and a flood of happiness and anticipation welled up in her heart—happiness for Cara and Edward, and anticipation for the child sitting full in her own belly.

"I expect you'll have to be content pursuing your

studies in fits and starts," Cara said, sliding a knowing gaze Millie's way.

Millie looked over her shoulder at Winston and hoped that Cara was right, and there would be many more babies interrupting her studies. She thought of the wonder that her life had become—the thrill of those months at the school, the blessing of Winston being hers forever. She had friends, a husband who loved her, more homes than a person had a right to…and soon, she would have a family.

It was everything she'd ever wanted, times ten. And it was perfect.

* * * * *

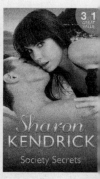

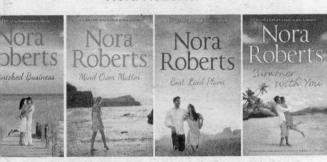

The World of
MILLS & BOON®